SECRETS

The Deeper You Dig a Web of Lies and Deadly Consequences

BY

CHRISTIE HENDRIX

TABLE OF CONTENTS

Dedication

This is for the people who have loved in secret, fought wars behind closed doors, and kept secrets that almost broke them. This is for the survivors, the dreamers, the hustlers, and the heartbroken. It's for the streets that raised us, broke us, and still taught us how to stand up.

To every woman who's ever felt unseen, and every man who's ever been misunderstood—You matter. Your voice matters. Your story matters.

And to my day ones—family, friends, and every soul who believed in me even when I doubted myself—

Thank you. I poured truth in every word.

Always follow your dreams and put your heart into everything you do—unapologetically.

With love,

Christie Hendrix

Chapter One

"Sin City Hustle: Love, Lust & Luck"

Vegas was hot that night, streets crowded with hustlers, tourists, and folks lookin' to make a fast come-up. The air was thick with smoke, spilled liquor, and bad decisions waitin' to be made. Girls posted up on corners, eyes scan-nin' for a payday, pimps posted up in the cut, clockin' they girls, watchin' every move. While undercover cops played it cool, tryna blend in, but out here, everybody could spot a badge a mile away.

I moved through the crowd, sidesteppin' drunks and dreamers, takin' in the scene like it was just another night. Livin' eleven minutes from the Strip meant I'd seen it all before—the game never changed, just the faces. Money, power, survival. Out here, you either played to win or got played tryin'.

My names Angel. My Mama and Daddy gave me that name like I was some kinda miracle sittin' in the middle of all they bullshit. Like outta all that powder, street money, and cheap motel linens, I was the only thing that ain't get touched by the grime. Mama swore when she laid eyes on me, Daddy broke down — first and last time she ever caught him cryin'. Said I was too pure, too good, to be stitched together from two folks the streets already chewed up. They really thought I was gon' be the one thing they ain't mess up. Their fresh start. Their clean slate.

But life don't honor good intentions. Out here, the streets don't give a damn what name you carry. And bein' born into the game don't come with no map or mercy. I was raised off dice games in pissy stairwells, clouds of loud rollin' thick in the hallways, old heads schemin' over spades and dominoes, and E-40 and Too Short blastin' outta busted speakers. Raised on arguments that sounded more like war cries, on promises made high and broken low.

Mama used to rub my cheeks with them cracked, lotion-slick hands and whisper, "You my Angel. Proof God forgave me for all the foul shit I ever did." She meant it. I believe that. Daddy did too, maybe. For a minute. But just 'cause you name somethin' after heaven don't mean hell won't claim it first.

They wanted better — they just didn't know how to be better. Kept hustlin', kept duckin' warrants, kept drownin' in the same cycle they swore they'd pull me out of. And I watched it all — eyes wide open. Soakin' up the bullshit, the quick flips, the smoke cloudin' up the air, and all them old regrets they couldn't hide if they tried.

I was supposed to be different. Special. Protected. But how you get a normal life when the ones raisin' you still out here battlin' the block just to breathe?

My bedtime stories was the sound of Pretty Tony slammin' dominos on the table, Mama cussin' him out while she counted their last dirty twenty, and the thump-thump-thump of some neighbor's headboard bangin' through the thin-ass walls. I used to shut my eyes so tight it hurt, wishin' for a different life. Wishin' for a house where Mama didn't gotta cry behind closed doors. Where Daddy ain't walk in smellin' like power, danger, and some high-price scent that couldn't cover what he'd really been into.

But when you born in the fire, you don't just survive it.

You learn how to spark your own flame and act like it don't burn.

Mama used to call it "hustlin'" like that made it holy, like grindin' on your knees was some kinda badge of honor.

But I seen the real. Seen her limpin' in at 3 a.m., wig crooked, lashes hangin' on by a prayer, heels in one hand, pain in the other. She'd slap them wrinkled bills on the counter like they meant more than what she gave to get 'em. And still, she'd lean down, kiss my forehead real soft, like broken was just how love looked in our house.

By the time I was ten, I knew how to keep quiet when the wrong folks came knockin', how to make a meal outta nothin', and how to lie to CPS with a straight face. Mama kept sayin' I was gon' make it out. That I was too pretty, too smart, too *somethin'* to end up like her.

But when you grow up watchin' your mama grind selling her body to survive, and your daddy break bread with killers like they play cousins, that shit get in your blood. And eventually... I let it take me.

I ain't jump into the life. I slipped.

Little by little. First it was just trappin' outta motels, runnin' errands for Daddy's girls. Then it was sittin' pretty at the bar while old men bought me drinks and whispered what they'd do with me if I was "naughty." I started lettin' them pay just to talk. Then talk turned to touch. Touch turned to tricks. And just like that... Angel ain't sound like no blessing no more. It sounded like a setup. By the time I turned 16, I made it my hustle.

People always ask how I ended up like this, and the truth is, I was raised by it. My daddy, Pretty Tony, was a pimp. My mama, Asia Dior, walked the blade for him…"

She was his bottom bitch, his bread and butter, the one who held it down before I even existed.

"Vegas wasn't where it started. I'm straight outta Long Beach…" But when I was young, my mama packed us up and dipped, chasin' money the only way she knew how. Hoein'. She swore it was just for a little while, just 'til we got straight. But this city? It'll swallow you whole. Before long, she was too deep in, lettin' tricks and fast cash write our story.

Mama never stayed still for long. She was always chasin' money, always where the big spenders were. One night she'd be on Sunset, heels clickin' against the pavement, and the next she'd be hoppin' a flight up to the Bay, maybe even Seattle if the money was right. She ain't care where she had to go—if the bag was there, so was she.

I remember watchin' her pack, slippin' tight dresses and high heels into a suitcase like she was headin' to a business meeting. And in a way, she was. Except her office was hotel rooms, strip club parking lots, and back seats of luxury cars. She'd come back days later, tired but smilin', droppin' money on the table before headin' straight to the bathroom to soak her feet.

"Seattle tricks break real bread," Mama mumbled, sittin' on the edge of that saggy-ass bed in our broke-down spot off 21st and Locust. Paint peelin' off the walls like even the building was tired of fightin'. Carpet so thin, you could damn near see the wood underneath. But Mama? She still latherin' up with cocoa butter like she a queen or somethin'. Like rubbin' them scars made 'em disappear.

"Seattle cool though," she said, side-eyein' that cracked mirror with a half-smile like she already been through it. "Best damn weed you ever touch. Tricks out there got long money — real loose with it too. You smile right, walk right, they'll hand over they whole check like you God's gift."

Angel was camped out by the heater, holdin' a one-armed Barbie like she was clutchin' hope, actin' deaf but hangin' on every word.

Mama's red-bottoms sat by the door, scuffed and tired, lookin' like they was too good for the dirt they rested on. Her feet was swollen from workin' the blade all night down Long Beach Blvd, stompin' between Anaheim and PCH, but she moved like pain didn't deserve her attention.

She snatched her wig off, tossed it lazy onto the nightstand next to Pretty Tony's sloppy stack of crinkled bills and an almost-dead bottle of Henny. Her real hair, sweated out and pressed flat against her scalp, clung to her forehead like memories she couldn't wash off — but her head? Still held high. Always.

Out in the front room, Pretty Tony and Big Smoke — the loudmouth pimp from 4B — was slammin' dominos like they was settlin' old beefs. The whole spot smelled like fried chicken, blunts, and cheap cologne — the official scent of broke dreams in the projects.

Pretty Tony cracked up from the kitchen, smackin' a domino down so hard it made Angel flinch.

"Folks up in Seattle be actin' soft, but don't let that fool you," he said, eyes sharp. "They got hitters up there that move quiet, real slick. Ain't nobody slow—slip once, and you gon' feel it in your chest."

Big Smoke leaned back, his gold tooth flashin' as he chuckled low. "Man, out here? These lil' cutthroats on Figueroa and Sunset'll line a nigga up quick. Bitches out here more loyal to the blade than they is to they own blood."

Mama let out a short, bitter laugh, still workin' that lotion into a fresh purple bruise climbin' up her thigh. "Ain't no loyalty in this game. Ain't never been. Long Beach, Compton, Watts... all that do is raise killers and hustlers. Make you cold before you even know what love s'posed to feel like."

She sat quiet for a minute, staring at the floor like it had done her wrong. Then she leaned in, voice barely above a whisper,

"But if that money call me up north? I'm on that Greyhound with what I can carry in a trash bag and my back against the wall. 'Cause out here? Love don't keep the lights on—money do."

Angel clutched her raggedy Barbie tighter, the little plastic legs bent and twisted, just like the world she was growin' up in.

Pretty Tony slapped another domino down hard, leaned back in his chair, and said, "Game don't hug you, baby—it size you up, spit you out, and charge you rent for the lesson. You don't play smart, you end up broke or buried."

Mama ain't even flinch.

She didn't have to.

Out here in Long Beach?

The hustle was the only one that ever showed love.

She pulled on that Newport slow, the tip burnin' red in the dark—same way that fire stayed buried in her chest. "Ain't nothin' like home," she said, rockin' that crooked smile—half hurt, half pride. "Sunset, Fig, Compton… them streets built a savage. Out here? You either eat or get ate alive."

She shifted slow, wincin' from the pain creepin' through her bones, but rubbed that lotion in like goin' numb was just how it go.

Angel soaked it all in that night, sittin' cross-legged on that old, crusty carpet, before she even knew survival was somethin' you had to earn.

My mama was the type to make a man drop a whole check just hopin' she'd remember his name. Skin like brown sugar, curves for days, and hair that stayed laid—even after three days on the blade.

She wasn't just out there—she *ran* that shit. Other hoes stayed clockin' her moves, tryna figure out what made her different, why the same tricks kept circlin' back like they ain't just drop a bag on her the night before.

But looks only got you so far, and Mama knew the game better than most. She had that sharp tongue, them slow blinks, knew just how to get in a man's head make him feel like the only one in the room. And if she could run up a bag without layin' down, best believe she was doin' just that.

From the moment I could talk, she was puttin' me up on game. "Mama ain't raise no fool," she'd say, eyes locked on her reflection while she lined her lips just right. "Keep your head high and your mouth shut—you watch more than you speak."

She taught me to watch everything and trust damn near nothin'. Told me folks'll smile in your face and snake you the second you blink. Said it's the quiet ones you gotta watch, and the loud ones usually ain't bout shit anyway.

Her love came in lessons, not hugs. Like makin' sure I never walked outside lookin' weak, or lettin' me sit in the room while she counted cash and cleaned her knife. She ain't say "I love you" much, but she made sure I knew how to move smart, talk less, and keep my eyes open even when I was laughin'.

But no matter how much game she laced me with, I always wanted more from her. More than just lessons on how to get by, more than quick hugs before she disappeared for the night. I wanted a mama that stayed, not one I had to share with the streets. But she was always chasin' money, always runnin' back to Daddy, handin' him her earnings like she owed him her whole existence. And when she wasn't around, she left me and my sister, Naliyah, with him.

Daddy wasn't no different. He was deep in the streets, but he made sure me and Naliyah had everything. I can't remember a time when we ever went without. We had the flyest clothes, the newest shoes, gold earrings that caught the sunlight just right. Birthdays? Christmas? He made sure we was laced, even if it meant somebody else had to take a loss for it. He was always fresh—tailored suits, gators on his feet, rings on every finger, nails clean and manicured like he ain't never put in no dirty work. But I knew better. He moved smooth, but he was a businessman before anything, and business in the streets meant somebody was always losing. It just wasn't gon' be him.

When we wasn't at Grandma's house, me and Naliyah spent half our childhood in the backseat of his car, watchin' the city blur past while he picked up and dropped off Mama and the rest of his girls. I used to press my face against the window, watchin' them walk to the car, legs long, outfits tight, faces painted like they ain't have a care in the world. Mama would slide into the front seat, perfume thick, eyes tired, lips still smiling for Daddy." He'd count the money, give a quick nod, and peel off like clockwork—same grind, different block.

I used to sit back there wonderin' if this was all life had to offer. If I was meant to follow in Mama's footsteps, to one day trade in my childhood for late nights and strange men. She always told me I was too smart for the game, too sharp to let it play me. But at the end of the day, smarts ain't got nothin' to do with circumstance. And circumstance had me right in the middle of it, whether I wanted to be or not.

Truth be told, I didn't sign up for this life—it came knockin'. I just got smart on how to stay ten toes down in it.

I'd say I'm well-prepared for this lifestyle. Tonight, I was on a mission...Not tryna get chose, that ain't me. I move solo, no pimp taxin' my earnings.

I love my money too much to let a man take a cut of what he ain't work for. Matter fact, I'm so slick with it, I can have a trick handin' over them blues without him even touchin' me.

These dudes out here? They hooked on chocolate, straight fiends for it. So why the hell would I ever waste time on a man tryna dig in my pockets when I can have one breakin' bread with no strings? I don't need no man to 'protect' me—I got my own back, and my money stay comin' in."

That's why my crossbody always on me—pepper spray, switchblade, lip gloss, and that *don't test me* presence. I ain't got no fancy training, but I grew up readin' faces and watchin' hands. I don't talk tough—I move silent, quick, and precise. Let somebody try it... I'll end the convo before a word leave they mouth.

First stop? I'm walking through the spot lookin' way too fly tonight —six-inch red bottoms, my most expensive perfume, and that signature red lipstick. Red meant I was on demon time. The Strip was packed, and I already knew these hoes out here played dirty. Ain't no loyalty in this game—if the price is right, anybody can get set up. But I stayed ready, always watchin', always alert.

The night was boomin'. One thing about Vegas? The Strip never slept, and neither did the paper. The high rollers was out, trickin' off like money grew on trees, and Angel? She was the one waterin' the roots.

Man, I ran that floor like it was mine. Heels clickin', hips swingin', whole casino watchin' but not sayin' nothin'. My phone? Lit. Regulars beggin' for a slot, new ones poppin' up like roaches when the lights off. They knew what time it was—tonight, I was taxin'. High demand means high price. Period.

First client, some thirsty trick near the high-limit tables. Told him I was free for thirty, he dropped a G like he was proud of it. Didn't even touch him—just let him talk while I sipped on my drink and played interested. Boom. 1K, no sweat.

Next up, private suite. Old dude smellin' like cigars and ego, fresh off a win. Wanted company. I gave him laughs, a light touch, a little neck—he was damn near throwin' hunnids just to hear me breathe. He ain't want sex. He wanted to feel young again. I can do that with my eyes closed.

Last one? Some corporate type frontin' like this was a "business trip." Please. Man booked a suite like that meant I was supposed to be impressed. I let him talk, let him vent, let my lips hush all that stress out his system. G for my time. Another G for the vibe. Two more for me to dip without leavin' a trace.

No trace. Not a hair, not a scent, not even a damn fingerprint. I ghosted that suite like I was never there—real slick, real silent. Slid them heels back on, fixed my bag, and hit the hallway with that don't-speak-unless-you-want-trouble energy.

Elevator ride down was quiet—just me and my thoughts, countin' bands in my head, plannin' my next move. Lobby was full of the usual late-night noise: drunks, lights, security actin' like they pay attention. I ain't make eye contact with nobody. Just kept it movin'.

Four bands, easy.

Split it up how I always do. Each one paid for somethin' different— but all of 'em paid to forget who they was, and I made sure they left rememberin' me instead.

This life ain't pretty, but I move smart. I stay watchin', stay two steps up. I don't gotta pull no gun—I'm the weapon.

As I walked down the street, my eyes caught a dark stain spread across the pavement, shining under them bright-ass billboards. A woman was huddled up in the fetal position, face lost in that city glow. My chest squeezed. Was she still breathin', or had the streets just claimed another soul?

Looked like some low-budget horror flick, except this wasn't no damn movie—this was real life, and out here, death was just part of the hustle. The only sound cuttin' through the night was the sound of sirens creepin' closer.

Word on the street was it started over a trick with deep pockets. Across the street, some dude in a designer suit sat in the back of a sleek black car, grippin' a fat stack of cash like it was his lifeline. Money was his shield, keepin' him untouchable while bodies dropped over the same paper he threw around like it was nothin'.

They fought over him, and in the end, neither one got the invite.

Me? I wasn't worried about bein' picked. My bag was already secured—four stacks in four hours. Ain't bad for a night's work. Some girls chase love, some chase dreams. Me? I chase money, and tonight, my bank account felt way fuller than my soul ever would.

Satisfied, I turned my attention to my next mission—food.

The moment I walked into the casino, the whole energy changed. Lights flickerin', dice hittin' tables, cash passin' quick—this wasn't no party. This was a jungle. Straight-up war zone. And everybody in it was out for their slice.

But tonight?

I wasn't nobody's prey.

I was the lioness. Queen of the whole damn game.

Across the room, I seen him—leaned up on that blackjack table like the whole damn casino was his playground. Tall, smooth brown, sharp as a razor in that tailored suit, rockin' a gold watch that ain't come from no outlet. He wasn't flexin', though. He just *was*—quiet power, like a storm waitin' on the right time to tear shit up.

I had a spot in mind for dinner, but my feet slowed. My eyes locked on his like they knew somethin' my body ain't wanna admit just yet. He caught me lookin'. Didn't flinch. Just smirked—head tilted, eyes runnin' down me like I was a bet he already won.

His stare? Dangerous. Deep. Like he seen every version of me in seconds but was still curious about what was hidin' underneath. He ain't just undress me with his eyes—he stripped the *mask*. That's what made my pulse skip.

I walked up to him, steady but with doubt stitched in every step. Didn't need to say much—just enough to keep things movin' and keep him wonderin'. My grin barely curled, like I knew too much to be too open. I kept that little distance between us on purpose— flirtin' with the flame but not tryna get burned.

"Damn," I said, eyes slow-dancin' with his, "you always this sharp, or you just tryin' to stunt tonight?"

He licked his bottom lip, slow and smooth. "Depends," he said, voice deep, cool like whiskey over ice. "You always step to danger, actin' like it's yours for the takin'?"

I raised a brow. "Only when danger got good credit and nice hands."

He chuckled, real low, leanin' in close—his cologne hittin' my senses like a sin I'd commit twice. "Mitch," he said, his tone all confidence and curiosity. "You?"

I leaned in just a touch, felt the heat flicker in that space between us. "Angel," I whispered, voice wrapped in silk. "But I only let certain people say it soft."

Mitch let his gaze slide down my body, then right back up—slow, bold, like he was tryna read what page I was on before he flipped it.

"Ain't nothin' soft about you, Angel. That name? That's false advertising."

"You'd be surprised," I said, eyes glitterin', "I got layers. But I don't unfold 'em for free."

He tilted his head, jaw set, eyes sharp. "I don't mind payin'. Long as the price don't leave me with no regrets."

I took half a step closer, let our energy tangle. My hand brushed his suit just enough to let him feel me without fully touchin'. "Regret's for people who don't know how to finish what they start."

He grinned—sharp, wicked. "So what you startin', Angel?"

I smiled without answerin', let the silence speak for itself. He watched me—eyes never blinkin', body still but charged, like he ain't wanna miss nothin'. That kind of attention? That's rare. Dangerous rare.

"You got a woman?" I asked, voice low. "Or just out here entertainin' anybody that look back?"

"Nah," he said, eyes lockin' with mine like truth lived there. "No woman. Just waitin' on somebody who know how to match my kinda crazy."

I tilted my head, serious now. "You sure? 'Cause I don't do halfway. I don't do pretty lies. You step in my world, you better be ready for the whole ride."

Mitch moved in, just close enough for his breath to brush my cheek. "I ain't scared of rides. I just like knowin' the seatbelt works before I hit the gas."

That got a smirk outta me. "Cute. But I ain't no test drive, baby. I'm the engine, the fire, and the wreck."

He looked at me like he already made up his mind. "And I'm the fool that'd crash just to say I touched it."

She slid her number across the table, smooth and slow, like it was something worth steal'n. "Here. Don't call unless you plan on showin' up right."

He grabbed it like it was gold, noddin' once, eyes locked on mine. "Angel," he said, rollin' my name off his tongue smooth, like a promise. "I'm callin'. And when I do, you better answer like you've been waitin'."

I didn't flinch. "We'll see."

I walked off, hips still swayin', his gaze heavy on me the whole way. Mitch? Nah, he wasn't gonna be the one that got away. This was just the warm-up.

- Chapter Two -

"Lust, Lies & Long Nights"

During the past few weeks, I've been keepin' it low-key, just steppin' back and thinking about how to flip my life around. I've been stacking paper, saving up to open my own hair and nail salon. Boss moves. Owning my own business has always been my vision.

I ain't tryin' to be out here sellin' my body forever. This whole pimp and hoe game? That's all my folks knew, and it's all they ever taught me. But me? I got bigger dreams and real goals that I'm about to make happen. Once I hit that mark and stack enough, I'll be done with all that.

While I've been chillin', I've been setting some goals, talkin' to loan officers, and hunting down some potential spots for my business. My credit score's solid, but that cash flow? It's a stretch right now. But I'm keeping that mindset right, saying my daily affirmations, and I know it's all gonna work out. "I'll get there. Good things take time."

Now, I can't lie, that run-in with Mitch a couple weeks ago? That's been on my mind heavy. I've been low-key waiting for his call. "Why ain't he called yet?" I'm startin' to wonder.

The more I think about it, the more curious I get. Part of me wants to roll up to the casino and see if fate brings us together again. But nah, that's a bad look. I can't be out here stalkin' him. I'll just play it cool.

And then my phone rings. Private number. Usually, I don't pick up unknowns, but something told me to answer. It was Mitch. Finally!

"Hey, beautiful," he says. I'm cheesin' like crazy, grinning from ear to ear.

"Hey," I reply, sexin' up my voice. "How's your morning going?"

I'm leanin' against the wall, twirling the phone cord around my fingers, just lettin' the flirtation flow. I'm still in my boy shorts, a little teaser shirt, hair bonnet on, and I hit him with that. "Better now that you finally put my number to use."

"So, any plans for tonight?" he asks, holdin' the phone up to his ear.

Why his voice give me that butterfly feeling in my gut? You know that feeling, like when you first got asked to prom? That soft puppy love vibe. For a second, I just pause.

"No plans. I'm free tonight. Ok, Mitch, can I expect you to pick me up?" I ask, barely containin' my smile.

"Nah, we'll be bussin' it. I'll meet you at the bus stop by nine. Nah, I'm kiddin'. I'll pick you up. Will you be ready by then?"

Alright, Mitch, I see you got jokes. I laugh.

"Yeah, I'll be ready," I say, and then I give him my address before hanging up.

Now, what am I gonna wear? I have no clue what we're doin' tonight, but I can't be out here lookin' basic. I dug through my closet like it was a treasure hunt. Finally, I found it: a sleek black mock-neck cut-out dress. That's the one. The dress hugs every curve and shows off this hourglass figure I've been workin' on. Paired it with some black Michael Kors pumps and a merlot Dede mini python bag. Lookin' fly, ready to slay.

I hit the bathroom, and it's go time with my hair. Took me an hour to get those loose curls right, 'cause my hair's past twenty inches now.

It's eight PM, and I'm in the shower, fresh out, lathering up with that Marshmallow Citrus whipped body butter. I'm smellin' sweet as hell, then I get my makeup on, slip into my dress, and hit it with that Love Don't Be Shy perfume by Kilian. The scent hits the air like a soft promise. That marshmallow and neroli mix got me feelin' like a whole vibe.

I'm gonna leave a trail of seduction wherever we go tonight.

I grab some water from the kitchen, only to knock it against the sink and spill half when my phone buzzes—Mitch. He's five minutes out. I toss the glass down, walk to the door, fumble for my keys, lock it up, then bounce to the parking lot to meet him.

I see him pull up in this turbocharged, candy red '68 Chevy Impala. Man, that thing is sittin' pretty on silver and red twenty-six-inch Forgiatos. The custom black leather seats with bold red stitching? Straight fire.

Mitch gets out, walks around to open my door. As I step into that flawless whip, the scent of incense fills the air, and I'm like, "What cologne you got on?"

"Aventus by Creed," he says.

Man smells as good as he looks. He's in a tailored two-piece Armani suit, black as midnight with ivory underneath, shining black leather shoes. Everything about him screams sophistication, class, and money. His hazel eyes? Lord, I could drown in them.

We cruise down the Vegas Strip, city lights bouncin' off the whip, colorful signs flickerin' like they tryna outshine the stars. Eddie Kendricks' Intimate Friends drifts through the speakers, smooth as the night air rollin' in. It's still warm, the heat from the day clingin' to the pavement, but that don't slow nothin' down. The streets stay packed—folks outside, music knockin', money flowin', and the whole city movin' like it got somewhere to be.

We talk, we laugh, and I'm enjoyin' the vibe. This man is somethin' else. I'm a sapiosexual—I love a mind that's sharp. Mitch? This man is a whole encyclopedia. He drops knowledge like it's nothin', and I'm sittin' there, hooked.

His voice lingers in my mind, and I know there's a deeper connection here. I can't wait to see where this goes.

As the wind blows through my hair, we pass by skyscrapers and city lights blur into streaks of color. I can't help but smile. Where's he takin' me tonight?

We pull up to this high-end restaurant. Plush red carpet, valet taking our car, the whole deal. This is a place that speaks luxury.

We step inside, greeted by a polished waiter, and I'm feelin' like royalty. The ambiance is on another level. Chandeliers glow softly, and the whole vibe feels timeless.

"This place is beautiful," I say, lowkey impressed.

"Well, there's a first time for everything," Mitch grins.

We're seated, and the waiter presents menus like they're treasures. When he asks what we want to drink, Mitch orders sparkling water, and I follow suit.

Then Mitch hits me with that smirk again.

"Did I tell you, you lookin' fire tonight?"

I let out a soft laugh, and he leans in closer, eyes locked on mine. "Damn, Angel, you so fine, I'm wonderin' if you taste as sweet as you smell."

I grin back, twirling a piece of my curls between my fingers. My lips glossed, I tease, "If I let you have a taste, just know you gon' be hooked for life."

He laughs, leanin' back in his chair. "Trust me, ma, if you on the menu, I'm eatin' every damn day."

We laugh, then flag the waiter down to place our order.

As the conversation flows, Mitch leans in with a curious look. "So, Angel, tell me about you. Where you from?"

I smile, real talk. "Long Beach, Cali. Grew up where everybody knows your mama, your business, and your favorite color." I pause. "Had to learn to move smart real early in age."

He nodded, eyes still locked on mine, his expression softer now. "I can tell. You got a story worth hearin'. Maybe one day, you'll let me in on it."

I smirked, playing it cool. "Maybe."

He leaned back real smooth, swirlin' them last couple cubes like he was thinkin' 'bout life or somethin'. "I'm from the Chi. Fast life, cold streets. But what about you, Angel?

What get you goin'?"

"Photography," she said, leanin' back too, matchin' his energy. "Snappin' life how I see it. Catchin' them little moments most folks overlook. That's my thing."

He ran a hand over his chin, real intrigued now.

"That's real dope. Mitch smirked, his voice dropping just a little. "Maybe one day, you'll catch a moment like this. Somethin' real. Somethin' you'll wanna remember."

I chuckled, twirling my straw in my drink. "Oh yeah? You think this a moment worth rememberin'?"

Mitch leaned in slightly, his voice low and smooth. "Depends. You tryna make it one?"

I smirked but didn't answer right away. I wasn't the type to gas a man up too quick. Instead, I took a slow sip of my drink, letting the silence stretch between us. Mitch watched me, like he was tryna read between the lines.

"So," I said finally, tilting my head. "Tell me more about Chicago. Not the tourist stuff—the real Chicago."

swirling the dark liquor in his glass. "The real Chicago? Man, it's two different worlds, dependin' on where you stand. Uptown, it's penthouses with skyline views, steak dinners at Maple & Ash, and designer bags that cost more than some folks' rent. It's brunches where deals get made over mimosas, private events where the right handshake can change your whole tax bracket. Money talk different up there—real quiet, real powerful.

"But cross the wrong block, and it's a whole different story. South and West Side? That's where the hustle loud. It's Harold's chicken after the club, dice games outside the liquor store, and kids pushin' packs 'cause school ain't payin' they mama's bills. Ain't no safety net, just survival. Out west, it's candy-painted whips, footwork battles, and legends still livin' off stories from back in the day. You either makin' it out or gettin' stuck. No in-between.

"Thing is, real ones know how to move in both. Money don't change the rules—it just give you more options."

I feel that. "Yeah, Long Beach the same way. You either catch on quick or end up learnin' the hard way."

Mitch studied me for a second, then grinned. "Yeah, I can tell you not new to this."

I smirked, settin' my glass down. "Never been."

The energy between us? Different. It wasn't just small talk—it was a vibe. The kinda vibe that made you forget where you were, like the rest of the room blurred out.

"So what you do for work?" I asked, raising a brow.

Mitch took a sip of his drink, his eyes still on me. "Let's just say I move in circles where keepin' your business low is key."

I laughed. "Oh, so you one of them mysterious types?"

He smirked. "Nah, just careful."

I wasn't mad at that. I understood the game—some things ain't meant for casual conversation.

He leaned in, his cologne hittin' just right. "What about you? You shoot the streets, but what else? What's the dream?"

I exhaled, thinking about it. "I wanna open a salon. Hair, nails, makeup—all that. Somethin' for the girls who wanna look good but don't wanna spend a whole paycheck doin' it."

Mitch nodded, lookin' impressed. "That's real. Ain't nothin' like a woman with a vision."

The convo kept flowin', easy and smooth. Laughs, little side glances, moments where the silence said more than words ever could.

Then his phone rang. He glanced at the screen, his whole vibe shiftin'. He answered, kept it short. "Aight. Bet."

I watched him carefully. When he hung up, he exhaled and turned back to me. "I gotta handle somethin'."

The switch-up was quick, but I peeped it.

"I'll take you home," he added, already standin' up.

I wasn't about to argue. He had that look—whatever was callin' him away wasn't small-time.

We hit the valet, and he slid the dude a bill without even glancin' at it. The way he moved. Like money wasn't a question.

When we pulled up to my spot, he put the car in park, then came around to open my door. Smooth. Gentleman-type. He took my hand, helping me out like I was something delicate.

"You good?" he asked, his voice lower now.

I nodded.

He pulled me in, his arms firm around me. Not too much, not too little. Just enough to make me linger. When he pulled back, his cologne still clung to me.

"Be safe, Angel," he said, eyes locking with mine.

I smirked. "Always."

As he pulled off, I watched his taillights disappear down the block, my heart beatin' just a little faster than before.

Damn. I mighta just got myself caught up.

Chapter Three

"Echoes of Power: T-Money and Mitch's Empire"

(T-Money)

T-Money's a beast. No way around it. The streets know his name like the back of their hand, and they fear it. Big man, broad shoulders, a presence that don't need no introduction. He's been in this game since he was a kid—twelve years old when he and Mitch started runnin' the block. Grew up in the gutters of Chicago, then bounced to Vegas to level up, and man, they been makin' moves ever since. Ain't no difference between the hustle on the Windy City streets and the neon lights of Sin City; just a matter of expansion. More money. More power.

T-Money's built like a wall, all muscle, all menace. His brown skin ain't just for show; it's a reminder to anyone dumb enough to step to him that they ain't got a chance. He ain't just a street king; he's a businessman, a sharp one at that. The dude's whole life revolves around numbers, flipping cash, and running his empire with a grip that don't loosen. Ain't nobody in Vegas who don't know T-Money. Ain't nobody who ain't got stories about him—stories that make you think twice about crossing him.

You don't get to T-Money's level without gettin' your hands dirty. He's the muscle, the one who makes sure everything stays in line. Debt collections? He's your man. Enemies? He's the one to make 'em disappear. The streets are his turf, and every step he takes hits hard—this game ain't never been fair.

Mitch and T-Money? They've been tight since they was kids. Ain't no loyalty like that kind. They've been building together, breakin' bread, and fighting their way to the top side by side. Ain't nobody got their back like family.

T-Money's like a shadow in the city—silent, deadly, but always present. And right now? Things are about to pop off.

"Yo, Mitch! Get your ass over here," T-Money growls, his voice low but thick with the kind of tension that makes the air feel heavy. Mitch turns fast, his brow furrowed as he walks towards him, pissed off like he's been dragged out of something important.

"What the fuck, T-Money? I was in the middle of a dinner date, nigga. This better be worth it!" Mitch snaps, his voice a mix of anger and confusion.

T-Money don't answer right away. He just motions for Mitch to follow him, down a narrow hallway that stinks of decay. The basement of a busted-down warehouse. That's the place. The smell hits Mitch hard—musty, old, like a place abandoned for years. Ain't nothing good down here.

They step through a door, and there's Billy. The man's tied up in a chair, blood dripping from his busted lip, a rag shoved in his mouth to shut him up. The sight of him makes T-Money grin, but it ain't a friendly grin.

"Look who I found, Mitch. Thought you was slick, huh?" T-Money spits on the floor like he's disgusted.

Mitch's eyes narrow. "You really thought you could fuck us over like this?" He walks up to Billy, grabs his shirt, and yanks his face up. "Where's our money, Billy? Where's the cash from last week's drop?"

Billy shakes his head, panic in his eyes. Sweat pours down his face as he tries to speak, but all you hear is muffled sounds through the cloth.

T-Money's grin fades into a cold, hard stare. He crosses his arms, watching Mitch work.

Mitch don't waste no time. He punches Billy straight in the jaw, the crack of the hit echoing in the dusty room. "Talk, Billy. Where's the fuckin' money?" Mitch growls.

Billy's eyes bulge, fear creeping in. Mitch gets in his face again, his voice dangerously calm now.

"I handed you a hundred keys. A whole mil. And now I'm sittin' here with nothin'—no product, no bread. Make that make sense."

Billy's lips twitch, sweat beading at his hairline. "The Russians… they took everything," he stammers, his breath coming in short, panicked bursts.

Mitch lets out a dry laugh, shaking his head like he just heard the dumbest shit in the world. "The Russians? You just let 'em take all my shit? No fight, no plan, not even a heads-up?" He leans in close, voice dropping to a dangerous low. "Tell me somethin', Billy. You workin' for 'em now, or you just that fuckin' stupid?"

Billy nods quickly. "We met at the spot, man. Everything was supposed to go smooth. But it went south—gunfight. I got out, but I had to leave everything behind... they set me up."

T-Money's jaw clenches. "This is bullshit." He's ready to end it right here, but Mitch holds him back.

"Hold up, T. We need more. Billy, tell us about the Russians. Who rolled with 'em? Who else was at that exchange?" Mitch presses, eyes blazing.

Billy wiped his face, voice shaky. "I don't know much… they pulled up deep, snatched the work. Ain't say nothin'—just took that shit like it was theirs."

T-Money grinds his teeth. "You better remember everything, Billy. Or this is your last fuckin' night on Earth."

Mitch looks at T-Money. "We need to find those Russians. Now."

Billy gave up as much as he could—names, faces, whatever he remembered. Mitch soaked it in, already plottin'.

The tension's thick as hell in the room. You can feel the weight of it in your chest. Mitch looks at T-Money, nods. "We goin' after them. Let's move."

Billy's ropes get cut. He stumbles, but Mitch's cold stare freezes him. "You move wrong, you're done. You gon' help us find them muthafuckas. This your one shot to fix the mess you made—don't blow it."

T-Money and Mitch step out into the heavy night air, the city alive with movement around them. Mitch looks at T-Money. "We need info, and we need it now. Reach out to the crew. We find these Russians first, or they find us."

T-Money nods, locking eyes. "Got it. Let's go."

Without another word, they split up, heading in different directions, each focused-on tracking down the lead. The city ain't no friend, but it's their playground, and they ain't about to let no Russians come up in their turf without payin' for it.

Weeks pass. Tensions rise. Mitch's crew's prepped, and they're ready. They know this mission's personal. They gotta hit the Russians before they think they can make a play. They ain't about to let some foreign hustlers snatch what's theirs.

On the night of the mission, Mitch's team moves like shadows. They hit the Russians where they're makin' a deal with another crew. The whole thing pops off in a split second—shots ring out, bodies hit the ground. The streets turn to blood. Mitch's crew? They ain't here to play. No mercy, no survivors. They hit fast, hit dirty, and take what they came for.

It's done in no time. Blood's all over the pavement, and the Russians' operation completely shut down.

But Mitch ain't done yet. Billy—he's next.

Mitch didn't play around when it came to mistakes. He was a man of action, and when someone fucked up, they paid for it.

Billy? He was hiding out in a shit-hole motel on the outskirts of town—one of those places where you slipped the clerk a few bills, and no one gave a damn about your name. The faded sign flickered weakly, barely lighting up the cracked sidewalk. Mitch and his crew rolled up, their steps heavy, the vibe tense as hell.

Inside, Billy was pacing, nervous as hell, sweat dripping down his face, eyes glued to the door every few seconds. He knew what was coming, and it wasn't looking good.

When that door flew open, he nearly jumped out of his skin.

"Mitch, wait! Hold up!" Billy's voice cracked, desperation written all over his face. "I did my part, man! We were good, right?"

Mitch didn't have time for that shit. He moved fast, grabbed Billy by the collar, and slammed him into the wall before Billy could even blink. His fist hit Billy's jaw like a sledgehammer. Billy staggered back, crashing into the chipped dresser behind him.

"Nah, man. You ain't off the hook." Mitch growled, shoving Billy's face against the wall. "You think 'cause you did your part that I'm just gonna forget you let them Russians steal from us? You dumb as hell, Billy."

Billy's eyes went wide, his chest heaving. "Mitch, please! I swear to God, I didn't know they were comin' for me like that! I was caught up, man. You gotta believe me!"

Mitch grabbed him by the throat and shoved him harder into the drywall, shaking with anger. "I don't give a fuck, Billy. You were supposed to be on top of your shit. You got too cocky. Now look what happened. You let those Russians walk away with our bread, our product, our muscle. And now you expect me to let you live? What the fuck world do you think you're in?"

Billy's breath came quick and shallow, panic written across his face. He dropped to his knees, begging, looking up at Mitch like a man already dead. "Please, Mitch. I'm begging you, don't do this! I'll disappear, you'll never hear from me again, I swear. Just let me go, man!"

T-Money stepped up, voice low and cold. "We told you, Billy— help us find them Russian sumbitchs. You helped, yeah... but you weak. You folded. Ain't no comin' back from that.

Mitch stepped forward, cold eyes never leaving Billy. "In this game, mistakes like yours get you buried. You let them take what's ours, and now you think you deserve to walk away? Nah. You think I'm gonna let that slide?"

Billy's voice cracked as he scrambled for any way out. "I didn't know they were coming, Mitch! I wasn't ready, it just happened so fast, please, man!"

Mitch's jaw clenched tight, the anger bubbling over. "That's the problem, Billy. You were supposed to be ready. You weren't and now you're gonna pay for it."

Billy's eyes widened as Mitch slid his hand into his coat, pulling out the cold steel of his gun. Billy's whole body trembled. "Please, Mitch! Don't do this! I'll vanish, you won't ever see me again, I swear!"

Mitch didn't even flinch, his eyes cold as ice. "That's the thing, Billy. I can't take that risk."

The shot rang out, loud as hell in the cramped room. Billy dropped to the floor, his lifeless body crumpling like a rag doll. Mitch didn't even look down at him. He turned to T-Money, voice like gravel. "Clean this up. We're done here."

The crew moved in, handling business without a word. Mitch straightened his coat like it was just another day, stepping out into the night air. They'd tied up Billy's loose ends, and the Russians had been dealt with. But Mitch knew it was never over. Another threat was always lurking, waiting for its chance to make a move.

As the crew piled into the cars and sped off, Mitch's mind was already on the next move. The streets were always hungry. And Mitch? He was the one feeding it.

The message was clear: cross him, and you die. No exceptions. No second chances.

Chapter Four

"Fast Life, Cold Streets: Angel's Hustle in the City"

Deep in the heart of the hood, where trouble stayed lurking and danger spoke its own language, Angel moved through the packed streets, steady and unbothered.

The night wrapped the city in a blanket of heat, and the streetlights above didn't make it any better, their cold glow hitting the streets in flashes. The tricks? They were always the same—looking for something quick, looking to bargain on everything, like they thought everything had a discount. They didn't care what was being sold as long as the price was right for them.

Determined to make a living, Angel distinguished herself from the challenges of these corners, holding her ground amidst the lowballing clients.

The gap between the struggle and the shine on the Vegas Strip was real—where the high rollers expected top-tier service, and the game was played on a whole different level. Angel stayed focused, stacking her bread for the salon she dreamed of, but no matter how much she tried to push it aside, Mitch kept creepin' into her thoughts. The man had a hold on her, and the fact that she didn't know where they stood irritated her.

The streets stayed loud, but inside, her mind was louder. That night, while the usual hustle played out, Angel ran into Latonya—another working hoe who'd been throwin' side-eyes at her success for a minute.

Latonya stepped in close, eyes low, her face set like she was tryna solve a puzzle. She usually kept her distance but tonight had her feeling bold. Her voice had a bite to it, laced with equal parts shade and respect. She cocked her head, sizing Angel up like she was tryna crack the code.

"So, you really out here actin' like you the one, huh? Pullin' all the big spenders while the rest of us gotta fight for the crumbs.

Angel, unfazed by Latonya's bitterness, responded with a calm confidence, "I ain't actin' like nothing, it's about knowing your worth. Angel went on to say "If you carry yourself like a queen, the tricks will treat you like one.

Angel barely moved, just lifted a shoulder, her face cold as ever. "Ain't nobody said life was fair. You don't pick your hand, but you better learn how to finesse it."

Latonya let out a dry laugh, sharp and mean.

"Real easy to talk that shit when you sittin' pretty with a stacked deck. While the rest of us out here tryna make rent with nothin' but scraps."

You really think these tricks care about anything past what's under that dress? "Listen, sis, They just see a pretty face and a fat ass, just someone to fuck."

Angel closed the gap, her voice smooth and low, like a warning. "See, that's where you trippin'. It ain't just about looks, it's about how you move. You gotta make 'em believe they can't find what you got anywhere else—make 'em think they'd be lost without you. Ain't about love, it's about control."

Latonya's jaw tightened, eyes narrowing as she shot a glance at Angel, clearly jealous. "So, what? You think you makin' all this money 'cause you just cute? I been on these corners longer than you, and I ain't seein' no stacks like that."

Angel's smile was cold, confident. "Mind your business, Latonya. I don't talk about my pockets to nobody. Just know, it's not luck, it's strategy. You gotta work the game, play it smooth. And you right about one thing—it ain't about love; it's about who's callin' the shots." She adjusted her bag, standing tall. "Now, you gonna keep askin' questions or let me get back to my grind? These heels cute, but they wasn't made for standin' 'round wastin' time."

Latonya paused, feelin' Angel's words hit her, makin' her rethink how she's been movin'. She rolled her eyes and mumbled under her breath, "Guess you think you runnin' shit now." Still salty, she slid back to her corner, but respect was all over her face even if she wouldn't admit it.

Despite the tension with Latonya, Angel continued to get her money. She tightened the strap on her luxury bag, a silent reminder of the life she'd created for herself. There would be time for doubts later, but for now, the night was young and there were tricks to turn.

The corners were full of drama, but Angel slid through 'em with her head up, all hustle and focus.. Night dragged on, she made it home, heavy with all the weight from them dim streets. The clock ticked slow, dawn colored the sky soft, and Angel found a little peace in her bed. Dead tired from runnin' them wild corners and servicin' tricks, she let herself catch some rest. The room stayed quiet, just city sounds sneakin' in through the window now and then. Angel lay frozen, lost in her mind, thinkin' 'bout all the wins and losses that shaped her. Moonlight crept past the drapes, throwin' down a low glow that held the weight of all she'd lived through. Angel soaked in the calm, knowin' the day would end with another long hustle. She slipped deeper, leavin' the city madness behind for a minute. Night moved on outside her window, but Angel grabbed them few hours to recharge, ready for whatever the streets threw next. When the morning light crept through the curtains, Angel dragged herself outta bed, her body feelin' heavy from the rest she barely got.

Angel unlocked her phone and scrolled through the messages, catchin' up on whatever slipped by. The room got a quick flash from the glow of her screen as she checked the time and what was poppin'.

Once she saw the missed calls and messages, she figured it was time to get it together and freshen up for the day.

She moved with purposeful grace, a routine established over nights spent traveling the city's rougher corners.

The sound of running water echoed in the small space as she indulged in a revitalizing shower, letting the warm cascade wash away the weariness of the night.

She slid into a red pencil skirt that wrapped around her body, the fabric catching the sunlight coming through the window, making it pop. The high waist gave her a bold look, showing off her shape with a little extra heat. She wore it with a white silk crop top, straps so thin they were almost invisible. The V-neck dipped low, just enough to tease, showing a little skin but keeping it mysterious. That outfit was all confidence, leaving you curious for more.

She wasn't just rockin' heels for the fun of it—those white joints were turnin' heads, gleamin' with every step. The straps were tight, holdin' her feet in place, while the stilettos had her standin' tall with that bold energy. The pointed toes brought the whole look together, clean and sharp, like she was ready to own the scene.

Angel flinched as soon as she hit the Vegas heat, the concrete burnin' up beneath her feet, makin' the whole street look like a heatwave fantasy. Even with her light crop top, sweat was already bead'n up on her skin. Ain't no shopping malls or museums gonna cut it—nothing but stress bottled up inside. Tonight? The casino scene didn't even tempt her.

She hopped in a cab, lettin' the neon lights of the Strip fade in the rearview. That's when a whisper from a late-night client popped into her head. When she reached her destination—an adult entertainment club—the driver, who was mute and weathered from life in the tough city, just nodded. This club wasn't the kinda place you'd expect to find out in the dry desert heat. It was tucked away, off the main strip, with windows covered up tight and a velvet rope keeping the riff-raff out. A spot where the good life and secrets went hand in hand.

Angel felt a cool breeze as she slipped past the rope. The joint was lit low, all moody vibes, with secrets hiding in every corner. The air smelled like bourbon and fresh leather, cutting through the quiet chatter and the slow, hypnotic thump of the bass that got under your skin.

Women glided through the room, their dresses hugging curves, their heels tapping against polished floors like a quiet warning—everything here had a price.

Angel eased into a booth, ordering a drink that burned just enough to remind her she was still in control. Here, she wasn't running, wasn't watching her back—she was whoever she wanted to be. A place like this didn't ask questions, didn't pry into why someone might need to disappear for a few hours.

The night moved in waves—glances exchanged, words left unsaid, flirtation used as currency. She played the game, cool and untouchable, keeping them intrigued but never too close. This wasn't about connection. It was about escape.

Then, just as the energy shifted, as the music deepened into something slow and dangerous, she felt a presence before she saw her.

"Enjoying yourself, Angel?"

The voice was smooth, dripping in amusement. Scarlet. Hair the color of warning signs, eyes that missed nothing. She leaned against the booth, a smirk playing on her lips.

Angel met her gaze, taking a slow sip of her drink before answering with nothing but a knowing look. She wasn't here to be figured out.

"Are you enjoying yourself, Angel?" the woman asked softly.

Angel recognized her – Scarlet, a regular at the club and a master of discretion. She offered a tight smile in return. "Just unwinding," Angel replied, her voice a touch guarded.

Leaning in, Scarlet's eyes lingered on the red skirt. "You know, there are a few gentlemen here tonight who would be more than happy to help you unwind in a more… private setting."

Angel pondered over this for a while, running her fingers along the edge of her glass.

The club's haze of secrecy only fed the emptiness that had been creeping up on her all day. Maybe a little company, a little distraction, wouldn't be the worst thing.

"Tell me about them," Angel finally said, her tone edged with curiosity and just a little challenge.

Scarlet's smirk deepened—she knew she had her. Leaning in, voice smooth as silk, she spilled the details. Who had money to burn, who liked to keep things quiet, and who came looking for something they couldn't get anywhere else.

Angel listened carefully, with a hungry sparkle in her eyes. This wasn't just about physical fulfillment tonight; it was a calculated game, an opportunity to gain knowledge, perhaps even leverage, behind the veil of secrecy.

Angel signaled her choice with a gentle nod. Scarlet walked her to a private back room, where the warrior in silk emerged again. The night was far from done, and Angel was ready to play by her own rules, taking advantage of the shadows of Las Vegas.

Scarlet led Angel through a tucked-away entrance, leavin' the loud energy of the main floor behind. The heavy bass faded, replaced by the low murmur of conversations and the shuffle of money bein' counted. The backroom screamed money—thick carpets that made every step quiet, velvet drapes hangin' like secrets, and the air rich with the bite of expensive cigars.

Kicked back in a plush armchair sat Mr. Thorn—silver-haired, sharp-dressed, with a goatee so sharp it looked carved. His icy blue eyes roamed over Angel, takin' his time like he was sizing up somethin' worth top dollar.

He was rockin' a suit that screamed money, clean cut, with just enough cockiness to show he knew he was top dog in this place. Scarlet dipped out without a word, leavin' Angel standin' there, alone with Mr. Thorn—the kind of guy who had power in his presence, no question.

He motioned to a plush stool at his feet, his eyes cold but sharp as they locked on Angel.

"Angel," he said, his voice smooth but low, the kind of calm that made you pay attention. "The talk out there don't do you justice."

'You mean "whispers?"' Angel replied, one of her eyebrows playfully lifted. 'Maybe you've heard there's a woman out there capable of making your night one to remember.'

Mr. Thorn laughed, but with a tint of sarcasm. 'Maybe. But I want you to tell me, Angel, are you just another pretty face or do you have something else in store,' he said with a teasing tone in his voice.

The undertone of the challenge in his voice provoked Angel's interest. Tonight was a long shot from just money, and she was looking to earn herself a new trophy to add to her extensive collection.

"Let's just say I'm a woman of many talents, Mr. Thorn," she said, her voice low and intimate. "But every talent has its price."

He leaned back, the chair creaking under his weight. "Alright, Angel. You want my money? Name your price. But I ain't paying for just the pretty face."

Angel stepped off the stage, letting the scarlet fabric slide down her body like it was nothing, but she could feel the weight of the moment, like she was treading water in way too deep. The beat of the music hit her chest, wild and fast, matching her pulse. She moved slow, but every step was deliberate, her hips rolling, each curve a magnet drawing you in. Her fingers teased the lace scarf around her neck before it slipped off her shoulders, the fabric falling slowly, almost too slow to handle. The dim lights hit her skin, tracing the smooth line of her back, making it all pop. That deep V of her top? Just enough to hint at what's underneath—enough to make him want more, but not enough to give it up.

Her eyes locked onto Mr. Thorn's, dark, intense, with something unspoken hanging between them. She took a step closer, her body heat closing the gap between them, and she could feel his stare burning her. She moved closer again, feeling the tension rise, that space between them charged. "Tonight's show?" she said, voice low, rich with promise. "It's just for you, Mr. Thorn." She traced a finger down his lapel, teasing. "The cost? It's more than what you can pay, baby."

As Thorn's eyes locked onto Angel, her top slid down her arms, exposing her big breast, and he couldn't help but drool. Her nipples were like two hard, brown bullets, begging to be sucked and licked. The lighting in the club made her shine like she was made of pure gold, with every curve practically yelling for attention.

Thorn's dick started to stiffen in his pants as Angel began to work her magic, her hips swaying to the music like a sensual snake. She let her skirt pool at her feet, revealing her smooth, shaved pussy, and Thorn's eyes almost popped out of his head. The lack of hair made her delicate folds and contours look like a perfectly manicured work of art, and he couldn't help but imagine his face buried between her legs, licking and sucking every inch of her.

Thorn was hooked, every movement she made making his body tighten, his breath coming quicker. A bead of sweat slid down his temple, the tension so thick you could cut it with a knife. The music shifted, the beat slowing, pulsing like it was keeping pace with his heart. Angel's crimson skirt twirled around her legs, flowing like fire as she moved. Every move of her hips was like she knew exactly what she was doing. Her eyes, deep and knowing, met his, and he couldn't shake the feeling. She wasn't just dancing—she was reeling him in, making him crave her, and there was no way he could fight it.

The dance reached its climax, and he was a mess of raw, unbridled desire. The dance hit its peak, and he was a damn wreck, all desire and no control. His fingers grazed her smooth skin, and she let out a deep gasp, the sound shooting straight to his dick.

He was already rock-hard, but now he was throbbin' like a motherfucker, dick strainin' against his pants like it was gonna bust free at any second.

Angel leaned in, her lips a whisper from his ear, and he felt his heart skip a beat. "Tonight, Mr. Thorn," she purred, her breath hot against his skin, "you got to see everything." Her fingers danced across his belt buckle, and he felt like he was gonna lose his shit. She rubbed against him, her body grindin' against his, and the friction was like a spark to gasoline. He was a goner, his orgasm buildin' like a freight train, and he couldn't do a damn thing to stop it.

He came hard, his cum spillin' into his pants like a damn fountain, and he felt like he was gonna pass out from the sheer intensity of it all. His body was shakin' like a leaf, his heart racin' like a jackrabbit, and he was pretty sure he was gonna die from pleasure overload.

Angel stepped back, a smile playing on her lips. "Was that worth more than a wad of crumpled bills?" she inquired, her voice seductive. Thorn was breathless, his chest rising and falling quickly as he tried to keep his composure. He couldn't help but start a slow clap, his voice barely a whisper as he spoke, "Damn, Angel. You're a hell of a woman."

He slapped his pocket, pulling out a thick stack of bills. "That was worth a heck of a lot more than I paid for it. Take this as a bonus."

Angel didn't hesitate. She took the money, her lips curling into a cunning grin. She'd played him just right, walked that fine line between power and mystery, and it had paid off. With one last look—quiet and almost mocking—she slipped past the velvet curtain, leaving Thorn still sitting there, stunned and alone. The weight of her presence lingered long after she'd gone.

Angel was owning the night. Everywhere she went, heads turned. The crowd couldn't get enough—her looks, her moves, all dripping with sex appeal. Every step she took during the rest of her table dances had the guys stuck, eyes locked on her as she worked the room, moving slow, smooth, and hypnotic.

By the end of the night, Angel was walkin' out with a fat stack of cash. She had danced for every high roller in the joint, the rhythm of her hips met with sharp claps and warm bills slipping into her palm. Mr. Thorn, her biggest fish, was there as usual, but tonight? Dude was extra generous. When he handed her the cash, Angel's eyes went wide. She couldn't believe the wad of bills he was pullin' out.

For her last table dance of the night, the crowd went wild. Angel flashed a grin, counting the bills that trailed the table, each one adding to the fat stack in her hand. The cash kept flowin', a loud reminder of how she had these dudes wrapped around her finger, runnin' the game like she owned it.

With her pockets heavy with cash, she slid outta the club, the bass still thumpin' behind her, but fading as she hit the cool night air. She stopped for a second on the sidewalk, just lettin' the world spin around her while she thought about what to do next.

Realizing she forgot to bring a change of clothes, Angel shrugged it off. Ain't no need to stress over it now. She'd just head home in the same outfit she wore to the club. It wasn't the best look, but damn, she was too beat to care about all that.

The streets were wild as ever, but Angel didn't mind. She felt good with the night's cash in her hands, knowin' she was covered for a minute. Even with the city buzzin' around her, she just kept movin' forward, head on straight, thinkin' about crashing on her own bed.

Finally, she hit her apartment building and let out a deep breath, glad to be home after that grind. She unlocked the door, stepped inside, and immediately felt the weight lift off her shoulders. Familiar sights, comfort. She kicked her shoes off and slumped onto the couch, the night's events already startin' to fade into the background.

Chapter Five

"Hood Harmony: Love & Loss in the Streets"

Mitch sat back in his chair, staring at the screen of his phone, trying to make sense of the mess swirling in his head. His feelings for Angel were real. The way her laughter hit him like a breath of fresh air, the way she'd opened up about her dreams, made him want something more. He'd never been the type to fall hard, not with the life he led. But Angel… she was different. She was like a bright spot in a world full of shadows. He needed to talk it out, though. T-money had been his right-hand man for years, and if anyone knew the game, it was him. So, Mitch dialed his number, waiting for T-money to pick up.

When the phone clicked, T-money's voice came through, low and steady, like he was waiting for Mitch to speak first.

"Mitch, what's good?" T-money asked, already sensing something was off.

Mitch took a deep breath, leaning back against the worn-out chair. "It's Angel, man," he started, voice heavy with the weight of what he was about to say. "I don't know what it is, but I can't shake these feelings. She's got me trippin', for real."

T-money didn't respond right away, just letting Mitch spill his guts. He already knew Mitch was caught up in something. He could hear the hesitation in Mitch's voice, the struggle. But T-money wasn't one to sugarcoat things. "Look, bro," he finally said, his tone measured and sharp, "I get it. She's real. You feel something. But you need to slow your roll, man. Get to know her for real before you let her in too deep."

Mitch shifted, fingers tapping nervously on the armrest. "I know, but there's something there. She's not like these other chicks. She's got her own hustle, her own dreams. She ain't about this street life, but she gets it. She understands the struggle."

T-money scoffed lightly, shaking his head even though Mitch couldn't see him. "Man, that's what they all say. But we ain't talkin' about just any woman here. We talkin' about your future. You're out here playing with fire, and you know it. The streets? They don't care about feelings. Trust? It's a luxury we can't afford."

Mitch closed his eyes, letting T-money's words sink in. He'd lived this life too long, seen too many people get burned by thinking they could mix business with pleasure. But there was something different about Angel, something he couldn't ignore.

"I hear you, bro," Mitch finally replied, voice softening, "but there's something about her. It ain't just about what she looks like. We've had real talks. Like, deeper than just surface level stuff, you feel me? And I can see myself with her. I ain't trying to mess it up."

T-money paused, then let out a long breath. He could tell Mitch was already too far gone, but he wasn't gonna let his boy make the same mistakes he'd seen too many others make. "Aight, but you gotta be smart, Mitch. Keep her out of your business. You can't be out here trying to save her or mix her in with your world. You get too close to her, and that could come back to bite you. The game's cold, bro, and you know that. So take your time, feel it out. Don't rush in like you ain't got a clue." "Everybody ain't always who they claim to be.

Mitch leaned forward, rubbing his eyes, already feeling the tension building. "I ain't rushing," he replied, but even to his own ears, he sounded like he was lying. "But I need to see her again. I need to know if this real. Ain't no turning back once I step in, man. You know that."

"Then take it slow. You know what's at stake. Angel ain't from where we come from. She don't know how the streets play. And you gotta ask yourself if she's really gonna be able to handle it if you let her all the way in."

The words lingered in the air between them, and Mitch knew T-money was right. He just didn't know how much longer he could fight what he felt for Angel.

Hours later, as the city settled into its familiar hum of nighttime chaos, Mitch found himself at a crossroads. His thoughts were tangled, but his gut told him he couldn't just let it go. He needed to see her again. And that was all he could think about.

With the streetlights flickering in the distance, he fired off a text to Angel, something simple, but enough to get the ball rolling. "Hey, Angel. Missed talking to you. You free tonight?"

A few minutes passed, and then his phone buzzed. "I'm always free for you, Mitch."

A smile tugged at Mitch's lips, but he forced it down, focusing on the drive ahead. He pulled up to her building just as the sky was turning that deep shade of navy, a perfect backdrop for the tension that had been building between them. When Angel stepped out, her smile hit him like a punch to the gut. He was done for. There was no way he was walking away from this.

"Hey," Mitch said, his voice low as she slid into the passenger seat. "You look good."

Angel smiled, her eyes lighting up. "Thanks, Mitch. You look pretty good yourself."

They didn't waste time on small talk. The moment they were together, there was this unspoken pull, a gravity that kept them locked in each other's orbit. He drove them out to the park, the one spot where the turmoil of the city felt far away.

The breeze through the trees, the soft rustle of the leaves—everything felt like it could be different. Like maybe this could actually work.

They walked down the winding path, quiet at first, just being there with each other. The noise of the city seemed to fade, leaving only the sound of their steps crunching on the dirt.

They kept walking, the silence sitting easy between them. Then, just like that, the words started spilling out. They talked about the type of music they liked, about how they were raised, about people they used to know and the ones they wished they could forget.

Mitch watched her as she spoke, the way she came alive when she talked about her plans. "I been thinking about more than just the salon," she admitted. "I wanna own shit—rental properties, maybe a little boutique. Something that's mine, you know? Ain't tryna work my whole life just to get by." Mitch nodded, impressed. "That's real. Ain't too many people think past what's right in front of 'em."

She looked at him then, eyes searching. "What about you? You ever think 'bout what's next?" He hesitated. "I mean… sometimes. Ain't like I don't want more. Just don't know what that even look like for me."

Angel didn't press him, just gave a small nod like she understood. And maybe she did. They found a bench, sat down as the air cooled around them. It was quiet, but not in a bad way. Mitch wasn't used to this—sittin' still, talkin' about shit that actually mattered. But with Angel, it didn't feel forced. For once, it didn't feel like he had to have all the answers.

For the first time in a long time, he felt like maybe he wasn't as alone in this world as he'd always believed.

As the night stretched on, Mitch and Angel finally walked back to the car. The drive back to her building was quiet, but it wasn't awkward. There was something comfortable about it, something familiar. When Mitch stopped the car in front of her building, he didn't want to let her go. But he knew better than to rush this.

"Thanks for tonight," Angel said softly, her voice low but sincere. "I needed this."

Mitch gave her a long look, his eyes heavy with emotion. "No, thank you. For making me feel like there's something worth fighting for."

With a soft smile, Angel stepped out of the car, the night air cool against her skin. She paused, glancing back at Mitch. "I'll see you soon, okay?"

Mitch nodded, watching her disappear into the building, his mind racing. For the first time in a long time, he felt like he might have found something real. Something worth holding on to. But T-money's warning echoed in his mind: don't rush. Keep her out of your business.

He knew he couldn't let her get too close — not yet. But damn, it was hard not to want her.

- Chapter Six -

"Big Boss Energy"

After chillin' all day with Angel, Mitch slid back to his crib—his lil' slice of high-rise heaven that looked like money walked in and never left.

Soon as he stepped in, the floors was gleamin' like they just got kissed by a maid with OCD. Everything open, modern, and smooth—furniture lookin' like it cost somebody's whole rent, but still laid-back enough to kick your feet up.

Dark wood under his feet, neutral colors on the walls—cool tones that made the place feel expensive but not loud.

Floor-to-ceiling windows showed off the city like a flex, lights from downtown bouncin' off the glass. And the soft lighting? Made the whole place feel like a late-night vibe—grown, sexy, and real bossed up. Mitch didn't just live here—he *arrived* here.

Mitch's spot wasn't just luxury—it was curated. Every piece of art, every sculpture in its place, like it belonged there. He didn't decorate for flexin', it was all about feelin' right when he walked in.

That black leather sectional? Centerpiece. Facin' a top-tier entertainment setup that could turn movie night into somethin' cinematic.

Fireplace glowin' soft in the background, givin' the space just enough warmth to balance all that clean chrome and glass.

Them tall glass doors led straight to his sanctuary outside—patio laid out smooth. Couch posted up for the best view of the backyard. Fireplace built into the stone wall, flat screen hangin' right above it. Spot was made for kickbacks or solo chillin'.

He sank into them cushions, poured up a shot of some top-shelf brown that hit smooth. Took a slow sip while starin' out at the backyard, the city lights twinklin' in the distance like Chi-Town itself was smilin' at him.

Then his phone lit up—T-Money.

T-Money: "Aye, big dawg! We out here posted at Vibe Lounge. It's lit, bottles poppin', music hittin'. You comin' or what?"

Mitch: "Man, I just touched down at the crib. Had a long day runnin' around, coolin' with shorty."

T-Money: "Oh, you was wit' Angel, huh? Aight, I see you, Mr. Loverboy. But tonight? It's up. We celebratin' the bag comin' in, and the whole crew slidin'."

Mitch: "Say less. Gimme like 30. I'ma throw somethin' on and slide through. Don't let nobody touch my section, ain't tryna fight no randoms for my spot." you feel me?

T-Money: "You already know what it is. "Money Mitch! Your seat already waitin'. Bring that same boss energy."

Mitch: "Bet. Keep my glass ready."

He knocked back the rest of his drink, that burn sittin' on his tongue like old regrets he still wrestlin' with. Angel stayed floatin' in his head—soft laugh, deep eyes, like she already knew the parts of him he ain't even shown yet. But this wasn't the night for gettin' lost in feelings. It was time to show face, handle business, flex a little.

He slid into his bedroom, opened up the closet like it was a vault. Picked out that midnight black tailored suit—the kind that hugged his frame like it was built for him and only him. Crisp white shirt, silk tie smooth as his talk. Every detail was intentional—cufflinks that whispered power, leather shoes that hit the floor like he meant every step.

Sprayed that cologne she liked—that deep, dark scent that made women stare and men step back. Buttoned up his jacket, checked himself in the mirror. Stared at a man who ain't just survive the game—he mastered it. Smooth. Solid. Scarred. Still standin'.

Out front, his all-black Bugatti Chiron waited, lookin' like a predator in the night. Doors lifted up like wings, inviting him back to the throne. Engine roared alive—deep, confident, unbothered. That sound didn't just turn heads—it *announced him.*

Streets turned into streaks, city glow flashin' past his windows like he was skatin' through a dream. He knew this rhythm. The pace. The pulse. The way the city moved at night, how it responded when real ones stepped out.

Pulled up to the club, slow and deliberate. Parked that Bugatti like he was leavin' art on the curb. Heads turned. Cameras flashed. Nobody said a word—they just *knew.*

Mitch stepped in low-key—no cap, chest tight like he walked through a spotlight he never asked for. The security doorman clocked him, gave a quick nod, and swiped him past—no line, no lame small talk. Real recognizes real.

He drifted into the club's heartbeat, bass rattling his ribs. Heads turned—some nods of respect, some side-eyes of envy. Sweat beaded at his hairline. Even he felt that pull, like the room was a magnet he couldn't switch off.

He half-smiled at the whispers—"That's him," "He runs this"—but inside, his stomach flipped. The streets never really let you go; they bounce back when you least expect it.

He cut through the sweat and smoke—shots of 1800 Silver tequila in a bartender's hand, the DJ mixing like the world depended on it, laughter bouncing off the walls. His palms itched at his sides—old habits dying hard.

When he reached the VIP rope—that velvet line and dim glow—his crew closed ranks around him, eyes sharp for any trouble. The energy jumped, and his breath caught for a second.

Mitch rubbed his wrist, reminding himself he wasn't untouchable. Just a man in a crowded room, chasing a high he knew could drop him at any second. But tonight? Tonight he'd lean into the chaos and hope it didn't swallow him whole.

Bottles already lined the tables—Ace, 1942, Louis XIII, Hennessy Paradis, a lot of rare shit folks took pictures of but never sipped. Cigars lit, thick clouds curling up like secrets. Perfume lingered off bad ones posted nearby, drawn in by money, power, and the kind of silence only killers carried.

T-Money leaned back, his chains catching the light, one arm slung across the velvet booth like he'd been born there. He took a slow pull from his glass, eyes scanning the scene with that crooked grin he always wore when he felt untouchable. "You see this, Mitch?" he said over the bass. "This us, bro. Whole damn city playin' catch-up while we chillin' in the penthouse."

Mitch ain't smile, but his stare said everything. Hazel-brown eyes, cold and calm, like he'd already mapped every exit. Dude was a storm behind them eyes—quiet, but you knew somethin' always brewin'. He held his glass like it owed him rent. "T, we came up from hand-me-down heat and dollar burgers. Now look at us. Whole scene watchin' like we the damn blueprint."

Big D chuckled, wide as a bear, blunt sittin' crooked between thick fingers. "Ain't nobody out here got our reach," he said, voice deep and scratchy from years of smoke and drama. "We got the bag, the firepower, and the respect. Anybody step wrong, they end up on a shirt or a story."

He hit the table with a flat palm, makin' the glasses jump like a warning shot. Heads turned. Not long, just enough to know they heard it. Respect came with noise.

Rest of the crew held their corners tight—jewelry swingin', eyes movin'. Ain't nobody slippin', not even on a night like this. Every toast came with a look over the shoulder. That's how it was. Party never meant peace.

Mitch leaned forward, elbows on knees, glass resting light between two fingers. "People love the crown 'til they feel the weight," he muttered, eyes locked on the dance floor. "You blink, and somebody already plottin'. Ain't no comfort in this seat. Just pressure."

T-Money smirked, swirlin' liquor like it was water. "You stay paranoid, fam," he said, laughing. "We ten toes down, every move calculated. Ain't no ghosts in this room."

Mitch gave him that look—half warning, half love. "I ain't scared of ghosts," he said low. "I'm watchin' the ones still breathin'. Them the ones who smile while loadin' clips."

That quiet came again—not awkward, just real. Like everybody remembered what it took to get here. Bottles poured, the music pounded, women kept slidin' in closer, drawin' near like moths to flame. But underneath it all, the weight stayed heavy.

T raised his glass again, eyes gleaming under the lights. "To the grind," he said. "To the ones that didn't make it, and the ones we still gonna bury."

They clinked glasses, the sound sharp over the music. They laughed, but not too loud. Celebratin' was allowed. Slippin'? Never.

It wasn't just a party. It was a pause between storms.

The night progressed with rounds of toasts and laughter. The crew recounted stories about street dealings, encounters, and close calls, instilling loyalty and brotherhood.

The club was mesmerizing, drawing Mitch into the rhythm of the night. The occasional flirtatious glances from the crowd heightened the exhilaration, turning their area into a nexus of excitement.

As the night went on, the music cranked up, and the crowd's energy kept building. The crew moved through the spot, all smooth and confident like they belonged in the center of it.

Mitch leaned back, taking it all in with a small grin on his face. His suit caught the light, clean as hell, standing out without trying. He didn't need to say a word. The way he carried himself? That spoke louder than anything.

The lights flashed, the whole place packed with life. The crew was surrounded now, all types of people drawn to their vibe.

T-Money was in his element, talking up the crowd and cutting through the music. Their section was poppin', groupies and hoes all around, trying to get their attention.

T-Money flashed a cocky grin as a couple of women walked over. "Look at this," he said, sizing up the scene.

The women giggled, throwing themselves at T-Money, eyes fucking devouring him, unable to hide how badly they wanted him. "Couldn't help ourselves," one purred, voice low and smooth, stepping real close. "Y'all are just too fucking fine to resist."

T-Money leaned back, smirking, all confident as fuck. "I feel that, gorgeous. We do have a way of turning heads."

T-Money felt a surge of heat as her stiletto heel tapped playfully against his chair. His eyes followed the line of the impossibly long leg, leading up to the hem of a dress that barely qualified as one. The absence of panties was a bold statement, and he couldn't help but appreciate the view.

"Hey, T-Money," she said softly and seductively. "Feeling a little frisky tonight? Maybe a glimpse at what's underneath this dress is just what the doctor ordered."

He leaned back in his seat, a sneer on his lips."I'm always up for a good time, especially when it's served up so... deliciously." His eyes darted across her, lingering on the bare flash of thigh."And you, my dear, are looking absolutely delectable."

Her heel crept up higher, giving him a clear glimpse of her pussy. "I'm the queen of temptation, T. This is just the appetizer. The main course? That shit will blow your fucking mind. I'll ride you so good, you'll be begging for more."

His heart pounded like a motherfucker. "I believe you, ma. I can already feel it." She leaned closer, her breath ghosting across his ear. "Then why don't you come find out?"

The room felt heavy, heat rising between them like a loaded gun. T-Money's heart raced, every nerve on edge. He leaned in, voice low and rough: "I'll hit you when it's time to dip." With a crooked grin, he added, "Trust me, this night's gon' stick with you."

Meanwhile, Mitch observed the scene with a hint of amusement, his eyes flickering over the interactions with a sense of detachment. He knew the power they held in their hands, the ability to command the attention of anyone in the room with a single glance. And as the night stretched on, he couldn't help but feel a sense of satisfaction at the sight of his crew basking in their celebrity status.

Feeling Mitch was holding back, T-money jokingly urged him to get in on the fun.

"Say, my guy, you better grab you one of these hoes; they're ready, Mitch," T-money grinned.

Mitch, however, shook his head, declining the invitation. "I'm good for the night, T. You be safe, though," he replied.

Mitch's lips curled into a sardonic smirk, watching T-Money stroll over to the group of women at the bar fluttering their eyelids. There was a time, back in the day, when he might have joined his friend. But the thrill of short-lived connections had long since faded, replaced by a weariness that mirrored the expensive liquor burning in his glass.

He took a slow sip, the burn of the liquor feeling more like a responsibility than a pleasure. "You gettin' old on us, Mitch?" Big D chuckled from beside him, his voice gravelly with amusement.

Mitch snorted. "Nah, Just got other things on my mind tonight. Besides," he leaned closer, his voice dropping to a conspiratorial whisper, "those ladies wouldn't hold a candle to the one I already got waiting."

T- Money's eyes widened in mock surprise. "Mitch, come on. You haven't slipped a wedding ring on it yet, have you?"

Mitch laughed, a rare sound that boomed across the club. "Nothin' like that, T. But trust me, she keeps me on my toes more than any woman at this bar ever could."

T-Money, all chrome grills and a booming laugh, raised an eyebrow. "You sure, man? You haven't gotten yourself out in, like forever."

Mitch smirked faintly. 'Maybe forever is exactly what I'm looking for. Besides, I gotta be sharp for that big client meeting tomorrow."

T-Money snorted. "Right, right. Mr. Serious Businessman. But hey", all work and no play..." He trailed off, the implication clear.

Mitch smiled faintly. "Maybe next time, okay? You know where to find me if you get lonely."

T-Money chuckled. "Yeah, yeah, buried under a mountain of paperwork. You take care, Mitch. Don't let those spreadsheets work you to death."

Mitch flagged down the bartender after finishing his own drink, which was a simple sparkling water with a lime wedge, while T-Money vanished back into the crowd. "Please just give me the check," he said. Outside, the city air was a welcome change from the club's stifling atmosphere. Mitch slid behind the wheel of his car, phone clutched in his hand. He wasn't looking for a ride-share or a date – his mind was set on something far more satisfying. He tapped open the app for his restaurant's new inventory management system, eager to see if the kinks had been ironed out. As he pulled away from the club, the city lights blurred into a comforting stream.

The aftermath of the party from earlier that night stayed with Mitch when he arrived home.With difficulty, he eventually unlocked his lavish bachelor home by fumbling with his keys—the cool metal a sharp contrast to the evening's warmth.

The air had a faint aftertaste of alcohol mingled with the scent of designer cologne. Mitch staggered a little as he made his way down the darkened hallway toward his bedroom.

As he entered the room, the mellow glow of the city lights streamed through the glass windows, creating a subtle mood over the modern furnishings.

The bed, covered with high-thread-count sheets, invited Mitch to surrender to its embrace.

With a weary sigh, he kicked off his shoes and collapsed onto the plush mattress.

The silence within the room created a serene retreat for Mitch to unwind, a welcome escape from the earlier chaos of the club. In the stillness, Mitch's mind began to drift, replaying the events of the night like a vivid dream.

The laughter, the music, and the vibrant scenes of the club gradually morphed into hazy memories as exhaustion claimed him.

The night, which had been full of temptation, gave way to the comfort of sleep. The world outside his windows continued its muffled symphony as Mitch gave in to the embrace of well-deserved rest.

Chapter Seven

"Grind & Dine: A Hustler's Kitchen"

Sunlight crept through Mitch's window like an uninvited guest, smacking him awake with a mean-ass headache. The night before had been one for the books—money flowing, bottles popping, women everywhere, and the city bowing at his feet. But all that came with a price, and this morning, that price felt like a pounding drum inside his skull.

He exhaled hard, rubbing his temples before dragging himself outta bed. Ain't no room for weakness in his world. Hangover or not, business don't stop.

First order of business? The cure. He made his way to the kitchen, body moving on autopilot. A steaming bowl of pho—his go-to fix when the Henny had him hurting—brought him back to life. A couple Excedrin on the side, a long sip of ice-cold water, and after ten minutes, he was feeling like himself again.

By the time he slid into his crisp, tailored suit, you'd never guess he spent the night celebrating like a king. The city was already in motion, the streets pulsing with that morning grind. Mitch maneuvered through traffic, watching the suits rush to their nine-to-fives, trapped in a cycle that would never touch the money he made in a night. They could keep that life.

But before he could hit *The Gold Room*, he had a sit-down on the other side of the Strip. Vegas money don't sleep, and this meeting had *big bag* energy.

He pulled up to a high-end hotel, real low-key and quiet. Upstairs in one of the private business suites, **Devon Triggs** was already waiting. Self-made. Self-taught. Self-paid.

When Mitch stepped in, Devon stood up looking just as sharp—tailored black-on-black suit, gold watch peeking from his cuff, and a diamond-studded pinky ring that said he wasn't new to this. But even with the polish, his eyes still held that hood fire—raw, alert, and unfiltered.

"Damn, fam," Devon grinned, dap already locked in. "You movin' like you still on last night's wave."

Mitch smirked. "Maybe I am."

They dapped up like brothers, real respect in the grip.

"I see you suited up today," Mitch said, eyeing his fit.

Devon chuckled. "Man, I had to put this tight-ass suit on so your rich friends ain't clutchin' they wallets soon as I walk in. But don't let the fresh cut and cologne fool you—I'll still body slam somebody in church shoes if my money look funny."

Mitch laughed. "Bruh, I know who I'm dealin' with. We come from the same struggle—same blocks, same hustle, same hunger. Ain't nothin' changed but the commas. Now let's get to it."

Devon pulled out his laptop and tapped a few keys. "First off, that inventory app you tested last night? It's solid now. That syncing issue? Fixed. Walk-in freezer readings, supplier receipts, product scans—all talking in real time."

Mitch pulled out his phone and tapped the screen, watching live updates scroll across. "Good. That glitch almost had Miguel ready to walk out."

"I know," Devon said, scrolling through logs. "That tomahawk ribeye order was misreading because the barcode was scanned with an old version of the supplier API. I rewrote that whole segment."

Mitch nodded. "You a beast."

Devon flashed a grin. "Always. But check this out—let's talk *real money*."

He flipped his screen to a dashboard showing analytics for *The Gold Room* app.

"I added VIP table bidding. High rollers can now fight for those prime booths like it's eBay. You let them bid when a reservation cancels—whoever pays more, gets the spot. That's new money for seats you were already givin' away."

"How much we talkin'?"

"Easy thirty stacks a month—*and that's lowballing.*"

Mitch's eyes narrowed, calculating.

"Wait—it gets better," Devon continued. "Chef cam. Real-time, in-kitchen feed. Guests get to see Miguel flaming the grill, Sofia slicing the sashimi—whole nine. It's exclusive content only app users can watch. You're not just feeding them food—you're feeding them *experience*."

"Chef cam, huh?"

Devon nodded. "Uncut. Authentic. Hell, Miguel's yelling gonna turn into a meme. Let that man go viral."

Mitch laughed. "You sick."

"And this feature here?" Devon tapped. "AI suggestions. The app tracks top-selling meals, peak hours, and even recommends wine pairings based on what's ordered. Imagine it knowing a customer's taste better than the server."

Mitch leaned back in his chair, impressed. "You built all this in, what, two weeks?"

"Man, I was broke five years ago, living off gas station sandwiches and coding on a busted iPhone. Now? I make more money on app licenses than some of these casinos do in a week. But this project? This one's personal. We build this right, your restaurant don't just serve food—it sets trends."

They shared a look. A real one. Two different streets, same grind.

"I want a beta ready in seven days," Mitch said. "Start with my Vegas crew only."

"Say less."

They dapped again. Mitch turned to leave, already imagining the empire he was about to scale with Devon in his corner.

By the time he hit the elevator, his mind was racing. Conversations like that always lit a fire under him.

Minutes later, the valet pulled up with his ride—gleaming under the Vegas sun, sleek and spotless. Mitch slid behind the wheel like he was slipping into power.

The city moved around him in a blur of color and motion. Billboards flashed, traffic pulsed, and people filled the sidewalks.

His car glided through it all, smooth and certain, until he pulled up to The Gold Room—his pride, the proof of everything he'd built. The place everyone knew.

Mitch stepped out, the warm Vegas air wrapping around him. He pushed through the heavy doors and walked inside, every step steady and deliberate. He wasn't just the owner—he was the heart of this place.

In the kitchen, he moved like a general on the battlefield, eyes sharp, peeping everything. New hires needed to be on point. Ain't no half-stepping in his house.

"Yo, Marco!" His voice cut through the kitchen noise like a blade. The young line cook, barely out of culinary school, damn near jumped, knife slipping dangerously close to his fingers.

"M-Mr. Thompson! Everything good?"

Mitch chuckled, low and steady. "Relax, youngin'. Just checkin' in. How's your first day on the hot line?"

Marco squared his shoulders, tryna play it cool. "Hot, sir! But I'm keeping up. Chef Miguel's been showing me the ropes."

Miguel—big dude, rough around the edges but loyal to the game—grunted in approval. He ain't play about quality, but if you was willing to learn, he'd school you right.

"Good," Mitch nodded. "Speed is key, but don't rush and mess up the sauce. Take your time, get it right. And if that Chilean sea bass don't show up soon… well, we gon' get real creative."

Marco swallowed, but there was determination in his eyes now. "Got it, boss."

Out on the floor, Sofia moved between tables, guiding customers through the menu with that effortless charm. A couple months ago, she was shaky, overwhelmed by the non-stop hustle. Now? Girl had rhythm, confidence.

She glided up to a table where a businessman was buried in paperwork. "Would you like to check out our drink menu this evening?" Her voice had that perfect balance—smooth but professional.

The businessman barely reacted, but the woman across from him smiled. "We'll take a bottle of your Malbec, please."

Sofia nodded, all grace. "Great choice. Pairs beautifully with our grilled selections." She scribbled the order down, smooth and practiced.

As she turned to leave, the businessman finally looked up—just a second too long. Sofia's neck flushed, but she kept it pushing. Mitch caught the whole thing, smirking to himself. His spot wasn't just serving up good eats—it was sparking a lil' something extra, too.

He made a mental note to pull Sofia aside later, tell her she was holding her own. Confidence like that? Priceless in this game.

Then his stomach knotted. The walk-in freezer loomed in the back like a bad omen. That missing sea bass? A whole problem.

The seasonal menu was built around it, and without it, they'd be scrambling.

Mitch locked eyes with Miguel, who was plating a dish with that signature focus. "Any word on the delivery?"

Miguel exhaled hard. "Nah, boss. Customs got it held up. Might be a while."

Mitch tapped the counter, brain moving fast. Ain't no way in hell he was about to tell customers, my bad, we fresh out. That wasn't how he moved.

"Aight, here's the play." He leaned in, voice low but sure. "We switch it up. That fresh red snapper we got in? Let's make it sing. Pan-seared, citrus glaze. We got them blood oranges, right?"

Miguel's brows lifted. "Red snapper, huh? Yeah… yeah, I can work with that." A slow grin spread across his face. "I'll throw in some fresh herbs, really make it pop."

The kitchen snapped to attention. Tension flipped from stress to focus. Sofia, still riding that earlier confidence boost, worked the floor like a pro. Marco, who had been fumbling before, now moved with purpose, his knife work sharp, steady.

That missing sea bass might've tripped them up, but it was bringing out something better—real teamwork, real hustle.

Orders rolled in. Pans hissed. The dining room buzzed. And Mitch? He stood in the center of it all, watching his people turn a crisis into a masterpiece.

The Marmalade Snapper—Miguel's last-minute remix—turned out to be a hit. Customers ate it up, raving about the flavors. Sofia was getting props left and right for her service. Even Marco, who started the shift shaky, found his groove.

By closing time, exhaustion hung heavy, but so did victory. Mitch wiped his brow, leaned against the counter, and let out a long breath.

"That was…" he started.

Miguel, rare smirk on his face, finished for him. "A wild ride."

Mitch chuckled. "A good one, though. That snapper? Straight magic."

Miguel shrugged, but his eyes gleamed. "A lil' improvisation, boss. We make it work."

As they locked up for the night, the restaurant sat quiet, but the energy lingered—the scents, the voices, the laughter.

Mitch took it all in. It wasn't just about food. It was about the people. The ones who showed up, put in the work, and turned a damn-near disaster into a win.

This wasn't just business.

This was family.

Chapter Eight

"Netflix & Chill: When the Grind Stops for a Minute"

Angel was done with the non-stop grind of Vegas. She needed a day to just vibe, forget the hustle, and focus on something that brought her peace—her photography. Her camera wasn't just a tool; it was a way to escape the chaos and see the world for what it really was. She walked through the city, the flashing lights of the Strip pulling her in, a stark contrast to the darkness she knew too well. The streets were packed with tourists and locals, each passing face and fleeting moment the perfect shot for her lens.

She zoomed in on the little things most folks missed—the small moments, the things that made the city tick. You had the hum of the crowds, the blare of traffic, the random bursts of laughter in the distance. Every click of her camera was like a silent acknowledgment of the beauty hidden in the madness. Vegas was a place of indulgence, where luxury rubbed shoulders with struggle. Bright neon lights blasted off massive casinos while folks stumbled through dark alleys, just trying to get by.

But Angel wasn't just about the flash. She knew how to stay cool when everything around her was fallin' apart.

As the sun beat down on the Strip, she noticed the hidden cracks in the pavement—discarded poker chips, old flyers, little signs of life that never left Vegas, even when the party was over. The desert sun made the city shine, but the cracks and shadows reminded her that nothing here came without a cost.

She stepped off the main drag and wandered into the quieter spots of town, places where the art on the walls told stories of survival. Every mural, every spray-painted word was like a message from the streets. Angel didn't just snap pictures; she captured the essence of the city—the resilience, the struggle, and the spirit that refused to fade.

As the sun started to dip, the whole city lit up in that golden hour glow, and Angel knew it was time to get that perfect sunset shot. The colors shifted in the sky, turning Vegas from a chaotic, restless beast into something calm and breathtaking. She wandered into the backstreets, away from the blinding lights, and found herself surrounded by crumbling buildings covered in street art. Those spots spoke volumes—about hope, about pain, about everything in between.

She caught a few portraits of the people she met along the way— folks whose faces told stories of their own. The lines in their skin, the tired eyes, the quiet strength—they didn't need words for you to know they'd been through it. Angel's lens didn't just capture images; it told stories, stripped of judgment, showing the humanity beneath the surface.

As the day slipped away, Angel found herself on a different kind of journey—one where her camera became a bridge, a way to reconnect with the side of the city she still loved, even in all its mess. It was a moment of peace before she had to dive back into the grind.

Finally, she stepped into a local coffee shop to chill. The strong scent of freshly brewed coffee hit her, and for a moment, everything felt still. She ordered a white chocolate mocha, the sweet flavor soothing her from the inside out. Sitting in a cozy corner with her camera still full of the day's shots, Angel took a slow sip, letting the warmth fill her up.

Her phone sat quietly on the table, buzzing every now and then. No calls, no texts, just silence. But she was patient—let him come to her when he was ready. The world outside was alive with the usual Vegas chaos, but in this corner of the shop, everything felt calm. Angel couldn't help but think about Mitch, though. He hadn't called, and she couldn't shake the feeling. It was like that quiet hum of anticipation, waiting for something to break the stillness. She stared at her phone, tapping it idly, wondering if tonight would be the night they reconnected.

Then, the phone rang. A blocked number flashed across the screen. Her heart jumped, and she picked up quickly. "Hey, Mitch!" she greeted, her voice warm and full of energy. She couldn't hide the excitement in her voice, laughing out loud as she spoke. The coffee shop around her quieted as people glanced over, but she didn't care.

Mitch: Yo, what's good, Angel? How you been?

Angel: I been good, you know, just handling my business. What about you?

Mitch: Same ol', same ol', just keeping it moving. But I been thinking about you.

Angel: Oh really? You been thinking about me, huh? Well, what took you so long to hit me up?

Mitch: My bad, Angel. Things got crazy, but I missed hearing your voice.

Angel: Aww, you missed me? That's cute, Mitch. What's up though?

Mitch: Ain't much. I was thinking we should link up tonight, chill for a bit. Netflix and chill?

Angel: (laughs) Netflix and chill, huh? That sounds like a plan. What you wanna watch?

Mitch: Whatever you feeling. I'm down for whatever.

Angel: I'm in the mood for a good action flick, or maybe a crime series. You down for that?

Mitch: Hell yeah. Crime series it is. Oh, and can you cook? Cause I was hoping for something homemade, too.

Angel: (smirking) Cook? Mitch, please, I'm a chef in disguise. What you want me to whip up?

Mitch: Surprise me. I'm sure whatever you make will be fire.

Angel: (laughing) You're laying it on thick, huh? But it's a deal. I got you.

Mitch: I'm looking forward to it. What time should I roll through?

Angel: Let's say around 8. Gives me enough time to get things ready. Sound good?

Mitch: Bet. I'll see you at 8.

Angel: Aight, cool. See you tonight.

Angel hung up, smiling wide. She couldn't help but laugh. Mitch had basically read her mind—she was gonna ask him over for Netflix and chill, too. What a coincidence. She started planning the night, her excitement bubbling up.

At 8 PM, Mitch knocked on her door, looking all cool rockin' a hoodie and some chill jeans—nothin' extra, just that laid-back fly he always kept. When Angel cracked the door, smilin' like she already knew he'd show, that home-cooked aroma smacked him in the face. His eyes lit up like a kid at the corner store. "Damn, this place smells good," he said, stepping in.

Mitch slid his shoes off at the door, peepin' the vibe—low lights, incense burnin', somethin' slow hummin' from her speaker, and that warm scent hittin' like vanilla and cocoa butter with a twist of somethin' grown. First time she let him through the door, and he knew that meant somethin'. Angel ain't the type to play house with just anybody.

Angel led him to the couch where a comedy show was playing on the big screen, setting the tone for a chill evening. "Yo, I like how you decorated this place," Mitch said, impressed. "It's got that warm, comfy vibe."

Angel smiled, pleased with his compliment. "Can I get you anything?" she asked. "Drink? On the house tonight."

She slid out the kitchen like it wasn't nothin', but that jumpsuit still sittin' right, holdin' every curve like it was custom. She ditched the heels, rockin' socks now, all cozy—still bad as hell. Mitch ain't even try to play it cool, eyes glued to that ass like it was talkin' to him. Hair still laid, face soft but beat just enough—like she wiped the day off but kept the attitude.

They curled up on the couch, plates in hand, movie playin', but they was locked in their own episode—laughin' loud, talkin' mess, throwin' jabs and low-key flirtin' like it was second nature—like they wasn't strangers, just two souls who already knew what came next.

He glanced over, catchin' her smirk as she twirled her pasta, lettin' that sauce drip. She looked real laid back, legs tucked up, leanin' into him like keepin' space wasn't even on her mind.

"You real cozy, huh?" Mitch said, bumpin' her with his shoulder.

Angel chuckled low, eyes half-closed. "Ain't no crime in finally breathin' easy."

Mitch watched her close. "You always on go, though. Bet sittin' still feel like you missin' somethin'."

She shot him a sideways glance, playful. "Can't be sittin' too long— life be waitin' to trip you up soon as you blink."

He nodded slow, eyes locked on her. "Yeah… life cold like that. Don't hit pause for nobody."

Angel wiped a lil sauce off her thumb with her tongue, then looked up at him. "That's why I grab moments like this, hold on tight. Like for real."

Silence settled in, heavy but warm. Mitch leaned in just a touch, voice dropped low. "I feel you on that."

Angel gave him a slow smile, head tilted. "Better be careful. Feel too much, you might not wanna bounce."

Mitch let a smirk spread. "Who said I'm tryna bounce?"

Her gaze stayed on his, voice soft but dead serious. "Then don't come at me halfway. I don't got time for games."

His voice dropped to a murmur. "Ain't no game here."

She leaned in, lips brushing his ear. "We gon' find out."

They spent the rest of the night laid up on the couch, talkin' mess, laughin' low, bodies inchin' closer with each story. Angel had her legs draped over Mitch's lap, one hand holdin' her wine glass, the other absently playin' with the gold chain around his neck.

"I ain't gon' lie," Mitch said, eyes locked on hers, "you feel like somethin' I ain't even know I needed."

Angel raised a brow, smirkin'. "Boy, don't gas me up if you ain't built to ride."

He chuckled, brushing his fingers along her thigh. "I'm just speakin' facts."

There was a pause—one of them heavy ones—where the room got real still, and all that tension that been floatin' between them finally landed.

Angel set her glass down, slid off the couch slow, like she was testin' him. "Come on," she said, voice low. "This way."

Mitch followed, heat sittin' in his chest, nerves mixin' with want. When they stepped into her room, the lights was low, candles flickerin' on the dresser like the whole night had been waitin' on 'em to show up.

Mitch closed the door behind him, eyes never leavin' her. His voice dropped, low and raw. "I ain't come here to play, Angel. You the only one ever had me pullin' up like this."

He stepped in, slow but sure, pullin' her close like the space between them had been lyin' all along. "So now that I'm here… show me what all that wait was for."

She tilted her head, eyes searchin' his. "Aight then… but if you fumble this? Don't act like I ain't give you the play."

Mitch smirked, slid a hand to the small of her back, pullin' her in close. "I don't drop nothin' I really want."

His eyes moved over her slow, voice low and rough. "You bad as hell, Angel… got me out here actin' like I forgot who I was before I stepped in this room."

Angel's lips curled into a slow grin as she traced his jaw with her thumb. "Mmm… you talkin' real bold," she said, voice like a tease. "Hope you move the same way you speak."

Mitch stepped in close, hands grippin' her waist hard, like he was tryna remind her who she belonged to—no words, just pressure and heat, like that grip said everything he didn't. His fade was fresh, lines sharp as hell, beard tight—man looked like he just stepped out the chair ready to snatch souls. His presence alone screamed alpha.

He smirked, voice low and heavy. "Ain't no time for games, ma. Let's get this shit movin'. And don't act brand new when you see what I'm packin'. My dick ain't small."

Angel raised a brow, lips twisting into a slick smirk. "Mm, we gon' see. But don't say I ain't warn you when I flip the script on yo' ass."

Mitch didn't waste no more time. He grabbed her jaw, pulled her in, and kissed her like he was claiming territory. Tongue deep, rough, not askin'—takin'. She gave it right back—nails in his neck, breath hot, kiss messy and full of heat.

"I don't do that weak shit," Mitch muttered against her lips. "I break backs and leave 'em thinkin' 'bout me every time they try to move on."

Angel moaned, grinding into him. "Good. 'Cause I don't want no weak shit. I want that real. That disrespectful dick. The kind that make me question my life choices."

He chuckled, dark and cocky. "You talkin' real reckless. But I'ma fix that mouth of yours—with this dick."

He carried her like she ain't weigh nothin', her legs wrapped tight around his waist, his hands locked under her thighs. They made it to the bedroom, door slammed shut with one heavy stomp. He dropped her on the bed like he couldn't hold back no more—rough, ready, and all in.

"Take that shit off," he ordered, standing over her, pulling his hoodie off slow. Tattoos laced his chest and arms, ink bold against his dark skin. His chain swung as he moved, heavy and real—just like him.

Angel peeled off her clothes, eyes glued to him, biting her lip. "Damn, you really built like that…"

Mitch yanked his jeans down, dick springin' free—thick and hard. He caught her eyes widenin' and smirked. "Told you I'm packin'."

Angel licked her lips, legs already trembling. "Bring that dick here, daddy."

He climbed on the bed, grabbed her ankles and spread her legs wide, eyes locked on her dripping pussy. "This mine now. You understand me?"

She nodded, but he gripped her chin, forcing her to look into his intense, dominant eyes. "Say that shit. I want to hear you say it."

"It's yours," she whispered, voice shaky but filled with desire. "All yours, daddy.

And that's when the feasting began. He started at her inner thighs, kissing and sucking, leaving deep, wet marks on her soft skin—like he owned it. He took his time, tasting her slowly, making her squirm and beg. The rough edge of his fresh beard scraped against her sensitive flesh, sending shivers through her with every drag. He bit and sucked, leaving hickies behind—marking her as his.

"Fuck, Mitch," she moaned, trying to grind against his face, but he held her hips down, keeping her still. "I can't take it... please, give me more."

He looked up at her, that wicked glint in his eyes sharp as ever. "Oh, you want more?" he growled, voice thick with control. "Good. 'Cause I ain't even close to done. I want you shaking, begging, and thinking 'bout this every damn time you close your eyes."

And with that, he dove back in, his tongue flat and wide, licking from her ass to her clit in one slow, agonizing stroke. He sucked her clit into his mouth, tongue flicking fast and relentless, while two fingers pumped in and out of her, curling to hit that spot that made her see stars.

Angel cried out, her back arching off the bed. "Shit! Right there, right there! Don't stop, baby, don't you dare stop."

He chuckled against her pussy, the vibration sending shocks through her body. "I got you, ma. I got you. You ain't goin' nowhere."

He added a third finger, stretching her, filling her, and she lost it. Her orgasm hit her like a freight train, her body trembling, her pussy clenching and releasing, gushing all over his hand and face. He sucked it all in, not wasting a drop, a savage look of satisfaction on his face.

"That's one," he said, his voice rough and deep, a commanding tone that made her body tense with anticipation. "But I'm not done with you yet, ma. We just getting started."

And with that promise, he went back in, his tongue and fingers not letting her pussy forget who was in control. He sucked and licked, his beard rubbing against her sensitive flesh, driving her wild. He flipped her over, grabbing her hips and pulling her up on her knees, her ass in the air.

He spat on his hand, stroking his thick dick, coating it with her juices. "You ready for this, ma? You ready for me to tear that pussy up?"

Angel looked back at him, her eyes wild with lust and submission. "Yes, daddy. Give it to me. Show me who's boss."

He didn't ease in—he slammed into her with one brutal thrust, stretchin' her wide, making her scream. "Good girl. Now take this dick."

He fucked her with power, hips snapping, his grip tight on her thighs. She clawed at the sheets, back arched, breath ragged. Mitch leaned in, teeth on her neck, biting and sucking until he left marks. His other hand slid to her throat, applying just enough pressure to make her gasp.

"You feel that? That's what real dick do," he growled, fucking her deeper with every stroke.

Angel was a mess beneath him—moaning, crying out, body jerking with every thrust. "Harder, baby. Choke me. Make me yours."

He flipped her over sudden as fuck, pulled her hips up and drilled into that pussy like a man possessed. His hand got all tangled in her hair, yanking her head back while he fucked her like there was no tomorrow, like the world was fucking ending and this was their last ride.

"You gon' be thinkin' bout me walkin' funny for days," he said through gritted teeth. "Ain't no other nigga gonna touch this pussy again."

She was screaming his name, her body bouncing with every thrust. Mitch reached around, rubbed her clit in rough circles while still hittin' it deep. She came hard, legs shakin', pussy clutchin' him tight.

But he wasn't done.

"You not tappin' out yet, are you?" he teased, smacking her ass. "We just gettin' started."

With one last deep, guttural growl, Mitch slammed into her, hips jackhammering like he was tryin' to claim her soul. He was in beast mode — no finesse, just straight savage. His balls smacked her clit with every stroke, the sound of skin on skin echoing off the walls like a war drum.

"Damn, Mitch!" she cried out, her whole body locking up, her walls grippin' him tight like she didn't wanna let go. "You feel so damn good. Too good…"

He let out a low grunt, jaw clenched tight, pullin' out just in time, chest rumblin' as he busted. He was on top, diggin' in deep, and she was takin' all of it—legs locked around him like she needed him deeper. His dick twitched, shootin' all over her stomach—hot, messy, claimin' her like she was his.

"Shit," he breathed, crashin' down on her, both of them sweaty and wrecked. "That was wild as hell. I ain't even done. You mine now, for real."

They laid there catchin' their breath, bodies stickin' from the heat. Mitch turned her face to his, pullin' her into a kiss that was all tongue and teeth, like he ain't care how messy it was. He wanted her to taste the both of them — raw and unfiltered.

He wrapped his arms around her, holdin' her close like she was his peace, like that spot on his chest was made for her.

"Damn," he panted, his voice husky. "You took all that like a real one. I'm proud of you."

She laughed weakly, her head on his chest. "Thank you, daddy… that was wild."

He kissed her forehead, still gripping her like she might disappear. "That was just round one," he muttered, brushing her hair back, breath still heavy. "Hope you ready, 'cause I ain't lettin' up anytime soon."

She bit her lip, half nervous, half excited. "Yes, daddy. Whatever you want."

He rolled her over again, this time pulling her up on all fours, her ass in the air. No hesitation, no mercy—he gripped them hips and went right back to work, proving he meant every word.

The next morning, sunlight filtered through the curtains, and Mitch kissed Angel's forehead as they lay together. Angel got up, showered, and cooked them breakfast, the aroma filling the apartment. They sat down to eat, talking like no time had passed at all.

"So," Angel began, her voice casual, "think you might stick around for a bit?"

Mitch smiled, a little guilty. "I could arrange it. Got a few things to handle, but I'll make it work."

After a few more laughs, Angel asked, "Can I ask you something?"

Mitch raised an eyebrow. "Shoot."

Angel sipped her coffee, watching him scroll through his phone. "Why you always calling from a blocked number?"

Mitch paused, looking at her with a soft expression. "It's not you, Angel. It's just... I deal with some shady folks. Gotta keep it low-key for my safety."

Angel didn't quite buy it, but she respected his honesty. "Alright," she said, "but next time, no blocked numbers."

Mitch nodded. "You got it. No more secrets."

As they shared the moment, Angel felt the crack in their connection begin to close, the trust slowly rebuilding. They didn't have all the answers, but right now, this felt good.

Chapter Nine

"Midnight Hustle: Playing the Game in the Dark"

Mitch slid into his crib, shutting the door behind him with a heavy thud. The weight of his life sat on his chest like a cinder block. He stood there for a second, eyes locked on the same four walls that had seen it all—money stacked high, bodies laid out, women coming and going, and the kind of silence that could only belong to a man with too much on his conscience.

He ran a hand down his face, letting out a slow breath. The game used to be sweet—money fast, respect given, fear automatic. But now? Now it felt like every move came with a shadow trailing behind it, waiting for the right moment to put him six feet under.

He thought about all the deals gone sideways, the bullets that barely missed, the homies he used to roll with now either locked up, dead, or moving different. The thrill had faded. The fast life didn't feel fast anymore—it felt like a damn treadmill, going nowhere, just waiting for him to trip.

He knew better than to get soft, but deep down, something was pulling at him. A different kind of hunger. A way out. But getting out ain't easy—everybody wants in, nobody just walks away. Not alive, anyway.

Later that night, Mitch pulled up to the bar where T-Money was already posted, chain heavy around his neck, a fresh bottle on the table. Mitch slid into the booth, his face set like stone.

T-Money peeped it right away. "Damn, nigga, you look like you seen a ghost."

Mitch leaned in, voice low. "I'm done, bro. I need out."

T-Money scoffed, shaking his head. "The fuck you mean 'out'? We built this shit from the ground up. You walk away now, it ain't just you who feel that heat."

Mitch exhaled, gripping the glass in front of him. "I ain't tryna die out here, T. Niggas getting locked up, killed over petty shit. The money ain't worth this paranoia no more."

T-Money leaned back, eyeing him like he was speaking another language. "You gettin' soft on me, Mitch? Cuz last I checked, we ain't come this far to be regular ass niggas."

Mitch didn't move a muscle. "This ain't me goin' soft, it's me peepin' game. You don't feel how different it is out here? Ain't no rules no more—just setups and backstabs."

Before T-Money could reply, some sloppy drunk stumbled up to their table, his eyes locked on the diamond hanging off T's neck.

"Run that shit, bitch ass nigga," he slurred, reaching for the chain.

The second his fingers grazed the ice, T-Money snapped. His fist connected with the dude's jaw so fast it sounded like a gunshot. The drunk hit the floor hard, groaning, but it didn't end there. Mitch and T were on him in seconds—kicks, stomps, hands flying. The bar went dead silent as the dude curled up, trying to shield himself from the punishment.

T-Money spit on him. "Who the bitch now, huh?! I should kill you, nigga!"

Mitch pulled him back before shit got too deep. "Nah, let's bounce. Ain't worth it."

T-Money muttered, " I shoulda put one in his head."

They left the bar, stepping into the hot night air. T-Money was still tight, mumbling under his breath. "That nigga really tried me…He don't even know how close he came to gettin' zipped up and tossed in the lake."

Mitch shook his head. "That's the shit I'm talkin' bout. One second you chillin', next second you gotta prove yourself. It don't stop."

T-Money let out a sharp breath, rubbing his hands together. "So what, you really done?"

Mitch didn't answer right away. He just looked up at the city lights, the streets stretching in front of him like an open wound. He had one foot in and one foot out, and he knew damn well hesitation could get him killed.

"Nah," he finally muttered, "but I gotta figure out how to be."

And with that, they kept walking, the weight of their choices pressing down heavier than ever.

As they headed to his car, Mitch could still hear the echoing sounds of that altercation at the bar. He was struck by the scene's intensity and the raw reality of street life. Their long shadows on the sidewalk as they walked under the fading streetlights reflected the uncertainty surrounding their choices. A biting reminder of the challenges associated with their hustle, the air tasted sharp, like danger.

When they finally reached the car, T-Money cracked a grin, breaking the tension. "C'mon, ghee, you moving slow as hell. Time is bread!"

Mitch smirked, pulling his keys out. "Chill, bro. Just making sure we ain't got eyes on us."

T-Money shrugged like it was nothing. "Man, we good. Ain't nobody coming for us after that."

"Maybe," Mitch replied, scanning the street. "But I'm not about to get caught slipping. You know how these streets play."

T-Money leaned against the car, grinning. "That's why you my guy. You cautious. Keeps me balanced."

Mitch laughed, shaking his head. "Yeah, someone's gotta even out your wild ass."

"Wild? Nah, Ghee, I'm just confident," T-Money shot back, hopping into the passenger seat. "Now let's handle this bread and wrap it up."

The whip slid through the Vegas streets like a shark in deep water, dark-tinted, engine humming low. Mitch and T-Money? They wasn't just part of the game—they *was* the game. Everybody ate off their plate, but nobody dared reach without permission. Their moves were silent, their money loud, and tonight was just another piece of the empire stacking itself higher.

They pulled up to Sacred Visions, one of them fake-deep spots folks ran to when they was tryna act like they on a spiritual journey—getting chakras "aligned" or burning sage to chase off bad vibes. The sign out front was all faded, talkin' 'bout spiritual healing like it was a sanctuary. But the real ones? They knew better. The only thing gettin' balanced in there was scales—and not the zodiac kind.

See, Sacred Visions was just the front. The real bread came from that white—big bricks of coke, pure as snow and twice as dangerous. Vic ran the shop on the surface, but in the back? That's where weight moved heavy. Cash got picked up there, product moved elsewhere. Jack and his truckers? Them boys stayed in motion—slidin' state to state with hidden compartments and clean papers. Sacred Visions handled the money. Vic made sure it stayed laundered and lookin' holy.

Mitch killed the engine, they slid out calm, like this was just another stop on a long list of dirty business.

Inside, the vibe was all fake zen—rows of candles promisin' love and luck, tarot cards stacked like lottery tickets, crystals that supposedly healed hearts. But they ain't pull up for no soul-cleansing.

Behind the counter stood Vic—solid dude, arms thick like he been liftin' engine blocks and pallets his whole life. Face carved from years in the game. No words needed. Vic slid the black duffel across the glass, packed with bands. Mitch stayed cool Vic wasn't reckless enough to short them.

T-Money knocked on the counter, grinnin'. "We straight, yeah?"

Vic grunted, strokin' his beard. "C'mon now. Don't insult me."

Mitch grabbed the bag, tossed it like it was filled with feathers. "You lined up for next week?"

Vic nodded. "Long as y'all keep Jack's wheels turnin', we good. Folks out here fiendin' heavy—ain't slowin' down one bit."

T-Money dropped a fat stack across the glass, bills crispy, blue strips peekin'. "Keep the work clean, Vic. Ain't nobody out here payin' top dollar for baby powder."

Vic smirked, tuckin' the stack under his hoodie. "Ain't no cut in my supply. Pure Peruvian. Always."

Mitch gave a sharp nod. "Good. 'Cause one misstep? We both outta business."

They dipped without another word, steppin' back into the dark like they was part of it.

The car glided down busted streets, headlights catchin' old graffiti and half-dead streetlamps. Mitch gripped the wheel, mind runnin' through the next moves. T-Money scrolled his phone, thumb movin' fast.

"Warehouse next," Mitch muttered. "We gotta prep them trucks. No delays."

T-Money sighed, eyes still on his screen. "Drivers been hit me all day. They impatient. Ask too many damn questions—'how much,' 'how long,' 'where to.' I told Jack to keep 'em in line."

Mitch swerved into a tucked-off alley, tires cracklin' over gravel. Warehouse looked dead, like a spot folks forgot. But inside? That's where the next stage got locked in.

They stepped in. Smelled like oil and hustle. Forklifts posted up like they was ready to move at any second. Boxes stacked high, each one holdin' more weight than it let on.

Jack was already there—lean, twitchy, smokin' a cigarette like it was his last breath. "Y'all ready for this next run?" His voice was scratchy, like his throat been through wars.

Mitch scanned the place. "Trucks movin' next week, right?"

Jack nodded, flickin' ash. "Yeah. Just don't keep my drivers on standby too long. They get jittery when shit ain't movin'."

T-Money chuckled. "We all do. Time is money. Ain't nobody clockin' in for free."

Mitch stepped in close, voice low. "No slip-ups, Jack. No bullshit. If one of your boys get caught ridin' with weight, that ain't just a lost load—it's a chain reaction."

Jack held his hands up. "I hear you. We ain't tryna catch heat. Last thing I want is them boys pullin' over my rig with a few keys sittin' under frozen chicken."

T-Money gave a cold grin. "They better hold they shit down. 'Cause if we catch a case 'cause y'all slippin', that's blood on yo' hands, no cap."

Mitch's tone sharpened. "We ain't playin'. This coke? Top-shelf—no fuck-ups allowed. We move clean, quiet, and quick. Anything less? Folks end up six feet under or behind bars."

Jack dropped his cigarette, crushed it under his boot. "Say less. Trucks'll be ready. Just don't have me waitin' on y'all. We all got skin in this."

Mitch nodded once. "Then let's keep it movin'. Ain't nobody tryna be legends in a courtroom."

With that, they dipped, the city swallowin' them up like it always did.

Back in the ride, Mitch let the engine growl low, his fingers drumming on the wheel as he checked the mirrors. "We settin' them drivers up tonight. No more light moves—we floodin' the city, keepin' the money flowin' heavy."

T-Money kicked back, scrolling his phone, a slick grin pullin' at his face like he was sittin' on a secret.

Mitch side-eyed him. "The hell you cheesin' for?"

T-Money let out a short laugh, shaking his head. "Just thinkin'—we might be some ruthless-ass fools, but we got this shit on lock."

Mitch huffed, focus back on the road. "Yeah? Let's just make sure we stay breathin' while we at it."

T-Money cracked his knuckles, voice ice cold. "Breathing's on you—I'm locked in on keepin' fools from testin' us. We baptized these streets in blood to mark our turf—ain't nobody movin' in on it."

Mitch nodded, foot pressing down on the gas. The tires bit into the asphalt as they tore through the streets, leaving behind heat and tension thick enough to choke on.

For a second, the thought of steppin' back crossed Mitch's mind—but just as fast as it came, it was gone. The money, the power, the loyalty to T-Money, all that ran too deep.

The city lights burned bright, throwin' glints off windshields and storefronts, makin' it clear—this was their world. And as long as the game kept callin', they was gon' answer.

Chapter Ten

"Tropical Retreat: Mitch and Angel Find Peace in Hawaii"

Mitch leaned back in his chair, thinkin' 'bout all the mess that came with the street life they was wrapped up in. He called Angel—just needed her voice. That steady tone, soft but grounded. They laughed, chopped it up, and vibed like they always did. Six months deep, and somehow, it still felt brand new.

During the call, Angel mentioned wanting a vacation—a break from the harsh reality they faced daily.

Recognizing the fatigue in her voice, Mitch offered, "How about we go on a trip? I'll cover everything. Where do you want to go?"

Angel, who'd never really traveled, lit up. "Hawaii," she said excitedly.

Mitch was burnt out too—didn't even hesitate. Next thing they knew, they was rollin' through the airport, tryna trade bright lights for some real peace.

Their excitement grew as they walked through the shining halls of the airport. At the gate, Mitch took care of everything, all smooth and steady like he'd done it a thousand times. Onboard, they kicked back, eyes forward, lettin' the silence talk for 'em.

As the plane climbed into the sky, Mitch glanced at Angel. "It's a whole new world up here. Enjoy the view."

Angel looked out the window, awestruck by the vastness below. The city's shadows faded behind them, replaced by sunlight and clouds. For a moment, their burdens were forgotten.

The flight became more than just a trip—it was a mental escape from the life they knew. The intimacy between them deepened, a quiet moment of normalcy far from the streets. As the plane neared the islands, Angel felt a rush of both excitement and nerves.

Upon landing, they were greeted by the warm embrace of tropical air and the sweet scent of island flowers—a stark contrast to the grit of the city. A luxury vehicle waited for them, far removed from their usual rides. The chauffeur, dressed sharply, welcomed them with a polite smile and opened the door to plush leather seats.

As they drove through Hawaii's streets, a new world unfolded— vibrant flowers, palm trees dancing in the breeze, waterfalls spilling down lush cliffs. It was paradise.

Reaching their five-star hotel, they stepped into elegance. Their suite overlooked an immaculate beach, the setting sun casting warm hues across the room. The transition from the concrete jungle to this tropical haven felt surreal.

Out on the balcony, the waves was doin' their thing—steady, calm, like they was tryna match the vibe. Angel leaned on the rail, just takin' it all in. "Yo, Mitch… this? This is dope," she said, her voice low, kinda caught off guard by how good it all felt.

Mitch stood right next to her, arms resting lazy on the railing. He wasn't even lookin' at the view—he was watchin' her. Her sundress was dancin' with the breeze, the sun hittin' her skin just right, like God put a filter on her or somethin'.

He tilted his head, real chill. "I been all over, seen some wild spots… but this? This hit different."

Angel shot him a playful side-eye. "Oh yeah? What makes this lil balcony moment so deep, Mr. Passport Stamps?"

He didn't blink. "You. You changin' the whole atmosphere."

She laughed, brushed a curl back. "Damn. That island air got you layin' it on thick."

Mitch smirked. "Nah, I been like this. I just say what's real. You movin' like a whole scene from a movie, and I'm out here tryna act like I ain't clockin' everything."

She turned her face, tryin' to hide that smile, but he caught it. He stepped in a little closer—not on no wild stuff, just enough to let her feel him there.

"I don't talk just to talk," he said, his voice dropping lower. "And I don't catch feelings easy. But you? Got me out here actin' funny."

Angel leaned into the rail, side-eyein' him. "You? Actin' different? That I gotta see."

He chuckled. "Then keep watchin'. I ain't hard to read."

Right then, he noticed two dudes down below lookin' too long in their direction. Without sayin' nothin', Mitch adjusted his stance, slid in front of her just enough to block their view. Smooth. Automatic.

Angel caught it, grinnin'. "Oh, so we movin' like that? You postin' up on protect mode?"

Mitch shrugged like it wasn't nothin'. "Ain't no shares on this."

She laughed, head thrown back. "Boy, stop. It ain't even like that."

He looked at her, serious but calm. "You sure?"

The way he said it made somethin' in her chest flip.

"You got mad confidence, Mitch."

He leaned in, close enough that his words hit her skin. "I don't usually miss. But you got me feelin' like I'm shootin' blind, just hopin' to hit right."

Everything got quiet—like the island gave 'em space to just *be*. They talked. Laughed. They was locked in, no stumbles, just flow.

When the sun dipped and the light turned low and easy, Angel caught herself feelin' too much—peace in her chest and questions in her gut. Angel felt an unexpected wave of gratitude—and curiosity.

Mitch had never done anything like this before. The luxury around them didn't match the life they led. It was beautiful. It was excessive. And it didn't quite add up.

She watched him sip his drink, calm as ever. "I gotta ask," she said finally. "How are you affording all this?"

Mitch smirked, not answering right away. "Angel, you act like I don't have a business."

She chuckled. "Come on. A restaurant? Sure. But this?" She gestured at the suite. "This is millionaire-level. And last I checked, you weren't on the Forbes list."

Mitch laughed, setting his glass down. "Maybe I'm just good at what I do."

Angel wasn't buying it. "This feels like more than restaurant money."

His eyes narrowed slightly. "Business is more than seafood platters and drinks. I made some smart moves. Got in with the right people."

"The right people?"

He met her stare. "Investors. Connections. It's all about who you know—and when to take risks." Then, softer, "Sometimes, it's better not to ask too many questions."

Something in his tone made her stomach twist. She wanted to trust him—but the evasiveness made her pause.

"So what?" she asked. "You expect me to just sit back and enjoy the ride?"

Mitch tucked a curl behind her ear. "Exactly. I brought you here to relax, not play detective."

Angel held his gaze. A part of her wanted to press him. But another part—lost in his touch, the warmth in his eyes—wanted to let it go.

Damn, this man is so sexy, she thought, a slow smile tugging at her lips.

This trip had revealed a different side of Mitch—quiet, powerful, magnetic. The way he moved, the way he looked at her, the way he carried himself—it was intoxicating.

She gave him a sultry stare, silently acknowledging the pull he had over her. She sipped from her glass, the sunset behind her, and thought:

How did I get so lucky...

The fine, chocolate, muscular man before her had a magnetic appeal that went beyond the physical. It was the combination of his looks and the way he handled business that created this spellbinding presence that captivated her completely.

She couldn't deny the attraction that pulsed between them. His presence was a potent mix of strength and sensuality, creating a magnetic pull she couldn't resist.

As the evening unfolded, Angel relished in the fact that this man had her wrapped around his fingers, and she reveled in the excitement of being drawn to someone who embodied both desire and determination.

Back from the balcony, Mitch and Angel knew they had to kick back and shake off that travel headache.

They jumped in the shower, warm water doing its thing, washing away the grime and tension from the trip.

Clean and fresh, they slid into some laid-back clothes and sank into the softness of their big suite.

Beat down and worn out, they stretched out on the massive king-size bed—finally feeling comfortable after those stiff-ass plane seats.

They hit up room service, hungry like they hadn't eaten in days. Wasn't long before a knock had 'em scooping up trays piled with hot plates. The smell hit hard—seasoned right, make-you-sit-up kind of good.

They started grubbin', forks tapping plates, trading laughs between bites. Mitch leaned back, arms stretched, finally feeling that pressure start to melt off him without sayin' a word.

Angel was curled up next to him, the flicker of the TV lighting her face soft. She was pickin' at her food, more focused on him than whatever was playin'. Every time their eyes caught, Mitch hit her with that slow grin—the kind that said, *Yeah, I see you.*

He reached over, brushed a stray curl from her cheek real smooth, like it wasn't the first time he wanted to. Then grabbed the blanket off the edge of the bed and draped it over her lap, careful, like she was something fragile and fine.

The luau outside kept doin' its thing—music, voices, laughter ridin' the wind. But inside? It was a whole different story.

Mitch leaned in, close enough to catch the scent of her skin, and kissed her forehead, soft but steady. Lips lingered like he ain't wanna let go. When he pulled back, his eyes locked with hers.

"You good?" he asked, voice low, got that gravel in it like he'd been holdin' back.

She nodded slow, a little smile creepin' up. "Yeah, I'm good," she said, barely louder than a breath.

He smiled back, hand slid around her waist, thumb drawin' slow circles on her side, fingers light but sure. They sat there, caught up in that stillness, blockin' out the noise, the world, all of it. Just them. Flawed, tired, but wrapped in a peace neither one could explain— and for once, that was enough.

The sun streamed through the blinds during the morning, lighting the room in warm, golden beams.

Mitch and Angel stretched and yawned, wiping the sleep from their eyes. A charge of electricity went through them as they realized– they were in paradise.

Hawaii, in all its beauty and promise, was just beyond the balcony doors.

Eager to begin their day. They chose to have a delicious breakfast, enjoying the hotel's tropical fruits, freshly baked pastries, and fragrant coffee. The flavors were a great introduction to the culinary delights Hawaii had to offer, setting a positive tone for the adventures ahead.

Angel stepped out, all sunshine and smiles, rocking a bright-ass bikini that hugged her curves just right, some daisy dukes that were way too short for anyone's good, and sunglasses that made her look like she was straight outta a music video. She looked like she was ready to turn heads and catch some rays.

Mitch, on the other hand, kept it chill but clean. He threw on a button-up shirt that was open enough to show he wasn't trying too hard, paired with some loose shorts that were comfortable but still had that "I got money" look. He wasn't really about the flashy life, but today he was feeling a little different—like he could use a change of pace.

Both of them had that restless energy in the air. They were geared up, ready to step out and see what the day had in store. With no real plan, just a little curiosity pulling them forward, they left the suite to see what trouble the day might bring.

The first destination on their agenda was to explore the pristine beaches that Hawaii is known for.

They walked down the beach, just talkin' it out,

Waves crashing off in the distance.

That turquoise water was shining so bright, they had to dip their toes, feelin' that cool Pacific chill hit 'em right.

After soaking up the sun, they bounced into the green, where flowers was wildin' out with colors all over the place, making the whole island feel alive. Palm trees swayed easy in the breeze, and the air smelled mad sweet with all those exotic blooms. The island was wrapping around 'em, putting 'em in that chill, island state of mind.

Hawaii's culture was pulling 'em in heavy. They hit up the local markets, talking to the friendly people. The handmade goods, the island clothes, and the bomb food gave 'em a taste of what the place was all about. Every moment added another layer to their Hawaiian story, making it something they'd never forget.

But they weren't just out here chillin'. They found some dope spots with wild views—green hills hitting the ocean, straight-up jaw-droppin'. Angel had her camera out, clickin' away, makin' sure they had shots to remember this trip forever. Island life was all about keeping it easy, so they went snorkeling in the clear waters and hiked trails leading to secret spots. They laughed their way through the villages, taking in that laid-back vibe that made Hawaii feel like a different universe.

The days kept throwing surprises—hidden coves, fire food, and the warm sun on their backs. The island's energy was all around them, and every laugh, every look, every quiet word under the stars made a memory that'd last forever.

Hawaii had definitely left its mark, but now it was time to bounce. They packed up their bags with souvenirs and memories, ready to fly back to Vegas.

As the plane took off, they looked out the window, watching the blue water and green hills fade into the city lights of Vegas.

It was like the world was changin', but the memories of Hawaii stuck with 'em. With a soft sigh, the airplane settled and caressed the desert pavement. Vegas welcomed them with the promise of a new kind of adventure and the comforting embrace of dry heat. It was a more mellow excitement, fashioned from the comfort of a life rebuilt and the rhythm of the waves, rather than the heart-pounding energy of their former existence.

Exiting the airport, they flagged a ride to take them home.

Rollin' through the lit-up streets of Vegas felt like snapping out of a dream. The car zipped past those neon signs, a whole world away from the chill of Hawaii.

Man, stepping off that island calm into this concrete jungle felt like somebody sucker-punched my gut—had me off-balance quick. One minute it's soft breezes, the next it's horns blarin', neon buzzin', and people sprintin' like they got no chill.

Riding through these streets at night, the city snapped me awake—like, damn, our whole world done flipped overnight.

The memories of Hawaii felt like a quiet escape from the madness of the city.

That week in Hawaii had brought Mitch and Angel even closer, leaving a lasting mark on their bond.

Back in Vegas, they kept that Hawaiian heat in their bones, the ocean's rhythm in their heads, and all the laughs they had, carrying those island vibes with 'em as they slid back into their usual grind.

The return journey marked not just the end of a vacation but the beginning of a new chapter.

Chapter Eleven

"Crossroads: When Truths Can't Be Avoided"

Mitch stepped into the restaurant, and as soon as the door swung open, the heavy scent of sizzling food hit him like a wave. The joint was buzzing with the usual late-night crowd, but it didn't faze him. His eyes locked on T-Money in the corner booth, hunched over a stack of cash, but the moment Mitch walked in, T's head snapped up.

"Mitch! Look who finally came back from his vacation! How'd paradise treat you, my guy?" T-Money tossed out the words, a mix of real curiosity and that signature sarcastic edge that only he could pull off.

Mitch gave a quick smirk, not giving too much away. "It was alright, man. Had to get away, clear my head for a minute."

T-Money cocked his head, brow furrowed like he smelled smoke. "Hold up—don't tell me this trip got you soft or some shit?" He leaned back, eyes sweeping over Mitch like he was hunting a lie.

Mitch chuckled low, playin' it off. "Ain't that. I'm just tryna catch my breath, that's all." But T stayed glued to him, not a muscle in his face twitching. Then, outta nowhere, Mitch's whole posture snapped tight. The easy vibe evaporated, replaced by a thick, heavy quiet that made every second feel like a promise waiting to break.

"Yo, T," Mitch said, voice dropping low enough to cut the room's buzz, "we gotta chop it up—private."

T-money shot Mitch a look, then nodded toward the back. "Let's bounce," he murmured.

They weaved through the dining room—servers gliding past, plates clinking, chatter buzzing—until they hit the door marked **"Manager's Office."** Mitch cracked it open and slipped inside. T-Money followed, closing it soft behind him.

Inside, the lights were dimmer, the air thick with fryer steam and late-night stress. Mitch shut the door, leaned against the desk, and pointed at the floor.

"Sit," he said, voice low enough that even the walls leaned in. "We gotta chop it up."

T-Money's eyes sharpened. "Aight, what's good? Something go down with Angel?" He threw the name out casually, but his gaze was intense, waiting for Mitch to crack.

Mitch shook his head, jaw tight as hell. "Nah, nothing like that," he said, but there was a beat, a hesitation before he said, "We just went on a trip, that's all." His words felt empty, like he was keeping something back.

T-Money raised an eyebrow, not buying it for a second. "A trip? Since when we taking hoes on vacations, Mitch?" His voice dripped with that trademark sarcasm, and the word "hoe" hit the air like a slap.

Mitch's face hardened, eyes flashing a warning. "She ain't no hoe, T. Don't disrespect her like that. She's different." He paused, trying to figure out how to explain what Angel meant to him without sounding weak. "Angel... she sees the world different. Makes you question all this... this life we lead." He growled, his voice low, like a threat that wasn't meant to be taken lightly. "If I thought she was a hoe, she'd be treated like one, you know how I roll."

T-Money didn't flinch, but his mind was working overtime, piecing things together, seeing a bigger picture than Mitch was ready to admit.

The whole thing with Angel wasn't as simple as Mitch thought. She wasn't just some girl he took to a fancy spot on the map. Angel had secrets, man. Big ones. Behind those soft eyes and that pretty smile, she was deep in a world Mitch had no clue about.

While Mitch was out there thinking it was all sunsets and romance, Angel was playing the game too. Vegas wasn't just a vacation to her—it was her second home. And in that city, the lights only covered up the shadows. She was out there running with people, handling business in the darkest corners of that world, where money and power spoke louder than words.

T-Money listened, more interested than ever, his gut telling him there was a lot more going on than Mitch was letting on. He leaned back in his booth, eyes narrowing as Mitch kept talking, oblivious to the bigger game. T-Money was smart—he knew that in their line of work, nothing was ever just what it seemed.

The streets of Vegas whispered about Angel long before Mitch even knew her name. She wasn't just a pretty face—she had a role, a purpose in the underworld. And now, somehow, Mitch had gotten tangled up in her web, thinking it was all innocent fun.

Mitch, still unaware, kept running his mouth, going on about the trip, the good times, the quiet moments with Angel. But T-Money? He could smell the trouble coming from a mile away. The deeper Mitch got into it, the more he realized that Angel was playing a game of her own, one Mitch wasn't even aware he was losing.

"Man, I don't know what it is, Mitch," T-Money said, shaking his head, his voice gruff. "But that wasn't ust a vacation to her, I'm telling you. She's got something else goin' on."

Mitch didn't wanna hear it. He was too deep in his feelings, too caught up in what he thought was real to see the cracks forming beneath him.

In the haze of smoke, as Mitch and T-Money sat there talking, the weight of their history filled the room. The walls, covered with faded pictures from their grind on the streets, told a story of loyalty, of struggles, of blood and sweat.

"You been my partner since we were kids, T," Mitch said quietly, the words heavy with meaning. "We came up together. Ain't nobody got my back like you. When the world goes sideways, I know I can count on you."

T-Money took a deep hit off the blunt, then exhaled, sending a thick cloud of smoke into the air. "You my brother, Mitch. Ain't nothin' changed. We been through it all, and I ain't goin' nowhere."

The bond between them was solid, built on years of loyalty, and the trust they shared was more than just business—it was family. They'd seen the worst of each other, the ugliest sides, but they'd always come out stronger.

Mitch's eyes softened a bit, his guard slipping for a second as he looked at T-Money. "From the block to this, it's been a ride. I trust you like no other, T. You family. And that shit don't come easy."

T-Money nodded, the two of them locked in a moment of shared understanding. It wasn't just about the money or the deals—it was about the life they had carved out together. They had each other's backs, no matter what.

The conversation turned back to business, but there was something different now, something deeper. Mitch and T-Money had been through hell together, and no matter what, that bond wasn't gonna break.

The smoke from the blunts burned down to a doobie, but the words they shared lingered in the air, an unspoken promise that no matter how many secrets got uncovered, they would face them together.

Meanwhile

Angel sat in the dark, just her and her thoughts. That silence? Loud as hell. Her heart beatin' like it knew time was almost up. She'd been sittin' on this heavy-ass secret for way too long, and it was startin' to eat at her from the inside out.

"I can't keep livin' like this," she muttered, voice barely a whisper.

Her chest felt tight. She'd played it cool for months, kept her hustle lowkey, but now? That guilt was creepin' in strong. Mitch was a good dude—damn near too good. And every time he looked at her with that trust in his eyes, it made her feel smaller, faker. Like she ain't even deserve him.

"I gotta tell him… eventually," she whispered to herself, eyes locked on the wall, hoping for some kinda sign.

But the truth? It was ugly. Raw. She wasn't proud of what she did, but shit, it paid the bills. Helped her stack bread for her dream. That salon wasn't gonna build itself, and journalism wasn't payin' nothing but stress and student loans. So she chose fast money, made her peace with it—until Mitch came along.

"What the fuck he gon' think about me?" she asked herself, voice crackin'. "He gon' look at me different... like I'm some type of trick."

That thought alone made her stomach twist.

What if he called her dirty? What if he couldn't see past the job, couldn't see the heart behind it—the grind, the dream, the survival? What if all he saw was what she did, not why she did it?

She felt stuck. Like every day she didn't tell him, she was diggin' a deeper hole. And every time he held her like she was somethin' special, the guilt hit harder.

"He gon' hate me," she whispered. "Or worse… he gon' pity me."

She rubbed her face, exhaled hard.

Angel was always calculated. She ain't jump into nothing without thinkin' it through. But this? This was different. You can't plan a heart reaction. Can't protect yourself from love turnin' into disappointment.

Truth was, she was scared. Scared he'd bounce. Scared he'd look at her like she was less. But the clock was tickin'. And no matter how tight she held onto the lie, the truth was comin'.

Ready or not.

She sat on her bed, stress written all over her face, then grabbed her phone and hit up her sister.

Naliyah answered on the second ring, voice all bright and bougie like always. "Hey girl, look who finally remembered she got a sister!"

Angel smiled. "Whatever. I miss you, damn."

"I miss you too… but what's up? You never call just to chat. You want somethin'?"

Angel laughed. "Can't I just call you 'cause I love you?"

Naliyah chuckled. "You can. But I still know you. So spill it."

Angel went quiet for a second, then sighed. "I been seein' this guy. Mitch. He's… different. Real good to me."

"And?" Naliyah pushed.

"He don't know what I really do for money."

Silence.

Then Naliyah hit her with it. "Girl, you still out here sellin' ass?"

Angel sucked her teeth. "Damn, can you not say it like that?"

"Well what you want me to say? You out here doin' what you gotta do, but you tryna play house with a man who don't know the half. That's not fair to him—or you."

"I know," Angel whispered.

"How long y'all been talkin'?"

"Seven months."

"Seven months?" Naliyah snapped. "You buggin'. That man been lovin' on a version of you that don't exist. You shoulda told him from jump."

Angel rubbed her forehead. "I was scared. I wanted him to see me as more than just… what I do."

"You *are* more, Angel. You smart, you got goals, you got that degree sittin' in a drawer you don't use. But you act like the streets gon' love you harder than your talent will."

"I chose fast money 'cause it gave me what that degree didn't—a way out," Angel said softly. "A way to build my salon."

Naliyah calmed a little. "I get it, sis. I ain't judgin'. But if he finds out from somebody else? That's gon' hurt way worse than the truth comin' from you. Tell him. Let him decide."

Angel nodded even though Naliyah couldn't see her.

Trying to change the subject, Naliyah added, "So what you been up to besides bein' sneaky?"

Angel chuckled. "Been pushin' my photography, savin' every penny I can. Tryna finally get that nail and hair spot poppin'."

Naliyah smiled. "Now *that's* what I'm talkin' about. I'm proud of you, for real. Just get that personal life together, too. Can't have your business boomin' and your heart in shambles."

They both laughed.

Then Naliyah's voice softened. "You know I love you, right? I don't always agree with what you do, but I'm always here. You ain't ever gotta go through none of this alone."

Angel closed her eyes, the lump in her throat growing. "I know. Love you too, sis."

That call wasn't just venting—it was everything. Naliyah had her own life, her own path. But when Angel needed grounding, needed truth with love, her sister never failed her. And that meant more than words could ever say.

- Chapter Twelve -

"Playing Both Sides"

Angel sat on the couch, eyes fixed on the ceiling, hoping for a clue, but all she got was silence. Her chest rose and fell slow, like she was trying to keep herself from drowning in thoughts she didn't wanna face. Naliyah's voice still rang in her head, that sharp mix of sisterly love and hard truth.

"You shoulda told him from jump."

Easy for her to say.

Truth never did Angel no favors. Every time she thought being honest would set her free, it just ended up cutting her deeper.

She let out a long breath, pressing her fingers to her temples. She knew what she had to do. Knew she couldn't keep dodging this. But knowing and doing? Two different things. And when it came to Mitch?

She just… wasn't ready.

Mitch wasn't like these other dudes she'd known—wasn't just another man passing through, looking for a good time with no real investment. He was different. Too damn smart. Too damn observant. He had this way of looking at her like he could see through all the layers, straight to the parts of her she didn't even wanna admit existed. That shit made her feel naked in a way that had nothing to do with taking her clothes off.

And Angel didn't do vulnerable.

Not after everything she'd been through.

She learned young that love was just another word for pain.

Her first real relationship had been a lesson in heartbreak—a man who knew all the right things to say but never meant a damn word. He sold her dreams and left her with nightmares. After that, she wised up. She built her walls high, kept her heart locked up tight.

Men always got what they came for—and not a drop more. Angel knew how to keep it business. Keep her heart out of it. Ain't no one gettin' close enough to flip her world. She played it smart, kept emotions on lock, and stayed focused on her grind.

That shit worked for years.

Then *he* showed up…

And messed around and made her feel something she wasn't tryna feel.

She hadn't meant to fall for him. Swore she wouldn't. But it happened anyway, slipping through the cracks before she even noticed.

At first, she told herself it was casual. That's how she operated— never too close, never too deep. But Mitch blurred those lines, made her question rules she thought were set in stone. He noticed little things, things most men overlooked. The way she chewed her lip when she was nervous. The way her laugh sounded different when it was real. He paid attention in a way that made her uncomfortable, like he actually cared.

And that was the problem.

Because if he ever found out the truth?

That look he gave her—the one that made her feel worth something—would disappear.

She closed her eyes, tilting her head back against the couch.

She'd spent months juggling both lives, keeping them separate like oil and water. But she knew better. Sooner or later, the truth was gonna come out.

Her phone buzzed.

She snatched it up quick, hoping—praying—it was Mitch. But the second she saw the name on the screen, her stomach twisted.

Not Mitch.

Just another client.

She deleted the text, like that would make it go away, then tossed the phone onto the couch.

Her chest felt tight.

How long could she keep this up?

Every night, she played her role, told herself it didn't matter. That she was just doing what she had to do. But Mitch had changed that. Made her want something real. And that scared the hell out of her.

Another buzz. Another text.

This time, she didn't even look.

She knew what it was.

Another reminder of the life she was still trapped in.

She ran a hand through her hair, pacing the room.

Two choices.

Keep pretending. Keep hoping she could balance both worlds without them colliding.

Or tell Mitch the truth.

And risk losing him.

She wanted to believe maybe—just maybe—he'd understand. That he wouldn't judge her. That he wouldn't look at her different.

But men didn't work like that.

She knew the game.

Men wanted the fantasy, not the reality.

And her reality?

That shit was ugly.

A knock at the door made her freeze.

Her heart jumped into her throat.

It was late. Too late for company.

She hesitated, every instinct telling her to ignore it. To act like she wasn't home.

But she couldn't.

Slowly, she walked to the door, her pulse hammering.

She reached for the handle, took a deep breath, and opened it.

Her stomach dropped.

Not Mitch.

Just a damn Amazon package.

She let out a bitter laugh.

The universe really had jokes tonight.

With a sigh, she kicked the box aside and shut the door, leaning against it for a second.

Disappointment settled deep in her bones.

She had let herself believe, just for a moment, that maybe he had come to see her. That maybe he felt the same pull she did.

But now, all she had was a package she didn't even remember ordering and the same heavy truth pressing down on her chest.

She walked back to the couch, picked up her phone, and stared at Mitch's name on the screen.

Her thumb hovered over the call button.

She should tell him.

She needed to tell him.

But the fear of what came next kept her frozen.

Because once the words left her lips, there was no taking them back.

And if she lost him?

She wasn't sure she could handle that.

She could already picture it.

Mitch rolling past her block one night, his car moving slow as he scanned the streets. Maybe he was coming from work, or maybe he was just out handling business. Either way, if he saw her standing there—under those flickering streetlights, looking like every other girl just trying to make rent—he'd know.

He'd know exactly what she was doing.

And the worst part?

She wouldn't even be able to explain it.

Because what could she say?

That it wasn't what it looked like?

That she didn't have a choice?

That this was survival?

None of that would matter.

Mitch didn't mess with women in the game. He didn't judge, but he had his boundaries. And if he ever saw her out there, working the corner, looking like everything she swore she wasn't?

That look—the one that made her feel safe, made her feel wanted—would be gone.

She could already picture the way his face would harden, the way his jaw would clench as realization hit him.

And that?

That would break her.

She could handle a lot. Rejection. Pain. Even betrayal.

But losing Mitch?

That was a whole different kind of hurt.

And yet, every night, she stepped out onto that street, knowing it was a risk.

Every time she leaned into a stranger's car, every time she put on that fake smile, she wondered if this was the night Mitch would see her.

If this was the night her secret would come crashing down.

And the worst part?

She didn't know if she'd stop.

Because the money was real. The security, the control—it was all she had ever known.

So maybe the truth wasn't what she feared most.

Maybe what she really feared… was choosing.

Because if it came down to Mitch or survival?

She wasn't sure she'd choose love.

- Chapter Thirteen -

"Hustle and Heartbreak: Truths We Can't Unsee"

As Mitch eased his foot off the gas, letting the car roll forward as his eyes locked onto the woman ahead.

Mitch pulled over, jaw tightening as his mind spun. What the hell is she doing out here? Dressed like that, moving like that—this wasn't the same Angel he remembered.

She approached a group of well-dressed men outside a club, laughing at something one of them said. A tall, smug-looking guy in a designer suit wrapped an arm around her waist. Angel didn't pull away.

Mitch's grip tightened on the steering wheel. A wave of emotions crashed into him—confusion, anger, something dangerously close to jealousy. He'd spent so much time caught up in the past, believing things were good between them. But now? She felt like a stranger wearing Angel's face.

He exhaled sharply, shaking his head. This ain't my business. Whatever Angel was into now, she'd made her choices. But damn, it didn't sit right with him.

Yet, he couldn't bring himself to drive away. Angel turned, as if sensing his presence, before slipping into the crowd. She was gone before he could be sure. Mitch hesitated, torn between chasing the truth or letting it go. The bright yellow lights altered reality and created illusions that frightened him.

Driving home, Mitch couldn't shake the image of Angel—laughing, pressed against that man outside the club. The city's usual hum felt different now, tainted. His grip on the wheel tightened, mind replaying the moment, questioning if his eyes had betrayed him. The thought of Angel hiding something this deep twisted his stomach.

Back home, Mitch dropped onto the couch, his mind a battlefield of doubt and frustration. He ran a hand over his face. "I can't deal with women who run the streets selling pussy," Ain't no way, he muttered, the words tasted bitter, like disappointment he hadn't prepared for.

Mitch had always been careful with women, avoiding the kind that brought unnecessary drama. He valued his peace, his stability. The idea that Angel might be living a double life threatened everything he thought he knew about her.

T-Money's warnings echoed in his mind, aggravating him more. "Take it slow, Mitch. Get to know her first before you start thinking about something real," T-Money had told him, weighing the pros and cons. "Not everybody is who they claim to be." Had he been played? Every moment spent with her, every ounce of trust he'd given—was it all bullshit? Embarrassment burned beneath his skin. T-Money had warned him, but he'd let himself fall too fast. Now, the thought that Angel had never been who she claimed to be gnawed at him like an open wound.

The anger rising within him wasn't just about Angel—it was about himself. He prided himself on being sharp, on reading people well. If this was the truth, he had failed to see it.

As the city lights flickered beyond his window, Mitch wrestled with his next move. Confront her or walk away? Either way, the trust between them was already shattered.

The next morning, Mitch didn't waste any time. He needed to talk to Angel, face to face. The text he sent was simple, direct: We need to talk. Face to face.

She didn't hesitate to reply. Okay. When and where?

Mitch's chest tightened with anticipation. He was pissed, and he had a lot to say, but a part of him knew that this conversation wasn't just about getting answers. It was about everything they'd built falling apart.

They met at his restaurant, exchanging hesitant greetings. Even the soft music seemed strained under the burden of their unspoken words.

The walk to Mitch's office felt long as hell, like every step was dragging some heavy truth behind it. His whole body was tight, fists clenched, jaw locked—He could already feel himself about to snap. Angel wasn't any better. Her stomach was in knots, nerves on edge, but she kept her face straight. She knew this was coming. Ain't no dodging it now.

Inside, the office was quiet, too quiet. The dim lights made everything feel colder than it was. Angel sat across from him, eyes narrowed, looking cautious but also strangely resigned.

"What is it you want to talk to me about?"

Mitch exhaled, watching her closely. "I need to ask you something, and I want the truth."

Her eyes narrowed slightly. "Go ahead."

"Were you on the strip the other night?"

A flicker of something—fear, hesitation—flashed across her face before she folded her arms. "Why are you asking me that?"

"Because I thought I saw you." His voice was calm, firm. "And if it was you… I need to know what you were doing there."

A tense silence stretched between them. Then, Angel swallowed hard. "And if I say yes?"

Mitch studied her, his jaw tightening. "Then I need to know if there's something you're not telling me."

A knot of fear tightened in her throat. She had spent so much time keeping this part of herself buried. But there was no use in lying now.

"I was there," she admitted, voice barely above a whisper. "Mitch, I've been trying to break free from that life, but circumstances keep pulling me back in."

Mitch exhaled sharply, rubbing a hand down his face. He had suspected it, but hearing it out loud made it real. "Damn, Angel. Why keep this from me? This feels like a betrayal of the trust we built."

Mitch leaned forward, his elbows resting on his knees, jaw clenched so tight it ached. His voice, when he spoke, was low and sharp, like a blade slicing through the thick silence.

"You fucking lied to me, Angel." His tone was cold, his eyes hard as steel. "You let me think you were different. That you were better than this street bullshit."

Angel flinched at the venom in his words, but she held his gaze. "I never lied. I just—"

"Cut the bullshit!" Mitch's voice erupted, his fist slamming onto the desk, making the lamp rattle. "You knew exactly what you were doing. You knew what I'd think. What, you thought I wouldn't find out? That I wouldn't see you out there?" His chest rose and fell with barely contained rage. "I feel like a fucking fool, Angel."

Angel swallowed hard, her fingers gripping the arms of the chair. "Mitch, I—"

"You what? Huh?" Mitch snapped, his hands balling into fists. He stood up so fast the chair scraped loudly against the floor. His body was tense, his muscles coiled with unspent anger. "I let you in. I fucking trusted you! And now, all I can think about is how stupid I was, walking around like some damn simp while you were out there selling your ass."

Angel's breath caught. "I didn't want this life, Mitch. I never did."

Mitch let out a bitter laugh, pacing the room like a caged animal. "That's the excuse? That's what you're going with? 'I didn't want this'? Then why the fuck are you still in it, Angel?" He shot her a look so sharp it could cut glass. "You had me out here defending you, thinking you were solid. But the whole damn time, you were just another bitch in the game, just another one of them."

"You sat there and fed me bullshit. I gave you my time, my trust. Hell, I took you to fucking Hawaii." His voice cracked with disbelief. "You think I do that for just anybody?"

Angel's breath hitched. "I never meant to hurt you."

Mitch let out a bitter laugh, running a hand over his face. "Yeah? Well, you did." His eyes darkened, his voice dripping with venom. "If I knew you was a hoe, Angel, I would've never even looked at you. Let alone fucked you. Let alone trusted you."

Angel flinched like he had slapped her. "I'm not a hoe, Mitch."

"Then what the fuck do you call it?" His voice rose, his patience snapping. "You let me believe you was worth something. You let me think I had something real with you. He shook his head, in disgust. Angel's eyes welled up, but she stayed silent.

"You know what the worst part is?" Mitch's voice dropped, his tone almost dangerous. "I don't let people in. I don't trust easy. But you? I did." He exhaled sharply, shaking his head again. Angel swallowed hard. "Mitch, I never wanted to lie to you—"

"But you did." He leaned in, his face inches from hers. "You let me take you places, spend money on you, lay up with you—thinking you were mine. All while you were out there, doing God knows what with God knows who."

Angel's lip quivered, but she squared up, throwing her shoulders back. She locked eyes with him, no flinch. "You wanna talk about lies, "Let's talk about the ones you been feeding me."

Mitch's stare turned cold. "The fuck you talking about?"

Angel rolled her eyes, a sarcastic laugh escaping her. "Please, Mitch. You ain't no regular dude making 'honest money.' You drop stacks like it's nothing. Expensive cars, top-shelf liquor, the finest shit at every restaurant. What, you think I'm stupid?"

Mitch's face darkened, but Angel wasn't stopping now.

"Word on the street? You ain't just slingin' food. You a damn kingpin, Mitch. That cash you flashing? Ain't from no restaurant. So don't try to act like you some legit businessman." She leaned forward. "So go ahead, Mitch. Say what you want about me. but you ain't fooling nobody. We both got skeletons. You ain't as clean as you want me to think."

Mitch's face twisted in disgust, and he took a step closer, looming over her. "Nah. You ain't like me, Angel. Don't even try to make that comparison." His voice dropped to a growl. "You let men put their hands on you for money. You gave yourself away. You really think that's the same thing as what I do? He shook his head. " I'm out here making moves, demanding respect. I don't sell myself short. And I sure as hell don't lay down with strangers for a fucking price."

Angel's fists balled up, her voice shaking with fury. "Mitch, you ruin lives. You spread poison through this city and act like you're better than me? You really think you're all high and mighty?"

Mitch let out a bitter laugh, his eyes flashing with anger. "I ain't perfect, Angel. But at least I don't pretend to be some innocent man."

Mitch held her stare, the air between them heavy, thick with things neither of them wanted to say out loud. He exhaled slow, like he was picking through his words before letting them loose.

"People love to talk," Mitch said, voice steady, but his eyes told a different story. "Rumors fly, but that don't mean they real. Yeah, I run my business, but the world I move in? It ain't simple. Shit ain't always what it looks like."

Angel didn't blink, her gaze locked on his, searching, waiting for something real. The silence dragged, tension pressing down on both of them.

Mitch rubbed his jaw, his voice carrying something raw. "You right, Angel. There's more to me than what I let you see. But don't let the streets fill in the blanks. Survival out here? It ain't as easy as just doing things the right way."

Angel scoffed, crossing her arms. "Man, stop playing. You wanted the truth from me, right? But now you feeding me this half-ass shit? Just say it, Mitch."

His jaw clenched. Another long pause. Then, he leaned in, voice low, eyes dark. "There's parts of my life I keep buried for a reason. Everybody ain't built to understand it. The world I'm in... it don't do black and white. It's all gray. And sometimes? The choices I make—" he shook his head, "they ain't clean, but they necessary. Yeah, I'm in some shit that ain't legal. But it's what keeps me breathing."

Mitch's expression shifted—anger, confusion, something else he couldn't name. He could see the weight of his words settling on her. He sighed, running a hand over his face.

"This ain't a life you need to get mixed up in," he said, voice calmer but firm. "It's the road I chose. And I ain't asking for approval. I don't need you to understand it, and I damn sure don't need your permission."

Angel's jaw tightened, her eyes sharp, burning. "Oh, so that makes it okay?" she snapped. "But I'm the one you got a problem with? You act like my life is too messy for you, but you out here poisoning the same streets I'm trying to escape. You don't see the problem?"

Mitch looked away, his mouth twisting like the words tasted bitter. "This ain't about what you want, Angel. It's about the risk. You put yourself in danger every day, and I can't afford to let your choices crash into mine. I built something. I ain't letting you or anybody else tear it down."

Angel scoffed, shaking her head, her pain buried under sharp words. "That's what this really is, huh? You ain't leaving 'cause of me— you leaving 'cause you too pussy to handle me. That's what it is, right, Mitch?"

His whole body went still. The room felt like it dropped ten degrees.

Mitch's jaw flexed, his hands curling into fists at his sides. For a split second, that dangerous glint flashed in his eyes—the one that made grown men watch their tone around him. He took a slow step forward, his voice low, edged with something lethal. "Watch your fuckin' mouth, Angel."

Angel swallowed, but she refused to back down. "Or what?"

Mitch let out a slow breath, forcing himself to loosen his fists. He wasn't gonna do it. Not to her. Not when he knew she was only saying that outta hurt. But damn, she was pushing him. Testing the very line most people didn't live long enough to cross.

Finally, he exhaled, shaking his head. "I ain't gon' do this with you." He turned away like he was done, like he was choosing to walk out before shit got worse. "Believe what you want, Angel. But I ain't stayin' for this."

The weight of his words settled in the space between them. The connection they once had—it was crumbling fast, slipping through both their fingers.

Angel's voice shook with anger. "Fuck you, Mitch. For real. You can stand there actin' like you better than me, but at least I own my shit. You out here livin' two lives, lyin' to yourself, actin' like you some businessman when we both know the truth."

Mitch stilled, his back still turned. Then, real slow, he turned his head just enough to look at her. His expression? Ice cold.

"You know what?" His voice was damn near a whisper, but the threat in it was loud. "You ain't my problem no more. Go do what you do best."

Angel's breath hitched. For the first time, her confidence wavered. "Mitch—"

"Get the fuck out." He didn't raise his voice. He didn't need to. The way he said it? It was final. "Before I do somethin' I can't take back."

Angel felt the shift. That was her warning. The last one she was gonna get. And she knew better than to push past it.

Still, when she looked in his eyes, past all the rage, past the street-made monster everyone feared, she saw it—that flicker of something else. Something real. He cared. That was the only reason she was still standing there.

But caring didn't change the facts.

The silence between them was suffocating. Angel searched his face, praying for some sign that this wasn't really the end. But she saw it. He meant every word.

Her throat tightened. Her pride wouldn't let her break in front of him, so she nodded once, turned on her heel, and walked out without another word.

The door slammed behind her, the sound slicing through the room like a bullet.

Mitch stood there, breathing heavy, his jaw clenched so tight it hurt. His fists stayed balled up, nails biting into his palms.

But he let her go.

Not 'cause he didn't care.

But because maybe caring too much was the real problem.

Outside, Angel moved fast, like she could outrun the weight in her chest. With every step away from his restaurant, something inside her cracked.

The streets, once familiar, once filled with memories of him, now felt empty as hell.

Tears burned her eyes, but she refused to let them fall.

How could he look at me like that?

Like she was nothing. Like everything they had didn't mean shit.

Yeah, she worked the night. But that wasn't all she was. She had dreams. Plans. She fought to survive, to build something beyond these streets.

But to Mitch? None of that mattered.

The city lights blinked around her, but they didn't do shit to push back the darkness creeping up inside. The farther she walked, the heavier that weight sat on her chest, pressing down like it was tryna break her spirit.

By the time she made it to her spot, her whole body felt drained—mind, heart, and soul all running on empty. She locked the door, let out a breath she didn't even know she was holding, and dropped onto the couch. The silence wrapped around her, thick and cold. What used to feel like home just felt... off now, like Mitch's words had sucked the life outta the place.

Was love really supposed to feel like this? Could it even exist without judgment, without somebody always holdin' conditions over your head?

Sitting there in the quiet, Angel faced the one truth she had been dodging all night—sometimes, no matter how deep you feel it, love just ain't enough.

- Chapter Fourteen -

"Club Drama: Livin' It Up, Drownin' Out the L's"

The music in the club was booming, bass heavy enough to shake the walls. Mitch was soaking it all in, feeling the beat take control as he stood surrounded by the madness of the night. His mind was far from Angel, After the breakup, he was out here livin' it up, doing whatever the hell he wanted.

The lights, the crowd, the energy—they all felt like a good escape.

With T-Money by his side, Mitch wasn't worried about much except the moment. He could hear T-Money laughing, cracking jokes, keeping the mood light. The world outside this club, with its drama and pain, seemed like a distant memory. But as the night carried on, he couldn't help but notice her—one of the groupies who had been eyeing him for years.

Baby wasn't shy about makin' her move—she was bold as hell, maybe a little too much, but Mitch wasn't in the mood to turn her down. The alcohol was flowin', the adrenaline was pumpin', and he was all in, ready to drown out everything with some distractions.

She was thick as hell, lookin' like a brown-skin model with long hair, full lips, and eyes that could stop traffic. She slid up on him, her body pressin' close, and he leaned in, feelin' the heat between them. She whispered something in his ear, but he didn't even catch it—didn't matter anyway. It was just a quick break from all the mess in his head. The guilt, the regret, the drama with Angel? That could wait. Tonight, he just needed to lose himself for a minute.

Unbeknownst to Mitch, Tia, Angel's homegirl, was in the club too. She'd heard all the gossip about Mitch and his reputation, but tonight, she was about to get a firsthand look. Tia wasn't one to keep quiet, and if her girl was out there getting played, she was the first one to step up and let her know.

She pulled out her phone, not thinking twice, and dialed up a FaceTime call. Angel's face popped up on the screen, her eyes lighting up as she answered, clearly not expecting what was coming next.

Tia didn't waste any time. "Yo, Ang, you good?"

Angel smiled, even though she wasn't entirely in the mood for a conversation. "Yeah, I'm good. Why?"

Tia's bubbly energy was impossible to ignore, and Angel could hear the playfulness in her voice, even if something felt off. "So what happened with you and Mr. Playerman?"

Angel paused. She knew exactly what Tia was getting at. She'd been dodging this question for days. "Why, what's up, Tia?"

"Ugh, men. Like clockwork, right?" Tia scoffed, clearly annoyed. "But hold up, boo. You deserve better. This nigga is a lying snake. Now, lemme show you somethin' real quick…"

Angel sat up on her bed, squinting at the screen. "Where are you?"

Tia swung the camera around, giving Angel a live look at the club. The lights pulsed, strobing in all kinds of colors, and the music was so loud it rattled through the phone. People were everywhere—dancing, laughing, living in the moment. But Tia's focus was on Mitch. Angel wasn't sure what to expect, but she wasn't ready for what came next.

Tia's voice cut through the noise, sharp as hell. "Girl, you see him? At The Beat Lab, lookin' lost like he ain't got a clue. And guess who he's with? This bad chick, fine as hell, like she just stepped off a magazine cover."

Angel squinted, trying to focus on the scene. Mitch was leaning way too close to this woman. She was hanging on him, hand on his waist, and the way they were standing… it didn't sit right. Angel's stomach flipped. She wasn't surprised, but the pain of seeing it with her own eyes felt different.

Angel's voice wavered slightly. "We broke up, Tia."

Tia paused for a second, then shot back, "Wait, what? That man really dipped on you? What happened?"

Angel let out a frustrated sigh. "He said I'm not the type of woman he can mess with. Said he can't be with someone who does what I do. I guess I didn't line up with his 'standards.'"

Tia chuckled, but it was empty, with no amusement behind it. "Boy, bye! Standards? Girl, that man was actin' like he was perfect or somethin'. Please. If he couldn't handle you, that's all on him, not you."

Angel rolled her eyes, trying to shake off the sting. "It just hurts, Tia. I thought he actually cared, but I guess I wasn't good enough."

Tia clicked her tongue. "Let me tell you, Angel. If he can't handle you, that's his problem. Ain't no way you need to change who you are for a dude like that. That's him lookin' for excuses to leave, not you."

Angel let out a shaky breath. "It's just… he didn't even try to make it work. He just walked away like it didn't matter."

Tia softened for a moment, then added with a little smile, "Girl, don't even trip. You're worth more than someone who can't see all that you bring to the table. Real talk, he probably scared you might be too much for him. Men like that don't know how to handle a strong woman."

Angel sniffled, then wiped away a tear. "You right. I guess I just gotta let it go. He clearly ain't the one."

Tia clucked her tongue. "Exactly! He wanna act like he's above you, let him. You're a whole damn queen, and that crown ain't for anyone who's too scared to wear it. We out here living our best lives, period."

Angel chuckled, feeling the fire come back. "You know what, Tia? You're right. I'm done with his ass. I'm gonna focus on my own happiness."

"That's my girl!" Tia cheered. "Now, forget him and all that nonsense. We out here in these streets, and there's a new spot on the strip that's poppin'. We about to show out and show them what a real queen looks like. How about we go handle this, get our vibe right?"

Angel smiled, the weight of the situation feeling a little lighter. "I like the sound of that. Let's go turn up and show these people what they're missing."

"Hell yeah!" Tia responded. "Let's go live it up! We ain't got time for no dude who don't appreciate us. You a whole vibe, girl!"

As they wrapped up their call, Angel took a deep breath. She was still hurt, but Tia's words really sunk in. Mitch and her just weren't on the same page, and that was okay. Tonight was about moving on, not holding onto someone who couldn't see her for who she truly was.

Angel stepped out, ready to hit the streets with Tia and forget all about Mitch's small-minded nonsense. Tonight was hers, and no one was gonna take that from her.

Chapter Fifteen

"Payback's a Bitch"

Mitch's phone rang, and without thinking, he answered, the weight of the moment already pressing down on him."Yo, Mitch, we got some serious heat comin' our way. Word on the street is the Russians ain't forgettin' what went down. They've been watchin' us, and they're comin' for everything — and everyone we love, bro."

A cold knot twisted in Mitch's stomach. "What the hell you mean, T? We smoked everyone that night, We handled our business, took back what they owed us. We've been stayin' low since then."

T-Money's voice dropped. "Vladimir wants blood. We didn't just take out his crew—we took out his family. Now he's coming for payback."

He exhaled sharply. "They've been watching us. If we slip, we're done."

Mitch leaned back in his chair, eyes narrowing as his fingers tapped the edge of the table. "Vladimir? Never heard of him. Mitch's eyes hardened. "I'm not worried about them. "We slid out clean before, we'll do it again. But we gotta play this smart, T. They really think they can pull up in our city and shake somethin'? Hell nah. We stay sharp. Always."

T-Money let out a low laugh. "I know how you move, Mitch. Always ten steps ahead. But this one? We keep it quiet. Too many folks watchin'. One wrong move, and it's a wrap."

Mitch got quiet for a second, thinking back on all the years they spent buildin' from scraps. Blood, sweat, long nights—none of it came easy. Now trouble was circling again, and this time, it felt close.

T-Money's voice softened but remained firm. "I'll gather the crew. We keep this tight, no loose ends. We can't afford no slip-ups now." The call ended, and Mitch scanned the streets. Every alley, every fire escape—either a way out or a decision he'd regret.

The city wasn't the same. The air was thick with something unseen, something waiting. The Russians was creepin' close—too close. One slip-up, and the whole block would be lit up like the Fourth. Mitch wasn't callin' no suits or boardroom types. Nah, he hit up the ones who still had dirt under their nails—the ones who bled for the turf and still owed him from back in the day. Favors stacked from backroom hustles and alleyway handshakes—it was collection time.

Burners was goin' off nonstop. Link-ups got set in shadowy spots— abandoned lots, back doors of corner stores, anywhere the streetlight don't reach. Word moved fast: Mitch and T-Money wasn't playin'. The city was theirs, and they was geared up for whatever smoke came with it.

Mitch stayed sharp—hood smart, eyes everywhere—but he was boxed in. He had to move quick before the Russians did, but not loud enough to bring heat down on the whole squad.

Every move felt like dancin' on a razor, tryin' to move silent while the wolves circled. One false step? That's a wrap—body bag or cell block. Either way, the clock was tickin'.

The game had changed, and now Mitch had to play it dirty, smart, and quiet all at once.

Meanwhile, Angel walked the streets, unaware of the storm brewing. And even though Mitch and Angel were no longer together, the danger closing in on her was still his burden to bear. If she got caught in the crossfire because of him, he'd never forgive himself.

And protecting her from a distance? That was the hardest thing he'd ever done.

- Chapter Sixteen -

"City of Suspense: Caught in the Crossfire"

As twilight draped the city in a cloak of inky darkness, Mitch and T-money ventured deeper into the night.

Every quiet meet-up, every secret message, told 'em something bad was about to pop off.

A little doubt crept in—was someone already switchin' sides? Had a snake slid into their crew, turning what was tight into a bomb ready to blow? Every handshake felt like a test, every look could cut deep.

The city held its breath. What was once a careful game turned straight-up war—one wrong move and you gone.

Angel used to be right by Mitch's side, ride-or-die, but things had shifted—quiet and heavy. Too many lies came to light, too many truths they couldn't unhear. What they had? It cracked under the weight of all that wasn't said before. Now, they moved like strangers with history—close enough to remember, too far to reach.

While Mitch and T-Money moved lowkey through the streets, the Russians closed in hard. Eyes everywhere—cameras, snitches, watchers tracking every move. They mapped Mitch's whole game— his crew, his weak spots—and then, they found Angel.

She was the key, the pressure they needed to break him down.

The night the Russians moved, the streets were alive, full of noise and people, but danger was close. Unmarked cars rolled through the block, ready to trap anyone tryin' to run.

Angel walked alone, the city's energy hiding the danger beneath. She moved through streets she knew, not knowing heat was closing in. The streetlamp flickered, casting shapes all around. Her phone rang, but she let it go.

Then—outta nowhere—a rough hand clamped over her mouth, cutting off her scream. Another grabbed her arms, twisting 'em behind her back like a ragdoll.

The man spun her 'round, grip tight. "Don't make a scene, doll," he hissed in her ear. Cold fear shot through her.

Panic tried to take over, but she clenched down. Tears stung her eyes, blurring the shapes ahead.

"Who... who are you? What you want?" she croaked, voice shaky, barely out 'cause of the hand over her mouth.

A dry laugh rumbled from the man. "Let's just say we wanna talk. You know a guy named Mitch?"

Cold hit her like ice in her veins. "Mitch? Who's Mitch?" she lied, voice trembling.

"Don't play dumb, sweetheart," he growled, menace thick in his tone. "We know you're close to him. And T-Money. We know everything – where they live, their whereabouts, their every move."

Angel's mind raced. Mitch. T-Money. They were in danger, and she was caught in the crossfire. She knew the risks of her world, but this felt different, more calculated, more terrifying.

"I... I don't know anything! I swear!" she pleaded, her voice cracking with a raw fear she couldn't mask.

The man with the cruel eyes studied her, with doubt crossing his face. "We'll see if you're telling the truth,"

The city, once where Mitch found his victories, now felt tainted by a creeping darkness. This hidden operation was a threat, quietly spreading like a shadow, ready to unravel everything Mitch had carefully built. The tension in the air grew heavier as the Russians set their sights on getting the information they wanted, with Angel as the reluctant key to unlocking the secrets of the mysterious duo. The gritty streets of the city were unnervingly quiet as Angel suddenly found herself trapped in a nightmare. What was supposed to be a simple late-night walk on the strip quickly turned into a terrifying ordeal. Despite her desperate struggles, their strength was too much, and she was shoved into the back seat. The car sped off, leaving the scene behind.

Inside the vehicle, Angel's fear intensified as a deep voice cut through the tense air, interrogating her about Mitch.

The city's vibrant glow filtered through the tinted windows of the car, casting a muted light on the tense scene within. The strangers remained hidden in darkness, their intent veiled by the mysterious atmosphere.

" I don't know who he is!" Angel pleaded, her tears mixing with the intense tension in the confined space.

The car reached a secluded destination, a looming building that appeared to swallow them into its ominous facade.

The Russians dragged her inside, the structure echoing with an almost perceptible sense of danger.

Deep within the building, Angel was firmly bound to a chair, encircled by a group of armed men whose faces remained hidden.

The room hummed with an atmosphere of covert dealings. Muffled conversations, like whispers echoing through a tunnel, bounced off the concrete walls, their content obscured by the din.

The Russian mobsters, dressed in sharp suits that seemed to belong in a crime drama, circled around her like hunters closing in on their prey. Harsh syllables, in a language Angel couldn't make sense of, snapped through the air. The men across from her leaned in, their faces barely visible in the dim overhead light. The only movement in the room was the frantic rise and fall of Angel's chest, each breath a battle against the crushing tension around her. The silence that followed each question felt like it pressed down on her, thick with unspoken threats. It was like a scene ripped from a mob movie. As Angel struggled against her restraints, the Russians pushed harder, their faces cold and emotionless.

Footsteps echoed faintly in the distance, and Angel could feel the tight grip of the maze-like structure surrounding her. The air was thick with a pulse of movement she couldn't quite see. Ghostly echoes—half-formed footsteps mixed with quiet murmurs—swirled around corners, their source unknown.

The Russians moved through the space with practiced ease, their every step revealing a familiarity born of countless operations within these walls. They had one goal: to extract the information buried deep within Angel, a prize they were determined to claim. Their tactics felt like a high-stakes chess match, playing out in the shadows, each move carefully calculated.

Angel was at the center of it all, her fate hanging by a thread. Unmoved by her pleas, the Russians pressed on with their unyielding interrogation, dragging her deeper into the darkness.

Chapter Seventeen

"The Devil's Deal: Lines Are Drawn"

<u>(Vladimir Kuznetsov)</u>

Vladimir Kuznetsov ran shit with a grip so tight, you either fell in line or got buried under it. He wasn't just some mob boss handed a crown—he took it, proved he was built for this. His bloodline was thick with mobsters, old-school killers who ran Moscow's streets like a family business. But he ain't ride off legacy alone. Vladimir earned his spot the hard way—playing the long game, outthinking, outmoving, and when needed, outkilling anybody in his path.

He came up in the cold, unforgiving streets of Moscow, where respect wasn't given, it was taken. The Kuznetsov name? It held weight from the gutter to the penthouses, had killers and CEOs movin' careful when they heard it.

You ain't make a move in the city without them knowing. They had hands in everything—legit businesses, underground markets, and pockets deep in dirty cops and politicians. If money moved, they got a cut. If power shifted, they were the ones shifting it.

Vladimir learned the rules early: trust no one, strike first, and never show weakness. His mind was a weapon just as deadly as his trigger finger. The empire his family built wasn't just about flexing muscle—it was about control, about making sure every move worked in their favor. The real money wasn't in petty hustles or taxing low-level crews—"Tossin' bricks 'round the map like he was playin' catch with the plug."

When he took over, he didn't just hold the throne—he expanded it, turned the game into something bigger, something untouchable. He wasn't the type to stunt in loud suits or flashy cars. That wasn't his style. He moved in silence, let his power speak without a single word. He was the kind of man you never saw coming until it was too late. A ghost in the underworld, a puppet master pulling strings while the city danced, never even knowing who was really running the show.

When Vladimir stepped into the room, his sharp gaze cut through the tension like a blade. The air thickened instantly as he turned to Angel, his expression cold and calculated, his tone laced with authority and quiet menace.

When Vladimir stepped into the room, his sharp gaze cut through the tension like a blade. The air thickened instantly as he turned to Angel, his expression cold and calculated, his tone laced with authority and quiet menace.

"Angel, sweetheart, you comprehend the gravity of this situation, don't you?" His voice, deep and commanding, reverberated within the confined space.

The walls felt like they were closing in as the Russian boss's presence grew heavier, pressing down on her like an unseen weight. Leaning against a table, the boss continued, "Your boyfriend has to pay for the lives he took—my family. Where is he?" His voice was tight with frustration, each word simmering with an anger that threatened to spill over.

Angel sat trapped in a cold metal chair, dread creeping through her like an unwelcome chill. The room felt suffocating, heavy with unspoken threats. Shadows swallowed the faces of the men surrounding her, their presence looming, watching. She strained to catch a glimpse of their eyes, to read something—anything—but all she saw were shifting outlines, the faint gleam of a silver watch, the dull glint of a gold chain. The silence stretched unbearably, broken only by the uneven sound of her own breathing. The building, an imposing structure with graffiti-covered walls, echoed with distant footsteps and the occasional creaking of worn floorboards.

The Russian boss circled Angel, his eyes never leaving hers. "Mitch owes a debt, and he will pay with interest.

"You can make this easy on yourself, or you can suffer the consequences of your silence," he said, his voice steady but firm, leaving no room for doubt.

The room was thick with tension as he waited for Angel's response. The only sounds came from the muffled hum of the city bleeding through the cracks, distant and indifferent to her fate.

The stark, windowless space offered no comfort, no escape. Reality crashed over Angel in waves—there was no bargaining, no illusions to cling to. Mitch, with his easy charm and reckless grin, felt like nothing more than a memory, a picture from another life. The security his name once carried now seemed worthless, as distant as the world outside these walls.

Her thoughts raced, searching for a way out, but every path led back to the same danger. The boss's gaze stayed locked on her, unwavering, his patience running thin.

"We know Mitch runs the Vegas streets," he continued, his voice cool and deliberate. "He can't hide forever. Tell us where he is, and maybe—just maybe—we'll reconsider what happens to those who align themselves with a dead man walking."

Angel's heart raced as the weight of her decision crashed down on her. Every part of her wanted to protect Mitch, to keep him safe, but the reality of what was at stake clawed at her. She knew that revealing his whereabouts meant risking his life, but staying silent could come with an even worse price. Her mind scrambled, torn between the loyalty she felt for the man she loved and the overwhelming need to survive.

The room felt small, suffocating, as the silence between them grew thick. The sounds of the city outside barely made it through the cracks, a faint reminder of a world that felt miles away. Across from her, the Russian boss remained unmoving, his gaze fixed on her like a predator watching its prey. His words, cold and calculating, pressed down on her like an invisible weight, making it harder to think.

Vladimir's anger was undeniable, but it wasn't just in his words—it was in his steps. He moved closer, each footfall heavy, as if the space around her was closing in. She tried to steady her breath, but her chest felt tight, each inhale a struggle.

The slap hit her with unexpected force, snapping her head to the side. The sting cut through her senses, leaving her dizzy and disoriented. Tears welled up in her eyes, not just from the pain, but from the crushing helplessness she felt in that moment.

And then the blows kept coming, one after another, relentless. Each hit was a painful reminder of how little control she had in this moment, how powerless she really was. The chair beneath her creaked, groaned under the pressure of her attempts to fight back, but she couldn't move, couldn't escape.

The room, which had once been cold and impersonal, now felt like a prison. The violence, the fury in Vladimir's eyes—it all blurred together, making her wonder how far he'd go to break her. It wasn't just about getting answers anymore; it was about forcing her into submission, stripping away everything she had left.

Angel's mind was spinning. Each wave of pain dulled her thoughts, each slap more distant than the last. She could barely think, just the pain and the overwhelming need for it to stop. Mitch's face, once clear in her mind, was now nothing more than a distant memory, a ghost fading further away with each passing second.

She couldn't hold out any longer.

In a broken, shaky voice, she finally gave in, the words tumbling out before she could stop them. "Okay, I'll call him."

The air around her felt colder now, as if her surrender had sealed her fate. The room was silent again, but it was a silence filled with the weight of everything she had just given up.

Vladimir leaned back with a sinister smile. "Smart choice, sweetheart. You'll save yourself a world of hurt." Struggling with the restraints, He gave Angel her phone, her hands trembling. She dialed Mitch's number, each ring resonating like a countdown to an uncertain fate.

Mitch, unaware of the unfolding nightmare, answered on the other end with his usual nonchalance.

"Angel, what's going on?" Mitch's voice carried a sense of calm, unaware of the turmoil brewing on the other end.

Angel hesitated for a moment, the weight of her decisions pressing on her. She took a deep breath and began, "Mitch, we have a problem. They've got me, and they want to talk to you."

Mitch, now alert, demanded, "Who got you? What's going on?" Angel could hear the concern in his voice, mixed with an undercurrent of worry.

Vladimir, having caught enough of the conversation to understand, stepped forward with calm precision and took the phone from Angel's trembling hand. His voice was cold, deliberate—without haste, but heavy with authority.

"Listen carefully, Mitch. We have the girl. If you want her alive and unharmed, you come to us. Alone. No police, no clever moves. You have twenty-four hours."

Mitch stood frozen, the weight of the words sinking in like stones. He wasn't just hearing a threat—he was staring down the consequences of every choice he'd made. Anger surged through him, colliding with a deep, gnawing fear he couldn't shake. This wasn't a game anymore. It never had been.

Angel, still and silent, waited—caught in the uncertain space between hope and dread. Her life now hung on Mitch's decision, and she knew it. Her breathing was shallow, her heart pounding in her chest like a countdown she couldn't stop.

Time felt cruel. Every tick of the clock echoed louder, each second peeling away her composure. The control she had clung to so tightly was slipping, like cracks forming in a dam that had held back too much for too long. She had tried to manage the lies, to hide the damage, to stay ahead of the fallout—but now it was all unraveling. And the closer the truth crept to the surface, the more she realized: this could destroy not just her, but Mitch too.

- Chapter Eighteen -

"Loyalty on the Line"

The Nevada sun beat down relentlessly, turning the cracked desert floor into a shimmering, unforgiving stretch of nothing. A faint haze hung in the air, thick with the sweet scent of marijuana, curling from the blunt in Mitch's weathered hands. The desert heat was unbearable, the kind that made you feel like you were breathing fire. Mitch leaned against his car, arms crossed, staring out as T-Money's truck kicked up a cloud of dust. It was all too quiet out here, just the sound of the engine and the relentless wind.

T-Money's truck came to a slow stop, the dust settling around him as he stepped out with his usual calm swagger, like he didn't have a care in the world. He wiped his brow with the back of his hand, the weight of the gold chains around his neck catching the light.

He didn't rush up to Mitch, though. He never did. Slow, deliberate steps. That was his style. He was a man who always had a plan—or at least, that's how he made it seem.

Without missing a beat, he snatched the blunt from Mitch's hand, taking a long drag. "Man, you know you're not the only one who needs to get high today," he muttered before handing it back.

Mitch took it back with a half-smile, trying to keep his nerves steady. "Damn, nigga, you ain't even put in on this." T-Money blew out a cloud of smoke, eyes narrowing. **"You're worried about that now?"** He handed the blunt back. **"Nigga, we got bigger shit to handle."**

Mitch's expression hardened. **"Yeah, you're right."**

T-Money took the blunt back, eyeing Mitch closely now. His gaze shifted as he leaned against the car, crossing his arms. **"Talk to me, Mitch. What the hell happened?"**

Mitch exhaled slowly, wiping his face with his sleeve. **"They got Angel, man. The Russians. They know she's tied to me, and now they think they got me right where they want me."**

T-Money let out a frustrated sigh, running his hand through his hair. **"Man, I *told* you the Russians was watchin'. Now they got her, this is fucked up."** He shook his head, pacing for a moment. **"Look, you know I got your back. Ain't no question.** Mitch looked at him, **"I know, T. I know. They're holdin' her hostage to get to me. They said I got twenty-four hours to show up if I want her back. I can't let them take her out, she's innocent in all this."** We both know that." "things didn't work out between us, but... she doesn't deserve to be caught in the crossfire. I feel responsible, T. We gotta get her out of this."

T-money raised an eyebrow, a mischievous glint in his eyes. "Hold up, are you telling me you ain't smashin' that fine thang anymore? Thought you two were gettin' serious."

With a grin Mitch chuckled. A hint of sadness lacing his voice. "Nah, nah. We were tight for a while," he admitted with a head shake."Life happens, you know? But none of that matters now. We just gotta get her to safety. T-Money exhaled deeply, looking out over the desert, like he was weighing his next move. **"Look, I'm skeptical as hell about this whole thing. But you're my boy. We've been through worse, right? If you're telling me she's innocent, then I'm down to roll with you. We get in, get her, and get out."**

Mitch gave him a nod, grateful but still tense. **"Appreciate it, T.** T-Money slapped him on the back, a dry laugh escaping his lips. **"Man, you're lucky we've been through hell and back together. You know I got your back, always. But don't be makin' no hero moves out here. You got one shot at this. We move quick, we move smart. If not... well, you know how that goes."**

Mitch shot him a look, eyes serious. **"I know. No mistakes."** We gotta get her outta Dodge after this is done."

T-money pondered this, his face etched with concern. "You've got a point, bro. But how are we supposed to pull that off? Mitch rubbed his chin, a frown creasing his brow. "I been thinkin' about that. Maybe we could stash her with Mama Rose.

She'd keep Angel safe, at least for a while." Mama Rose, a fearsome woman who ran a hidden speakeasy on Chicago's Southside, was one of the few they could trust implicitly.

"Mama Rose, huh?" T-money chuckled. "That old woman could probably take down a whole squad of Russians herself. But yeah, that might just work."

Mitch leaned back, rubbing his jaw as he let the words settle. The weight of what they were about to do hung heavy in the air.

"Look, we gotta figure this shit out," Mitch said, his voice low, like he was talking to himself as much as to T-Money. "Getting Angel back ain't gonna be no easy job."

T-Money grinned, but it was more of a cold, calculating look than anything friendly. You worrying too much, Mitch. We handle this like we always do—calculated, ruthless, and we keep the crew tight. G? He's a tech genius, but when shit hits the fan, he's got the street instincts that'll keep us all alive. You know he ain't no stranger to a fight. He's just got a different way of handling business." He tapped his fingers on the table, the sound sharp and steady. "You're right about one thing, though—this time, it ain't gonna be easy. But when has it ever been?"

Mitch paused, his voice dropping to a low growl. "Yo, T, we gotta talk before this shit blows up in our faces."

T-Money took a long drag, the cherry glowing like a warning in the dying sunlight. His eyes were sharp, calculating. "Spit it out, man. We ain't strangers to this life. We've been through hell and back. We know how this game plays."

"Man, we been brothers since sandbox days, built this empire together, side by side. If one of us goes down..." Mitch paused, the words catching in his throat.

"Say it, man damn," T-money urged, his voice uncharacteristically soft.

"Just know I love you, homie. More than this life, more than this hustle. You ain't just my partner, you my family."

Silence stretched between them, heavy with unspoken sentiment. A faint smile flickered across T-money's lips.

"Love you too, man," Mitch said quietly. "We can't dress it up. Things might get ugly. But if we go down, we make sure it leaves a mark." Chicago raised, remember? Ain't no surrender, no backing down. We go down loud, together."

That old spark lit up in they eyes for a split sec—like nothin' ever changed. Fist bump was quiet, but it hit deep. Years of blood, losses, and loyalty in one move. They both knew the streets don't give do-overs. Stakes was life or death. But scared? Hell nah. Not tonight.

Mitch leaned back, that crooked grin playin' on his face. "Just imagine the headline, bro—'Chicago legends go out in flames.' Better than some weak-ass obituary actin' like we ain't never shook the city."

T-money chuckled, the sound rough but honest. "Yeah, they'll remember us all right. Not as victims, but as kings who went out on their own terms."

"Remember that time we got chased by the cops through half of the park, just for that damn hot dog?"

T-money chuckled, the memory softening the grim lines on his face.

Mitch snorted. "Man, you almost lost your shoes that day! And I swear, Officer Williams had a personal vendetta against us."

They shared a laugh, the sound echoing hollow in the cavernous space. The levity, however, was a fragile thing, easily shattered by the reality of their situation.

"But hey," T-money continued, his voice turning serious, "we always made it out, one way or another. And we ain't done yet."

"Hell no we ain't," Mitch declared, his eyes hardening with determination. "We got unfinished business, gotta see this through."

Damn right," T-money agreed, his fist bumping Mitch's. "We built this kingdom by blood, sweat, and tears. We earned our stripes and we ain't going out like punks."

Silence fell again, heavier this time. The weight of their shared past, the burden of the lives they'd taken, pressed down on them.

"Look," Mitch finally said, his voice low, "I ain't preachin', but I just want you to know... I ain't proud of everything we did."

T-money nodded slowly, understanding etched on his face. "Me neither, man. But sometimes, the streets leave you with hard choices. We made the ones we had to, to survive, to protect the ones we loved."

"Yeah," Mitch sighed, the weight of it all settling into his chest. "But that don't mean we gotta keep walkin' down the same road. If we make it outta this, maybe..." He trailed off, unsure of how to put into words the faint hope that flickered in him, a hope he wasn't sure he deserved.

T-money picked up the thought, finishing the sentence for him. "...Maybe we find a way to step out, do something different. Leave this life behind, build somethin' real, somethin' clean." He paused, but then the air shifted. "Right?"

Mitch looked at him, a tired smile tugging at his lips. But before he could say anything, T-money's voice cut through the silence.

"Hell no, Mitch! I ain't ready to leave the game yet, bro!" The words spilled out faster than he meant, but they were the truth. He wasn't sure what life looked like without this, without the crew, without the grind.

A spark of light danced in Mitch's eyes. "Yeah, maybe. We deserve that, man. A chance to rewrite our story, not just for ourselves, but for the kids comin' up. Show them there's more out there than this."

"You serious, Mitch?" T-money finally spoke, his voice a low growl.

He exhaled a cloud of smoke that dissipated into the night, his eyes narrowed in a mixture of disbelief and simmering anger.

Mitch remained silent, the weight of his unspoken desire heavy on him. T-money scoffed, a harsh, humorless sound.

"Picket fence, dreamin' 'bout the suburbs now? You think that kinda life's gonna be all sunshine and roses? They got problems out there too, just a different kind."

The anger in T-money's voice landed like a punch, completely at odds with the casual way Mitch had proposed the idea.

He gestured around the grimy desert area, a sardonic smile twisting his lips. "This life, it ain't pretty, I know that. But you think we got here by wishing on stars?"

Mitch finally met T-money's eyes, a spark of defiance igniting in his own. "I know what it took, T," he said, his voice gruff. "But there's gotta be more. This constant struggle, always looking over your shoulder..."

"Don't you see?" T-money interrupted, his voice escalating. "This ain't some nine-to-five, Mitch. This is who we are." "It took us years to get to the top," T-money said, his voice thick with the weight of it all. "Remember those nights, man? Huddled up on a park bench in Chicago, freezing our asses off, with nothin' but a dream and a pocket full of dime bags?"

Mitch felt the wave of memories hit him like a freight train, raw and unfiltered. He could almost feel the cold, the hunger, the burning desperation that had driven them both. They'd been nobody, fighting for scraps in a city that had no room for them.

T-money's words cut through the haze of those memories. "We clawed our way up, Mitch. Fought for every inch, every dime. Ain't no easy handouts. We ain't no damn boardroom players. We built this shit on sweat, blood, and sleepless nights. This wasn't handed to us, bro. We made this, piece by piece, on these streets."

There was no illusion between them now. No sugarcoating. Just the truth—dirty, brutal, real.

He jabbed a finger at Mitch's chest, the blunt forgotten in his hand. "You wanna walk away from that? From everything we built together? From the blood, sweat, and tears we poured into this life?"

Silence descended, heavy with unspoken words and a lifetime of shared history.

The anger in T-money's voice had softened, replaced by a profound sadness. He understood Mitch's yearning for a different life, but leaving it all behind felt like a betrayal, a disrespect to the path they had walked together.

Mitch let out a slow breath, feelin' the weight of T-money's stare. The heat in his eyes, the anger wrapped in that betrayal, hit him like a freight train. "Yo," Mitch started, voice calm but the storm in his gut barely held in check, "I ain't tryna downplay what we been through, man. You're my brother, my ride or die. Ain't no way I'd be here without you, we built this shit together."

T-money's scowl softened just a little, the edge in his eyes startin' to ease up, but the tension was still thick between them.

Mitch took a drag off his blunt, the smoke driftin' up in the air like the silence between them. "But there comes a point, T," Mitch continued, his voice gruff, "where this shit don't hit the same. Maybe it's age, maybe it's seein' too many young niggas get swallowed up, lost to the streets that don't give a damn. Or maybe it's too many body counts, too many faces buried in the dirt for us to just keep movin' like nothin' happened."

He paused, thinkin' carefully before speakin' again. "Look, I ain't sayin' you gotta walk away with me. This life's in your blood, loyalty deeper than the desert dirt. But if you ever get tired of it, if you ever feel like you want something else, something clean... you know I'm there. No questions."

The air between them was thick now, the silence loaded with everything they'd been through. There was no easy answer, no quick fix, just the weight of all those years in the game—what it had cost them, and what it still might.

T-money didn't respond, but the tension in his shoulders eased slightly.

Mitch knew his friend wouldn't change his mind overnight, but planting the seed, letting him know he wasn't alone – that was the first step.

"We ain't gotta be on the same page, T," Mitch finally said, a hint of a smile tugging at the corner of his lips. "But the page next to you, that's mine. Always will be."

"Alright," he said, his voice low and gravelly, "let's get back to the Russians."

T-money sat up straighter, the playful banter momentarily forgotten.

He pulled a crumpled map from his back pocket, slapped it on the hot hood of the truck. "Word is, they got Angel stashed in some old military site, way out past where GPS stop workin'. Used to be a Cold War arms spot—left to rot."

Mitch leaned in, bare arms catchin' sun, brows low as he followed the route. Sweat beading, jaw tight. "Desert dry, middle of nowhere. Figures they'd pick a place nobody looks twice at."

T-Money shook his head, lips twisted. "Quiet? That place damn near a bunker. Fences high, wire sharp, cameras posted up like hawks. We ain't just walkin' in."

"And how many trigger-happy guards do you think they'll have stationed there?" Mitch asked, a glint of steel in his eyes.

T-money shrugged. "Enough to make things interesting. But hey, that's what we do best, right? Walk into trouble and stir the pot."

Now that she was being held captive by a ruthless Russian mob outfit with a reputation for brutality. They couldn't leave her there.

"We need a plan," Mitch said, his voice firm. "Something precise, something that gets us in, gets Angel out, and gets us the hell out of there before the whole city's crawling with Spetsnaz."

The next few hours felt like a haze—half-focused planning, a blur of maps, scribbled notes, and talkin' through every move like their lives depended on it. They went over the guard routes, plotted every entry and exit, but it still didn't feel like enough. Mitch could feel the weight of it, but there was no turning back now.

He slung his duffel bag over his shoulder, the familiar weight of his customized Glock comforting, even though he hated how much he relied on it. It was always there, ready.

"Time to get Angel back," Mitch said, his voice low, rough, like he was trying to convince himself just as much as he was convincing T-Money. Doubt was there, lingering, but he shoved it down. Not now. T-Money met his gaze, something in his eyes flickering— determination, maybe desperation, but most likely a little of both. "Let's do it," he muttered, his smile sharp but tense. It wasn't confidence—it was the kind of grim resolve that came from knowing they didn't have a choice, not if they wanted to make it out alive.

Chapter Nineteen

"No Mercy: Streets of Vengeance"

In the dead of night, you could hear Mitch and T-Money loading their guns, the sound sharp and cold. The smell of gun oil mixed with the thick, uneasy vibe, almost suffocating. Their hands moved with the precision of men who'd been down this road a thousand times, but tonight felt different. There was a weight to it, heavier than the usual job.

T-money checked his rounds, methodical, making sure each bullet was accounted for. His eyes flicked to Mitch, his face hard, but there was a flicker of doubt behind his cold stare. They knew the risks, but there was no turning back now. Not when Angel was on the line.

Mitch gave a low grunt as he slid his Glock into place, the gun feeling right in his hand. "Tonight ain't about the usual shit. We ain't just movin' weight. We're goin' in deep, into the heart of enemy turf. Angel's gotta come back with us, no matter what. We've taken these fuckers down before, we can do it again."

T-money gave a half-smile, but there was no humor in it. "You think they can handle us a second time? Last time, they didn't see what was comin'. This time, we're makin' sure they never forget us."

Mitch's eyes hardened, his voice colder now. "It's personal. Ain't no petty beef, no street bullshit. These guys took somethin' that's ours. We're doin' this for respect. For the code we live by."

T-money nodded, but his expression didn't change. "Yeah, well, just make sure this don't turn into a one-way trip. We get in, we get out. We don't lose anybody tonight. You hear me?"

The room fell quiet. It wasn't a speech. It was a warning. No one said a word.

Mitch broke the silence, his voice steady but heavy with meaning. "Alright, here's the play. We got two ways in: front and back. Dru and G, y'all take the front. Cause a distraction. Keep them busy. You shoot anyone who moves, don't think twice."

Dru cracked his knuckles, the sound like thunder in the still room. "No problem, boss. We'll light this shit up."

Mitch turned to G, eyes narrowing at the blade hanging from his belt. "Leave the knives tonight. We need firepower, not toys. You got that silenced piece I gave you?"

G grinned, sliding the switchblade away. "Always, boss. Silenced nine, ready to put in work."

T-money's eyes flashed with approval. "That's what I like to hear. Me and Mitch'll take the back. We'll disable their security, make us a clean exit. Fast and quiet. That's how we move."

G tapped his silencer. "Ain't no one gonna hear us coming."

Mitch shot him a look. "Good. Now listen up. When we're inside, no heroics. No one's out here for glory. We stick together. If someone goes down, we drag 'em out. No exceptions."

Dru raised an eyebrow. "What about Demitri? That big Russian? Dude's a freakin' tank. Word is, he can take a bullet and still keep moving."

Mitch's lips curled into a grim smile. "Demitri ain't shit. We take him down the same way we take everything else. We fight like there's no tomorrow. Fear's a luxury we ain't got. You worry about him, I'll worry about the rest."

T-money slammed his fist onto the table, his voice like a war cry. "Tonight, we show these fuckers what happens when they fuck with us! They ain't ready for this shit."

The crew nodded, a chorus of silent agreement. There was no fear here—just resolve. Just a family bound by blood and bullets.

"Bet," Mitch grumbled, his voice low, but full of heat. "Let's go remind these motherfuckas who the fuck we are. They got the numbers, but we got the heart. Tonight, they 'bout to see what real fear look like."

"Let's show these mothafuckas who they fuckin' wit." They moved out, slipping into the night like shadows, the air heavy with the weight of what was coming. Mitch and T-money took the lead, guiding the crew to the ride, the engine growling in the dark, ready for the storm ahead.

The city was alive, but tonight, it felt like the calm before the storm.

Mitch slid behind the wheel, his fingers tight on the leather. T-money was already deep into the blueprint of the building where Angel was locked up, his mind working over every detail. The crew was scattered, each man in position, ready for the signal.

The streets were their battleground now. Mitch could feel the adrenaline kicking in, a cold rush as he imagined every way this could all go wrong. He could see it in his mind—the bodies, the chaos, the sirens. But Angel's face was in his mind too. Her eyes, scared and desperate. He wasn't leaving without her.

T-money's eyes never stopped scanning the dark streets, his hands never still. The tension was thick in the air, but they knew this dance. They'd done it a hundred times. No talking, just the quiet hum of the engine and the steady beat of their hearts.

When they hit the main road, Mitch gritted his teeth. It was now or never. His grip tightened. The city passed by like a blur, but everything felt too real. They were stepping into the unknown, but that was just another night for them.

They didn't need to say anything. The plan was set. They had one job tonight—get Angel back. And make sure these Russians never forgot who they were fuckin' with.

Chapter Twenty

"In Too Deep: The Last Stand"

The flickering glow of the security monitor threw erratic shadows across Vladimir's face, his eyes narrowing as the grainy images shifted. For a moment, his usual suspicion gave way to something darker, something more dangerous. A twisted smile curled his lips.

"Looks like the rats are finally here," Vladimir muttered under his breath, his voice rough, like someone who'd been grinding their teeth for too long. He didn't even look away from the monitor as he spoke.

Dimitri didn't react at first, his gaze fixed on the screen, studying the shaky image. His jaw was tight, but he wasn't showing any outward signs of tension. He'd been in enough of these situations to know when to keep his cool. His fingers drummed absently on the edge of the table, a quiet rhythm that betrayed a little more anxiety than he wanted to admit.

The figures in the car were barely distinguishable, just blurry shapes in the darkness, but Dimitri knew that walk. The stiff, deliberate movements. The way they didn't look like they were just out for a casual drive. No, these guys were here with purpose, and that alone told him they weren't playing around.

He shifted in his seat, glancing at Vladimir, who had already turned back to the monitor. "This is it, huh?" Dimitri said quietly, his voice low but tinged with something like resignation. He wasn't afraid, but there was that nagging feeling that they might've underestimated what was coming.

Vladimir's grin spread slowly, like he was enjoying a moment he knew would come. His eyes burned with something cold and dangerous. "Let's see if they've got the heart to finish what they started."

Suddenly, he slammed his fist down on the table, making the whole room rattle. The sharp crack echoed through the air as he yelled, his words in Russian heavy with venom: "Думали, могут играть с нами? Глупцы. К утру от них только воспоминания останутся." "Get Petrov and his boys on high alert. Let them know the entertainment has arrived early." His breath came heavy, chest rising and falling with the intensity of his anger. There was no more playing. His mind was already two steps ahead, calculating the damage, and nothing would stop him from seeing it through.

Dimitri grunted, his voice thick with exhaustion and a touch of impatience, as if the weight of the world hung on every word. He muttered a quick series of commands into the hidden mic, each one sharper than the last. Then, silence. The kind of silence that presses down on you, thick and suffocating, turning seconds into endless minutes.

Outside, the night was still, save for the occasional gust of wind scraping across the barren desert. The secluded building stood like a forgotten ghost on the edge of nowhere, far from the bright lights of Vegas—so far that the world felt like it didn't even remember it existed.

Rain started to fall, hot and relentless, lashing against the corrugated metal of the warehouse. The storm felt like it was ripping through the desert itself—each crack of thunder a punch to the gut, each flash of lightning a jagged tear in the sky. Vladimir stood still, his gaze fixed on the windows, watching the rain turn the dust into mud. The isolation was heavy, but it didn't bother him. This was where things went down—where no one would ever look. And the storm outside? It wasn't nearly as wild as the one brewing inside.

He reveled in the chaos, the thrill of the hunt that coursed through his veins.

Years of smuggling and black-market dealings had transformed the once-abandoned building into a fortress.

Steel shutters secured the windows, and a multitude of hidden cameras provided a 360-degree view of the surrounding yard.

The warehouse floor was a museum of violence. Decades of weaponry, from antique rifles to modern assault weapons, lay stacked together, each a testament to a different era of conflict.

Vladimir, a man who thrived in his territory, had thoroughly prepared for this eventuality. He knew Mitch wouldn't back down, not with Angel's life hanging in the balance.

"It was a game of chess, and Vladimir was already several moves ahead, controlling the board with calm precision. The game had begun. He grabbed a heavily modified AK-47 from a hidden rack, the weapon a familiar weight in his hands."

Tonight, the building wouldn't just be a battleground; it would be a graveyard for Mitch and his foolish crusade.

As Mitch and his crew arrived, the headlights flickered, sputtering out one last weak glow before plunging them into darkness. The warehouse loomed ahead like a black abyss, swallowing sound, light—everything. Inside the car, the air was thick with tension. Mitch tightened his grip on the wheel, his pulse hammering. He could feel it—the weight of the moment pressing against his chest.

No one spoke. The doors swung open in near silence, the crew moving like predators into the night. T-Money adjusted his jacket, the metal of his gun catching a faint glint from the distant streetlight before disappearing into the fabric. Dru and G flanked them, their breathing steady, eyes sharp.

Then—from inside the warehouse—a laugh. A deep, guttural chuckle that slithered through the darkness and coiled around Mitch's spine.

The Russians knew they were here.

"Shit," T-Money hissed.

Mitch's fingers flexed around the grip of his Glock. No time to rethink. They had to move.

"Spread out," he ordered, voice low but firm. "Keep your backs to the walls."

They slid through the busted door like ghosts, movin' fast but quiet. The warehouse was big, empty, and gave off that don't-get-too-comfy energy. Smelled like grease, metal, and somethin' foul—like bad business went down here and never left. One weak-ass bulb hung from the ceiling, swingin' like it was nervous too, throwin' jumpy shadows over old crates and jacked-up pallets. The silence? Thick enough to choke on. Then—footsteps. Heavy. Purposeful.

Mitch barely had time to react before a figure lunged from the darkness. A Russian goon, massive and built like a battering ram, came at him fast. Mitch twisted, ducking the wild swing that sent a metal pipe crashing into a crate behind him. Splinters flew. The impact echoed.

T-Money's gun barked—two sharp pops cutting through the tension. A scream followed.

No time to look. The goon swung again. Mitch feinted right, then drove a knee straight into the man's ribs. A grunt. A stumble—but not enough. The Russian recovered fast, shoving Mitch back with brute force.

Mitch hit the ground hard. Pain burst through his spine. The goon loomed over him, fists raised, ready to cave in his skull.

Then—A shot.

The Russian jerked violently, a crimson mist spraying from his throat. He staggered, gurgling, hands clutching the wound. Another shot—this one tearing through his temple. He crumpled like a puppet with its strings cut.

T-Money stood over him, smoking gun in hand. "You good?"

Mitch coughed, pushing himself up. "Yeah."

No time to process. Another shout—Dru's voice.

Across the warehouse, Dru was locked in a brutal struggle. A Russian had him pinned against a stack of crates, knife flashing in the dim light. Mitch raised his Glock, but the fight was too tight— one wrong shot and Dru was dead.

Dru grunted, the blade inching toward his throat. In a desperate move, he drove his forehead into the Russian's nose. A sickening crunch. The man reeled, blood pouring from his shattered nose. Dru didn't hesitate. He grabbed the Russian's own knife and buried it under his ribcage. A wet gasp. Silence. The body slid to the ground.

T-Money wiped the sweat from his brow. "This is getting messy."

Mitch scanned the room. "Where's Vladimir?"

As if in answer, gunfire erupted from the second floor. Bullets tore through the railing, sending sparks flying. Mitch ducked behind a crate, cursing.

Vladimir stood on the balcony, a pistol in each hand, grinning like the devil himself. "You American dogs don't know when to quit."

Mitch's jaw clenched.

"We gotta move," T-Money said. "Now."

They split, darting between cover, dodging the hail of bullets raining down. Dru and G laid down fire, forcing Vladimir back toward an office door.

"He's running!" Mitch shouted.

They charged up the stairs. Mitch reached the office door first—just in time to hear the lock click.

T-Money didn't wait. He kicked the door in. The wood exploded inward.

Inside, Vladimir stood near a desk, blood smeared across his lip. Behind him, two more Russians flanked him, guns raised.

The room exploded in gunfire.

Glass shattered. Walls chipped. T-Money took one goon down with a clean shot to the throat. The second rushed him, slamming him into the desk.

Mitch wrestled with Vladimir. Fists flying. He felt the Russian's knuckles crack against his ribs, pain flaring, but he didn't stop. He drove his own fist into Vladimir's stomach, then smashed his elbow into the man's jaw. Vladimir stumbled, wiped blood from his mouth with the back of his hand.

Then he laughed.

"You don't have the balls," Vladimir sneered, his smirk sharp, taunting.

Mitch raised his gun. "Try me."

Vladimir moved—fast.

His hand darted under the desk.

Steel flashed.

The knife sliced through Mitch's side, hot pain tearing into his flesh. He grunted, stumbling back, but kept his gun trained.

Vladimir was already moving.

"Motherf—" Mitch growled, gripping his side as Vladimir yanked open a hidden panel in the wall.

Dru snatched up a crumpled paper from the desk. "Bastard had an escape route ready."

Mitch wiped the blood off his palm. "Not today."

They caught a glimpse of Vladimir's shadow disappearing into the tunnel.

"No way he's getting outta here," T-Money muttered.

Without hesitation, they bolted after him.

The tunnel swallowed them in darkness, their heavy boots thudding against the floor. The scent of damp earth mixed with something foul, something rotten.

A dim bulb buzzed overhead in the back, strugglin' to light up the place.

Gunshots cracked through the silence—loud and mean. That janky bulb kept hummin', throwin' just enough glow to stretch the darkness thin, leavin' the edges lookin' like trouble was waitin' just outta sight.

Then—G dropped.

No scream. Just the sickening thud of his body hitting the dirt floor. The sound was quieter than it should've been—almost peaceful, like the world had paused for just a second. Blood spilled from his chest, dark and slick, seeping into the dust. His gun slid away, forgotten, useless.

Mitch took a step forward, but it was already over. Too late.

G's eyes stared up, wide, lost. His mind still trying to figure out what just happened. Blood poured from the hole in his chest like it was trying to drown him in it.

T-Money's voice snapped Mitch out of the fog, rough with disbelief.

"Shit, Mitch… he's gone."

They had no choice but to keep moving. Keep going.

Vladimir's voice tore through the tension, like a whip crack in the chaos.

"Now, you idiots! Get here now!" His words cut through the madness, demanding, hard as steel.

Behind him, shadows shifted. More of his guys, closing in.

Mitch didn't hesitate. He raised his gun—And all hell broke loose. Bullets ripped through the air.

T-Money dropped the first guy, a clean shot to the throat.

Dru put two in another's chest before he could fire back.

Mitch charged forward, bullets screaming past his ears. He took cover behind a stack of crates, then popped up and let off three rounds—one, two, three. Bodies hit the ground. Silence followed. Vladimir stood alone now, he turned slowly, his blood-stained suit a reminder of how far he'd fallen. That usual cocky grin? Gone. His face was stiff now, colder than before—like he'd crossed a line and knew there was no comin' back.

He stood there, chest rising and falling with each breath, but his eyes... his eyes were steady, like a man who'd already come to terms with what was coming.

"You think this ends with me?" His voice was rough, almost tired, like he'd said it a thousand times before. "You think you can just walk away from this? No... you're a fool if you think that."

Mitch didn't flinch. He didn't have time for Vladimir's games anymore.

"I know I am," Mitch replied, the words as cold as the barrel of the gun in his hand.

Vladimir looked down at his hands, the blood staining them like a final mark of everything he'd done. He exhaled like it was all too much, then let out a bitter laugh. It wasn't a victory laugh. It was something darker.

"You think I'm afraid of death?" he muttered, shaking his head as he stared at the blood. "I've been dancing with death for years... death ain't the enemy, Mitch. It's the living that hurt you." He looked up, locking eyes with Mitch. "I ain't scared of it. I welcome it. But you? You're just a man who thinks he won. This ain't over."

Mitch stepped forward, his gun aimed steady at Vladimir's head.

"You done fucked up, Vladimir. I told you, you wouldn't walk out of here." Vladimir's face softened for a second, almost like he was respecting Mitch for getting this far. Then, he went quiet, his lips curling into a faint, almost resigned grin.

Mitch didn't wait. He squeezed the trigger. The shot rang out, and Vladimir's head snapped back, a final, harsh punctuation to the game that had gone on too long.

Mitch exhaled, lowering the gun.

T-Money kicked one of the dead men's rifles aside. "Damn. About time."

Dru rolled his shoulders. "Let's grab Angel and G and get the hell outta here."

Mitch wiped sweat from his brow, already moving. "Yeah. We're done here." They left the bodies where they lay.

Blood in the dirt. Silence in the air. And Vladimir? Just another dead body in a city that never did, and never would, belong to him.

They went back for G's body, the air thick with the weight of what they'd just lived through. Angel was still tied to that chair, her eyes wide, full of a mixture of fear, confusion, and relief. Mitch cut the ropes, his movements mechanical, as though he was trying to move through the haze of everything that had happened.

The fight wasn't over, but they'd won. The enemy had fallen.

But the aftermath was always worse.

They had to move fast, before backup showed up or the law came crashing down on them. They weren't invincible; the odds were still stacked against them. Bruised, bloodied, but alive, they lifted G's lifeless body, the weight of their fallen brother pulling at them with every step.

Mitch said nothing as they walked. There wasn't much to say. The silence between them was all the acknowledgment they needed. They'd honored their promise to G, but the cost of it gnawed at their insides. There was no triumph here, just survival. The weight of their actions would stick with them.

Back at the hideout, the reality set in. Time didn't heal anything, but it gave the wounds a different shape. Grief turned from sharp pain to a dull ache that lived in the back of their minds. They buried G quietly, no grand ceremony—just the sound of dirt hitting wood, the last of the fight leaving their veins.

But even in the silence of that moment, Mitch knew it wasn't over. There was always more to lose, more to fight for. They couldn't rest. Not yet. They'd keep their eyes open, their guards up. Retaliation was coming, no matter how much they wanted to ignore it.

Mitch wasn't ready to let everything they'd fought for fall apart. They'd made it this far, and that wasn't something you could just walk away from.

- Chapter Twenty-One -

"New Chapter, Same Hustle: Gettin' Out"

As the dust settled on the aftermath of the violent war with the Russian mob,

Angel sat cross-legged on the floor of her apartment, staring at the half-packed suitcase in front of her. A pair of heels rested on top of a pile of folded clothes, and she been sittin' there for damn near five minutes, stuck on whether to bring 'em or not. They was broke in just right, yeah—but they also came with baggage. Nights walkin' the blade, flashin' fake smiles under them Vegas lights, creepin' in and outta rooms with dudes she ain't even look at twice. That life? She was done wit' it. But lettin' go wasn't ever easy.

With a sigh, she shoved them into the bag and zipped it up.

She should have been used to leaving by now. Her whole life had been a series of transitions, running from one place to the next, trying to outrun the past. But this time, it wasn't just about starting over. It was about survival.

The Russians wouldn't forget what happened, and neither would she.

A knock at the door pulled her out of her thoughts.

"Angel, you packed, or we gotta drag you outta here?"

T-Money. Of course. "Come in," she called, rubbing her temples as she stood.

T-Money pushed the door open, stepping inside like he owned the place. "Damn, girl, you look like you been stressin'. What's takin' so long? We gotta hit the road before Mitch starts actin' like a parole officer."

Angel rolled her eyes but smirked. "I needed time to make sure I wasn't leaving anything important behind."

T-Money scanned the apartment. "Important like that dead plant in the corner?"

She swatted at him, but he sidestepped, laughing. "I see why it died. Even your threats weak as hell."

Before she could come up with a comeback, another voice interrupted.

"You ready?" Mitch's voice was steady, He stood in the doorway, leaning against the frame, arms crossed. His expression was unreadable, but his presence filled the room like a shadow stretching over her. It always did.

Angel cleared her throat. "Yeah, just about."

Mitch nodded, stepping inside. He took a slow look around the apartment, his gaze settling on the empty walls. "Didn't think you'd actually leave this place."

She crossed her arms, mirroring him. "Didn't think I'd have to."

Something flickered in his eyes, but he didn't let it settle. Instead, he picked up one of her bags, testing the weight. "You pack bricks or clothes?"

T-Money snorted. "Man, you know women pack their whole damn life just to go 'round the corner. She probably got her high school yearbook in there too."

Angel pointed at the door. "You can leave now."

T-Money grinned, grabbing a suitcase of his own. "Nah, I think I'll stay. This is quality entertainment."

Mitch shook his head, adjusting his grip on the bag. "Let's get moving."

As they carried her things out, Angel took one last look around the apartment. It wasn't much—just a place to sleep, eat, and exist. But for a while, it had been hers.

Now, it was just another chapter closing.

The SUV was already stuffed, engine lowkey growlin' while Mitch tossed her bags in the back. The Vegas night was thick and heavy, city sounds rolling in from the strip, restless and loud.

Angel slid into the passenger seat, while T-Money took his rightful place in the back, sprawling out like he paid for extra legroom.

"Alright, road trip rules," he announced. "Number one—whoever's driving controls the music."

"Wrong," Angel said immediately. "Whoever's in the passenger seat controls the music."

"False," Mitch said, putting the car in drive. "Driver has final say."

T-Money groaned. "This some dictatorship-type shit. Y'all ever heard of democracy?"

Mitch smirked. "Yeah. I just don't believe in it when it comes to my car."

Angel flipped through the playlist on her phone, ignoring their back and forth. "As long as T-Money doesn't start playing old-school slow jams like he's trying to set the mood, we're good."

"Excuse you," T-Money said, clutching his chest. "That's art, sweetheart. You ever heard of Luther Vandross? That's music that feeds the soul."

Angel glanced at him over her shoulder. "I don't need my soul fed at two in the morning on a road trip with y'all."

Mitch chuckled under his breath, but it faded quickly. The humor was a brief distraction, but reality pressed in on all sides.

They were leaving for a reason.

An hour into the drive, the neon lights of Vegas were long behind them, replaced by the darkness of the desert highway. The city had a way of pulling people in and never letting go, but Angel wasn't looking back.

She could feel Mitch's energy beside her—silent, controlled, but always on high alert. He drove like a man who didn't trust the road ahead or the people behind him.

"You really think they'll come after us?" Angel asked, breaking the silence.

Mitch kept his eyes on the road. "I don't think. I know."

T-Money let out a dramatic sigh from the backseat. "Man, y'all ever think about just joinin' a book club or somethin'? Might be less dangerous."

Angel smirked. "You think the Russians got a book club?"

"Probably," T-Money said. "But instead of readin', they just stab the pages with knives to make a point."

Mitch shook his head, but the corner of his mouth twitched like he was fighting a smile.

Angel exhaled, staring out the window. "I don't like running."

Mitch glanced at her. "This ain't running. It's resetting the board."

"Feels the same to me."

He didn't argue, because maybe it did.

Angel wasn't naive. Leaving Vegas didn't mean they were safe. It just meant they had a head start.

And the thing about running was—you always had to stop eventually.

Somewhere along the highway, they pulled into a gas station. The fluorescent lights buzzed overhead as Angel stretched her legs, breathing in the hot desert air.

Mitch leaned against the SUV, watching the parking lot like a hawk. He never truly relaxed.

Tucked away, unseen, lay a hidden arsenal, a precaution taken by Mitch and T-Money. They wouldn't underestimate the dangers of the open road. A small duffel in the trunk held a .45, extra clips, and a sawed-off shotgun—just in case. Underneath the driver's seat, a switchblade rested within easy reach. Mitch had been in the game too long to take chances.

T-Money came out of the store holding a bag of snacks and two scratch-off tickets.

Angel raised an eyebrow. "Really?"

"Hey, you never know," he said, scratching furiously. "I could be a millionaire in the next five minutes."

Mitch snorted. "And what? Retire from talkin' too much?"

"Nah," T-Money grinned. "If I win, I'm takin' y'all on a cruise. Y'all ever been on a boat with an open bar? I'd be legendary."

Angel shook her head, but for the first time in days, she felt lighter.

Maybe it was the absurdity of the moment, or maybe it was just T-Money's ability to make anything feel less heavy than it really was. Either way, she wasn't complaining.

As they got back in the SUV, she glanced at Mitch.

"You okay?"

He met her eyes briefly before looking back at the road. "Yeah."

But they both knew that was a lie.

There was too much unsaid between them, too many wounds that hadn't healed.

She didn't know what Chicago held for them, but she knew one thing for sure.

They weren't done with each other.

Not yet.

As the SUV pulled back onto the highway, Angel settled into her seat, the road stretching before them like an open question.

And for the first time in a long time, she was willing to see where it led.

Chapter Twenty-Two

"Chicago Bound: The Quiet Struggles We're Hiding"

The road stretched long and unbroken before them, a ribbon of asphalt winding toward a future neither of them could fully see. The rhythmic sound of tires against pavement filled the car, an unspoken metronome measuring time in miles rather than minutes.

Vegas was behind them. But the past wasn't as easy to leave behind.

Mitch could feel it sitting between him and Angel, an unspoken weight pressing down on every silence, every stolen glance. He knew he should say something, but words had never been his strength. Handling problems? That was easy. Talking about them? That was different.

Angel sat in the passenger seat, arms crossed, her gaze fixed out the window. She hadn't spoken much since they left, and though Mitch wanted to believe she was just tired, he knew better. She was still processing everything—the Russians, the kidnapping, the escape, the fact that despite everything, they were still here. Together, in some twisted way.

And yet, they weren't together.

Not like before.

Mitch flexed his fingers on the steering wheel, gripping it tighter.

She had every reason to shut him out. And yet, she was still here.

"Long drive," he said finally, his voice cutting through the silence like a dull blade.

Angel didn't turn to him. "Yeah."

It wasn't cold, but it wasn't warm, either.

Mitch sighed, focusing on the endless stretch of highway ahead. "You sure about Chicago?"

Angel hesitated, then finally turned slightly toward him, her expression showing a mix of uncertainty. "Are you?" He held her gaze for a beat before turning back to the road. "Yeah."

"And after that?"

His jaw tightened. "We figure it out."

A small, tired smile flickered across her lips. "You always say that."

Mitch smirked despite himself. "Because it's true."

From the backseat, T-Money let out a loud snore, mumbling something about chicken wings in his sleep.

Mitch shook his head. "Man, he could sleep through the apocalypse."

Angel actually chuckled—soft, almost reluctant, but real. The sound sent a strange warmth through Mitch's chest, but it didn't last. The tension between them was still there, a quiet undercurrent neither of them knew how to address.

So much had been left unsaid.

Maybe because saying it would make it real.

Maybe because neither of them knew what to do if it was.

The highway signs blurred past them, but Mitch barely saw them. His mind was too tangled in thoughts he couldn't escape.

Angel had been through hell.

And he had put her there.

He had sworn to protect her, and yet she had needed saving because of him. The Russians hadn't come after her by accident. They had used her to get to him.

No matter how much blood he had spilled to get her back, it didn't erase that fact.

Sorry wouldn't change anything.

And yet, here she was—still in his car, still close enough for him to hear her breathing, still not completely gone.

That meant something.

Didn't it?

Angel finally broke the silence. "Why do you still feel responsible for me, Mitch?"

His fingers flexed on the wheel. "What kind of question is that?"

"A real one," she said, turning toward him fully. "We're not together anymore. You don't owe me anything."

Mitch scoffed. "That's not how it works."

Angel let out a sharp breath, shaking her head. "Why? Because you're some kind of protector? Some knight in shining armor?"

Mitch gave a low, humorless laugh. "You know damn well I ain't no knight."

Angel held his gaze, something flickering in her eyes before she looked away. "No. You're not." Her voice was softer this time. "But you did save my life."

Mitch glanced at her, his expression guarded, a moment of vulnerability in his eyes. "You saved mine first."Angel frowned. "What?"

Mitch kept his eyes on the road. "You think I don't know what I was before you? I was just another street nigga playing the game, stacking money, making enemies. That was it. I never had a reason to be better."

Angel blinked, caught off guard by the raw honesty in his voice.

"I didn't think about shit outside of myself," Mitch continued, his voice steady but low. "Then you came along, and for the first time, I started thinking about something bigger. Something more."

Angel swallowed, her throat tightening.

"And then I lost you," Mitch admitted. "Not just because of the Russians. Before that. The breakup, the secrets… I pushed you away."

Angel looked down at her hands, struggling to keep her emotions in check.

She had loved him. Deeply. Maybe too much.

But love hadn't been enough.

She had lived her own double life, one Mitch hadn't been able to accept.

When the truth had come out—about her past, about the choices she had made to survive—he hadn't looked at her the same.

And she had hated him for that.

"I don't know if I can ever forgive you," Angel admitted quietly.

Mitch nodded, his chest tightening. "I don't expect you to."

They went quiet again, but this time it wasn't so heavy.

Ain't no changing what's done.

But who knows—they might still find a way to fix what's next.

Somewhere around the halfway mark, T-Money finally woke up, stretching in the backseat.

"Damn, I slept good," he mumbled, rubbing his eyes. "Y'all didn't crash or nothin', right?"

Mitch smirked. "Not yet."

T-Money yawned. "Good. 'Cause I got dreams, my boy. Big ones. Like startin' a food truck. Call it 'T-Money's Taste Test.' Sell soul food with a twist. You ever had fried chicken with a hint of cinnamon?"

Angel turned in her seat, giving him a look. "Cinnamon?"

T-Money nodded seriously. "Just a sprinkle. Trust me, it's hella good."

Mitch shook his head, chuckling. "You should stick to running your mouth."

"Y'all laugh now, but when I got a line wrapped around the block, don't ask me for no free plates," T-Money warned.

Angel smirked, shaking her head.

The laughter felt good. It cut through the tension, even if just for a moment.

But underneath it all, the reality remained.

Chicago was their fresh start. Their escape.

But it wasn't a guarantee.

Mitch tightened his grip on the wheel, his mind racing. There were still too many threats out there. Too many unfinished stories.

He couldn't afford to lose Angel again. Not after everything.

Not now.

Chapter Twenty-Three

"Homecoming: Reuniting with Momma Rose"

(Momma Rose)

Momma Rose wasn't your typical old lady. At 70-something, her gray hair and weathered skin didn't fool anyone. She was still a force to be reckoned with in Chicago's criminal underworld, a woman whose reputation stretched through the South Side like a shadow you couldn't outrun. Even if she'd stepped back from the game a few years ago, she had that look — sharp eyes, a quiet smile that hid steel, and a walk that still carried the weight of someone who'd survived battles most folks didn't even know existed.

Raised on the South Side, Rose learned early that survival meant playing the game with no mercy. Childhood dreams had no place in a world where you had to be tough just to make it another day. By the time most girls her age were dreaming of love and family, Rose was already deep in the drug trade, carving her path in a world where respect had to be taken, never given.

She'd once been the queen pin, her empire spreading across Chicago, where loyalty meant life or death. Cross her, and the consequences were swift and unforgiving. But Rose had always operated by a code: loyalty, respect, and integrity. She wasn't the type to backstab or double-cross; you knew where you stood with her. She'd cut you out or cut you down, but never without reason.

Years later, she had slowed down. The game was risky, and the rewards didn't match the price anymore. So she opened a speakeasy. It had that old-school charm, the kind of joint where you could get a drink and talk business, or just find a little peace. Still, people remembered who she was, and they respected it.

Momma Rose had seen all kinds of people come through her speakeasy—old-school pimps, washed-up dealers, functioning addicts, men with stories to tell and regrets they drank away. The place wasn't just a hideout; it was a confessional. A history lesson. And Mitch and T-Money? They had a front-row seat to it all.

They were just kids when they first started sneaking in, barely out of elementary school but already drawn to the energy of the place. They'd slip through the doors, hiding in the corners, soaking up game from men who had lived fast and lost hard. The OGs never sugarcoated anything—if anything, they talked too much after a few drinks, passing down war stories like bedtime tales.

At first, Momma Rose would run them off. "Get your little asses outta here before I tan your hides myself," she'd say, waving a hand at them like they were stray cats. But no matter how many times she kicked them out, they always found their way back. She started to notice how they listened—not just hearing but really listening. The way Mitch studied people, how he caught things most grown men missed. The way T-Money had that quick wit, always cracking jokes but never losing track of the bigger picture.

One night, she had enough. She could keep tossing them out, or she could make sure they learned the right lessons. Lessons that might actually keep them alive. So, with a long sigh and a shake of her head, she let them stay.

Rose never coddled them. She didn't have time for that. Instead, she put them up on real game—not just how to make money but how to survive. How to spot a setup before it happened. How to tell the difference between loyalty and convenience. How to walk into a room and know exactly who was the biggest threat without saying a word.

Mitch and T-Money became more than just a couple of kids hanging around—they became hers, in a way. She didn't call them sons, but the bond was there. They weren't blood, but blood didn't mean much in a world where your own kin could set you up for a dollar.

Still, Rose never stopped watching them. She knew how the streets could change a person, how power could twist a good heart if you weren't careful. Mitch had something in him—something dangerous, something calculated. And T-Money? He hid his sharp mind behind jokes, but she knew he was always thinking, always scheming.

She'd given them a foundation, but she also knew one truth better than anyone: No matter how much you teach someone, you can't control what they do with the knowledge.

And that's what scared her most.

Momma Rose looked up from her spot in the kitchen, a grin spreading across her face. "Well, well, look who finally decided to show their faces!" she called, her voice rough but warm. "You boys been avoiding me?"

T-money grinned. "You know how it is, Momma Rose. Always got something to chase."

Mitch added with a half-smile, "Yeah, but you're right. Ain't nothing like coming home."

Momma Rose chuckled, tossing her hands up. "Damn right! Now get over here and give me a hug. I've missed your asses."

They shared a moment, a tight hug full of old memories and unspoken words. For a second, it felt like time had stood still.

T-Money wiped his hands on his jeans as they stepped back. "So what's good, Momma Rose? Anybody out here actin' wild that need to be checked'?"

She waved him off, a little smirk on her face. "Same old foolishness. Nothin' I can't handle. But what about y'all? You back in town just to visit, or you plannin' on stirrin' the pot again?"

Mitch stood with his arms crossed, eyes movin' around the room like his thoughts wouldn't settle. "Ain't made no moves yet. Just watchin' how things play out. But if it feel right… we might jump back in the game."

T-Money grinned. "You know how it is, some folks just don't know when to quit."

Mitch laughed. "True that. But for now, we good. Ain't nothin' like your cooking, Momma Rose."

She smiled and turned back to the stove, her voice softer. "You boys always knew how to make an old lady feel good. Now sit on down. Dinner's almost ready."

As they sat down around the table, the conversation shifted easily from one topic to the next. Stories, jokes, old faces. It was like no time had passed at all.

"Uh-huh, I see you brought a lady friend back with you, Mitch," Rose said, her voice heavy with curiosity. "Go on, don't be shy. Introduce me to her."

Mitch stiffened, and for a moment, a flicker of hesitation crossed his face. "Uh, yeah. Momma Rose, this is Angel. She's... been through a lot, and I thought it'd be best if she stayed here for a bit."

Angel smiled nervously, her voice soft. "It's nice to meet you, Momma Rose. Mitch speaks very highly of you."

Rose studied Angel's face. Her eyes lingered a little longer than necessary, scanning for any cracks in the surface, any sign that Angel wasn't who Mitch said she was.

Rose wasn't a fool. If Mitch trusted her, then fine, she'd accept that for now. But trust was earned, not just given. And Angel? She was a question mark.

Still, Rose gave her a warm smile, though it didn't quite reach her eyes. "Well, darling, any friend of Mitch is a friend of mine. But I've lived long enough to know that people ain't always who they say they are. So we'll see. You're welcome to stay, but you better not be playing any games. Ain't nobody got time for that around here."

Angel gave a quiet nod, appreciating the warmth. "Thank you."

Momma Rose eyed Angel for a moment longer than most would, the look sharp and discerning. Her intuition had always been spot on. Something about Angel didn't sit right — but she wasn't about to make a scene. Instead, she offered a genuine smile.

Momma Rose waved a hand. "Dinner's getting cold. Come on now."

They sat down to a spread that made Mitch's stomach growl. Fried chicken, collard greens, macaroni and cheese, cornbread. Momma Rose's cooking was legendary, and there was something about it that made you feel like you were back in your grandma's kitchen.

"Dig in," Momma Rose said, leaning back with a satisfied sigh. "It's just like how I used to make it back in the day."

Mitch and T-money dug in first, the tastes familiar, comforting, a reminder of better days. Angel followed suit, savoring the warmth in each bite, feeling something like hope settle in her chest.

As they ate, the noise of the world outside faded. For a moment, there were no worries. No threats. Just good food and people who cared about you.

After dinner, Mitch and T-money stood, ready to head out. The day's worries were still waiting for them, but the comfort of being home — even just for a short while — was enough to ease some of the tension in Mitch's shoulders.

"Thanks, Momma Rose. You always know how to take care of us," Mitch said, clapping her on the back as he turned toward the door.

T-money nodded. "Yeah, this was the best part of our trip, no doubt."

Momma Rose gave a knowing smile. "You two take care of yourselves out there, now. And Angel, you're always welcome here. You're part of the family now."

After they left, Momma Rose made sure Angel was settled into the room she'd prepared for her. The fire crackled softly in the living room, and as Angel sat on the plush bed, the weight of the past few days seemed to lift just a little.

Momma Rose checked in one last time before heading off to bed herself. "You need anything, you let me know, alright?"

Angel smiled softly. "Thank you, really. You've already done so much."

As the door closed behind her, Angel sank into the bed, the soft linens and warmth of the house a stark contrast to the harshness of everything that had come before. For the first time in what felt like a long time, she let herself relax. In this home, with people who'd been through hell and back, she knew she was safe.

And tomorrow? Tomorrow was a new day.

Chapter Twenty-Four

"Through the Lens of Change"

A month slid by in a blur—liquor pourin', smoke sittin' thick in the air, and that gritty jazz hummin' through the floor at Mama Rose's.

Chicago wasn't Vegas. It didn't burn quick and loud—it crept. Slow. Like pain you tryin' to shake but it won't let go. The city got memory. Streets lined with buildings leanin' in like old heads whisperin' secrets you don't wanna hear. Bricks worn down from weather, time, and stories nobody got the heart to retell.

Sky stayed on gray, like even it was fed up. Wind cut through corners and cracked windows, movin' like it knew everybody's business but kept it to itself. The air felt old, like it'd seen some shit and wasn't impressed no more.

Inside, them heavy curtains deadened the world. Everything sat in a soft, dusty glow, like time moved crooked in there—slow, off-beat, like it ain't follow the same clock as everybody else.

Angel slipped behind the bar like she belonged there. Her dark brown hair blended into the dim, amber lighting, and even though she was new, she had a knack for it—the careful pour, the way people leaned in a little when she set their drink down. Mama Rose had that face that been through storms—deep lines that held stories, eyes that missed nothin'. She didn't ask Angel no questions when she showed up, just opened the door like she already knew the weight she was carryin'. Maybe she saw a reflection of her younger self, or maybe she just understood—some folks don't need to explain nothin', they just need somewhere to land.

She was tough, but wise with it. Taught Angel more than how to pour a smooth drink—she taught her how to read the room, feel the energy, know when to speak and when to let silence do the talkin'. Sometimes comfort came in a nod, a word, or just lettin' folks sit with their pain without judgment.

Still, as much as the speakeasy had its pull, it wasn't enough. The city was callin' Angel louder than the jazz in the back room. On her days off, she'd grab her granddaddy's old Nikon—beat-up but still snappin'—and roam the streets, lookin' for… somethin'. She couldn't name it, but her lens caught pieces of it—truth in alleyways, beauty in broken things, stories in the cracks of the city.

Millennium Park became one of her favorite haunts. The Bean—its polished surface reflecting the ever-changing sky—fascinated her. The park was a blend of energy and stillness, tourists snapping photos while locals sat lost in thought beneath the golden afternoon glow. Her camera clicked in steady rhythm, preserving the fleeting magic of the city: the laughter of a child chasing pigeons, an elderly couple holding hands on a bench, the towering skyscrapers framing the whole scene like sentinels of time.

One blustery Wednesday, she found herself in Pilsen, a neighborhood bursting with color and culture. The air was thick with the scent of sizzling carne asada, mingling with the fresh paint of sprawling murals that stretched across brick walls. She roamed through art galleries filled with bold strokes and social commentary, pausing to snap a photo of an elderly woman weaving tapestries, her weathered hands moving with practiced grace.

The city's unpredictable weather mirrored the turbulence inside her. Unlike the relentless desert sun of Vegas, Chicago's moods shifted on a whim. One day, sunlight filtered through the clouds, painting the streets in gold. The next, a bitter wind sliced through the city, forcing her to wrap herself tighter in a coat that felt foreign against her skin. Yet, strangely, she welcomed the cold. It sharpened her senses, keeping her tethered to the present.

But for all the excitement of exploration, a restlessness gnawed at her. The speakeasy was an adrenaline rush, but it didn't fulfill her. She missed the feeling of accomplishment, of using her mind in a way that mattered.

One night, after watching Mama Rose expertly handle an unruly patron, Angel blurted out her desire to find something more.

Mama Rose, perched on a stool, polishing a glass with slow, methodical swipes, glanced up with a knowing smirk.

"The city's got plenty of opportunities, kid," she said, her voice rough but kind. "But don't go rushing yourself out the door. This place is a safe haven when you need it."

Angel nodded, warmth spreading through her chest. For all her bluntness, Mama Rose had become an unexpected source of stability.

Determined, Angel spent the next few days scouring job listings, dusting off the journalism degree she hadn't thought about in years.

She sent out applications—to newspapers, online publications, even a quirky travel blog that caught her eye. Each rejection email stung, but she refused to let failure define her.

Then, while browsing a dimly lit bookstore, a flyer caught her attention: Photography Workshop—Capture the Soul of Chicago. Led by a renowned street photographer, the workshop promised to explore the city's lesser-seen beauty.

A spark ignited in her chest. This—this could be the bridge between her past and her future.

She used her meager speakeasy earnings to pay the registration fee, a small but significant investment in a dream she wasn't quite ready to let go of.

<u>A New Perspective</u>

On Saturday morning, Angel found herself huddled with a small group of aspiring photographers, bracing against the biting November wind. Their instructor, Ezra, was a wiry man with a shock of white hair and eyes that held a lifetime of stories. His voice, surprisingly strong for his frail frame, carried over the group.

"Today, we're not just learning about shutter speeds and f-stops," he declared. "We're learning how to capture the soul of this city."

He led them through hidden alleyways and vibrant neighborhoods, pointing out a faded mural protesting gentrification, a lively tamale stand where children giggled between bites of warm masa, the glowing red lanterns of Chinatown swaying in the breeze.

Angel was captivated. Ezra's passion was contagious, his critiques pushing her to see beyond the obvious. She experimented—angles, shadows, fleeting expressions. She became obsessed with the contrasts: the sleek modern skyline towering over the weathered faces of street vendors.

As the day stretched on, they arrived at a quiet park, where golden leaves blanketed the ground like a tapestry of autumn. Children shrieked with laughter, weaving between the falling foliage.

Angel's gaze landed on a lone woman sitting on a bench, feeding sparrows. Her face, lined with years of experience, held a gentle peace. Angel lifted her camera. This wasn't just a picture of an old woman with birds. It was a portrait of solitude, of quiet joy in a chaotic world.

The shutter clicked.

Later, in a cozy coffee shop, Ezra reviewed their work. When he reached Angel's photo, his eyes crinkled with delight.

"This," he said, tapping the print. "This isn't just a picture. It's a story. You've captured something real, something felt."

Angel's heart swelled. Maybe photography wasn't just a hobby. Maybe it was a way to carve out something new.

As she walked home that evening, the crisp autumn air filling her lungs, the city lights ahead felt less like a blur and more like a promise.

For the first time in a long while, she felt hope.

Shadows of the Past

Yet, beneath the liveliness of her new life, a darkness loomed. The memory of the Russian mob clung to her like a shadow.

Word had spread through Mama Rose's network—Vladimir was dead. But paranoia was a stubborn thing. Vegas had been a stage where danger lurked behind velvet curtains. Chicago was different. The threat was less immediate, but the unease remained.

Walking home alone at night, every rustling leaf sent her heart racing. Streetlights cast long, distorted shapes, twisting into the ghosts of old fears.

Mama Rose noticed.

One slow evening, as Angel wiped down the bar, the older woman leaned in. "Still jumpin' at shadows, kid?"

Angel exhaled, tension sagging from her shoulders. "Vegas... it gets under your skin."

Mama Rose nodded, her voice a low rumble. "Ain't stupid. It's survival. But you gotta learn to control it, or it'll eat you alive."

Angel hesitated, then met her gaze. "I can do this," she said, voice steadier than she felt.

Mama Rose studied her for a long moment before offering a faint smile.

The night still held its chill, but as Angel sat across from the formidable woman, the city's hum no longer felt like a threat.

For the first time in a long time, it felt like a lullaby.

The lights in the speakeasy barely did their job—just enough glow to see the bar, not enough to tell who might be lurkin'. Smoke sat heavy in the air, mixin' with the sting of cheap whiskey and worn-out stories soaked into the wood. Angel sat across from Mama Rose, watchin' her count that stack like every dollar had a story. Nails hittin' the paper in a rhythm, like she'd done this a thousand nights before and knew the sound by heart.

Mama Rose's eyes—usually sharp enough to slice through a lie—went soft for a split second. She didn't ask no questions, didn't need to. She saw what Angel was holdin' in, the kinda fear that don't always show up loud. Just nodded a little, like, *"I see you, baby."*

"You alright, kiddo?" Mama Rose finally asked, her voice a gravelly rasp that somehow managed to be both comforting and sharp.

Angel hesitated, then took a deep breath. "Thinking about getting a gun," she blurted out, the words tumbling out before she could stop them.

Mama Rose's brows jumped like she wasn't expectin' that one, her fingers pausin' mid-count. The clack of cash stopped cold. Even the room seemed to catch its breath—just the low moan of a blues record scratchin' from the corner.

"A gun, huh?" she said, voice low like thunder before a storm. "You think that's gon' fix what's broke? That metal don't come with no instructions for what it do to your soul."

Angel kept her eyes locked on hers. Her voice steady, but the fear was tucked just beneath it. "I ain't tryna be no shooter, Rose. I just ain't tryna be caught slippin' either."

Mama Rose eyed her hard, then leaned back on her stool, that usual steel in her stare givin' way to a hint of respect.

"Look here," she said, voice low and a little worn, "I ain't sayin' keepin' a piece don't got its place. In the right hands? It'll shut a fool down fast."

Angel straightened up, her red stare catchin' fire, curiosity peekin' through. Mama Rose had walked through storms out here—she ain't just talk, she lived it.

"But you can't be out here playin' tough," Rose went on, leanin' closer like she was slidin' some truth across the table. "That thing ain't for show. You carry it, you carry weight with it."

Angel nodded slow, feelin' the knot in her chest twist tighter. "Then show me," she said, voice rough with honesty. "I'm done feelin' powerless."

Mama Rose's eyes mellowed, them hard years carved deep in her face. "I get it, baby. I know you ain't playin' with this kinda thing. But it ain't just 'bout squeezin' a trigger. It's 'bout what you might gotta live with after. That weight don't just vanish."

She sat quiet for a beat, not sayin' it out loud, but her mind drifted. She'd seen what that steel life could do—how it tore folks apart, snatched up people she loved, even made her take some out along the way. That mess stuck to her like smoke in old clothes.

The air between 'em got heavy with what wasn't said. Angel knew the cost too. She'd watched that same kind of pain unfold before. Now it was her fear to carry. Still, holdin' power in her own hands? That idea gave her just enough strength to sit with it.

Momma rose stood up from the stool, her movements surprisingly agile for a woman of her age.

Mama Rose slipped behind the bar, diggin' through a hidden spot under the counter. A minute later, she came back out holdin' a worn leather case.

"Here," she said, settin' it down with a quiet thump. "Take a look."

Angel eased the case open, and inside, wrapped in red velvet, sat a shiny revolver. The sight hit her—cold, heavy with power and danger.

Mama Rose's eyes, sharp like a hawk watchin' its prey, didn't miss a move Angel made. "That's a Smith & Wesson Model 10. Been ride-or-die with me through all kinds of trouble." Her finger traced the smooth barrel, a little shake betrayin' stories she never said out loud.

"But don't touch that beauty till you know what you doin'," Mama Rose warned, voice steady. "If you serious 'bout protectin' yourself, I'll school you. It ain't just about pullin' the trigger — it's knowin' your piece, how to clean it, how to aim right."

Angel's eyes sparked with fire. She didn't wanna be some scared girl hidin' behind a gun, but havin' that knowledge? That power to stand her ground? That was real.

"Aight, Mama Rose," she said, voice strong. "Teach me."

Mama Rose cracked a slow smile, that old fire burnin' bright. For weeks, tucked away where nobody could see, Mama Rose took Angel under her wing. The clinks of drinks swapped for the sharp pops of bullets in a soundproof room. Patient and tough, Mama Rose drilled her on gun safety, takin' care of the piece, and how to hit her mark. The weight of that revolver in Angel's hands turned from scary to steady — a tool to respect, not fear. More than that, she learned how to read a room, spot trouble before it found her. The fear that once squeezed her chest started to fade, replaced by a quiet confidence, like she finally held the reins of her own story.

One night, after a hard session, Mama Rose sat across from Angel, a worn bottle of whiskey between 'em. Ice tinkled soft in their glasses as they soaked in a tired but real kinda peace.

"You're alright, kiddo," Mama Rose said, swirling the amber in her glass.

Angel lifted hers, the golden shine catching the dim light. "Thanks, Mama Rose. More than you know."

Quiet settled in between 'em, just the city hum outside. Angel felt something new — a bond to this woman who'd become like family, a guide, a real one she could trust.

For the first time in a long while, she didn't feel powerless.

- Chapter Twenty-Five -

"Forgiveness in Full Bloom"

As Mitch slowly picked through the flowers, trying to find the perfect arrangement for Angel. The weight of their past fallout pressed heavily on him, and as he carefully chose each petal, it felt like he was trying to piece together something broken—maybe even more than just their relationship. His thoughts were tangled, as if his mind couldn't decide whether he was seeking forgiveness or just trying to feel like he was doing something, anything, to fix the mess between them.

He ran back their last convo in his head on loop—every sharp word stuck like splinters, every pause between 'em draggin' him deeper into doubt. Was she even down to hear him out again? Or did he mess it up for good? That fear of gettin' curved ate at him heavy, but still, he knew he had to shoot his shot. The flowers were a risk, a quiet, almost desperate attempt at reaching out. Maybe it would show her he was tryin', even if he'd fumbled before. Maybe it would chip at them walls she built.

Inside the speakeasy, the soft clink of ice in the shaker cut through the haze. Angel, locked in on her martini, shook it like muscle memory, not even peepin' the storm brewin' on Mitch's end. Across the bar, Mama Rose clocked it all, leanin' with that slow grin that said she'd seen this kinda thing before.

Then the door jingled, breakin' the moment. A delivery guy stepped in, lookin' like he took a wrong turn somewhere, eyes squintin' through the dim light.

Mama Rose, sharp as ever, stood up straight and made her way over. "You bringin' somethin'?" she asked, voice smooth like a shot of top-shelf bourbon.

The delivery dude gave a nervous nod, holdin' out a bright-wrapped bouquet. "Uh, yeah. For Angel?"

Mama Rose's eyebrows shot up. "Angel? Who's sending you flowers, girl?"

Angel, mid-shake, froze. She hadn't even realized someone had been sending anything her way. "Flowers?" she said, her voice tinged with disbelief. "For me?"

Mama Rose chuckled lowly, her eyes narrowing at the massive bouquet. "Look at these. I've never seen flowers quite like that. It's like a whole damn garden in there."

The delivery guy, clearly nervous, fumbled with his clipboard. "I just need a signature, ma'am," he said, shifting uncomfortably under the sudden attention.

Mama Rose snatched the clipboard, eyein' Angel and the flowers like she was piecin' somethin' together. "Alright now, spill it. Who out here tryin' to shoot they shot?" she joked, voice light but her eyes lowkey diggin' for answers.

Angel squinted at the bouquet, confusion writ all over her face. "Shoot they shot? I ain't got a clue. Might be somebody playin' games." Still, even as she said it, her mind spun, tryna figure out who'd send her somethin' sweet outta nowhere. Ain't like she had folks knockin' down her door.

Mama Rose let out a dry laugh, her grin creepin' in. "Playin' games with them kinda flowers? Girl, please. That's somebody layin' they heart on the line." She threw a nod at the delivery dude, who looked like he couldn't tell if he should laugh or run.

Angel approached the young man, her curiosity getting the better of her. "Can you at least tell me who sent them?" she asked, her voice tinged with a hint of desperation. "Please, there's got to be something you can tell me?"

The delivery boy shrugged helplessly, glancing between Angel and Mama Rose. "Sorry, ma'am. The instructions were real specific. Just deliver, get a signature, no names."

Mama Rose lifted her brow, grinning as she nudged Angel toward the flowers. "Look like your night just flipped a page, huh? You better find out who sent this before your drink go flat."

Angel sighed, reachin' out slow to grab the bouquet, her fingers grazin' the bright petals. That sweet smell hit her, bringin' a mix of jitters and a weird kinda hope that somethin' was 'bout to change. Was this really happening? Could it really be Mitch? She couldn't picture him sending something so... extravagant. It didn't feel like him, not at first glance. But who else could it be? The flowers, with their daring red rose amidst the sunflowers, felt like a swirl of emotions in a single bouquet—familiar, but still somehow unexpected.

"Alright, Mama," Angel said, managing a small smile. "I'll finish the martini lesson after I figure out who this mysterious Romeo is."

Mama Rose let out a throaty laugh. "There you go, girl. Just remember, whoever sent 'em obviously has some taste. So, get on with it!"

Angel's fingers trembled slightly as she dug deeper into the bouquet, her eyes widening as a small, crisp white card appeared from beneath the flowers. Her heart skipped a beat. Could it be Mitch? She could feel the flutter of anticipation in her chest. Was this the apology she had been hoping for?

"There's a card," she murmured, her voice barely audible as she pulled it free.

Mama Rose leaned in, her voice practically humming with excitement. "Well, go on. Open it already!"

Angel hesitated for a moment, her breath catching in her throat as she turned the card over. The handwriting on the front was elegant, simple – her name in bold script. She exhaled slowly, flipping the card open, unsure of what to expect but certain that her heart was already pounding in anticipation.

Inside, the words seemed to reach out to her, each line carrying a weight of emotion that was hard to ignore:

Dear Angel,

In the dance of life, you're the melody to my song,

With you, each moment is like where I am meant to belong.

From the bright lights of Vegas to beaches in Hawaii,

We've loved and laughed and so much more.

From that first meeting of us in the casino's glare,

To walks on trails, hand in hand, like a dream.

Remember our Netflix nights, just the two of us?

Hanging out and laughing, feeling wild and new.

Your loveliness, your power, they never end to surprise,

When you're around, my concerns always tend to disappear.

I treasure what we've experienced, oh so precious,

And I hope to be forgiven, I keep hope in reserve.

So tonight, let's lay the past behind,

And usher in the future, with our hearts aligned.

Dress up to the finest, for a chauffeur will guide,

To whisk you away, my lovely, have no need to be afraid.

I do hope you'll say yes, and travel with me,

For a flight of friendship, under starlight.

I miss your smile, your laugh, your grace,

Let's together build a sweet home.

With love and affection, now and forever,

Mitch

The words settled into her chest, and she felt something stir inside her—something she hadn't felt in a while. Was it hope? Or just disbelief? Either way, the card, the flowers, Mitch's heartfelt (and somewhat theatrical) apology—everything about it felt too personal to ignore.

She met Mama Rose's eyes, a playful smile creeping up her lips. "Well, this certainly changes things."

Mama Rose, her eyes twinkling with amusement, leaned in closer. "Oh, plans, huh? Care to share with the old bat exactly what this 'sunset' will interfere with?"

Angel laughed, though it was more of a nervous chuckle. "Nothing important, just my usual routine." She shifted uncomfortably, not sure how much she should reveal. "I'll clean up, get some sleep, you know."

Mama Rose scoffed playfully, shaking her head. "Sleep? Angel, sweetheart, don't you know a chance like this—sunset, apology, the whole nine yards—is way more important than a few hours of sleep?"

Angel let out a quiet laugh, the truth of it sinking in. "Yeah, you're right. A sunset with an apology sounds pretty good right now."

"Well, go on, then," Mama Rose urged. "Get yourself ready. Looks like Mitch is pulling out all the stops for you tonight."

Angel's gaze flickered to the flowers again, a small smile tugging at the corner of her lips. "Fancy, huh?" she said softly, her voice teasing, but with a hint of something else—maybe excitement.

Mama Rose chuckled, the sound rich with knowing. "Fancy car, fancy clothes... sounds like someone's pulling out all the stops for this apology. Let's just hope it's as good as it looks, huh?"

Angel hesitated for a moment, her fingers still resting on the bouquet, before she stood a little straighter, heart beating a little faster. Tonight, maybe, just maybe, things could start to feel right again.

Chapter Twenty-Six

"Rewind and Press Play"

The chauffeur swings the door open, letting Angel step out in front of the upscale jazz lounge. Instantly, she feels Mitch's eyes on her, like she's the only thing that matters in the whole world. The night is full of anticipation, and as soon as she steps out, she knows she's caught his attention. She wore that skirt like it came with a warning label. Didn't flash no grin—her walk said enough to quiet a whole sidewalk.

It had been too long since she'd dressed up like this, and she couldn't help but feel a sense of pride as she watched Mitch's eyes linger, as though she'd pulled him back into a memory he hadn't realized he missed.

"Damn, Angel," Mitch said, his voice low, admiration slipping into the words. "You look... incredible. I ain't expectin' all this when I asked you out."

Angel couldn't help but grin, tossing her hair over her shoulder as she caught Mitch's gaze. "Had to keep up, Mitch. You've been working for it, so I figured I'd provide you with something to look at," she said, her voice a mix of teasing confidence and uncertainty.

Mitch laughed, leaning back against the car in a casual stance, his smile making her heart skip a beat.

There was something about the way he looked at her—like he saw more than just her exterior, like he was remembering everything that had passed between them."Well, damn, I'm glad I did. I wanted to show you a good time, and trust me, I won't let you down."

Angel's eyes twinkled with amusement as she walked up to him, teasing, "You better not. I might just walk out of here if you do."

He grinned, his lips curling up, and together, they walked toward the entrance of the club, the soft hum of the jazz spilling out into the cool night air. Angel took in the place around her. The inside had a cozy, intimate vibe, bathed in soft lighting. The polished wood floors gleamed underfoot, the rich leather seats giving it that timeless, smooth look. The walls were covered in vintage jazz posters, and the stage was set for a night of smooth Neo-Soul vibes. Angel could already feel the groove in the air.

Mitch brought her to the bar, and they sat on tall-backed stools. He ordered them their drinks, his eyes scanning the room before he turned to her. "So, what do you think? Pretty decent place, huh?"

Angel nodded, her eyes glittering. "Yeah, it's got that retro vibe. You know I adore places like this." She took a deep breath, filling her lungs with the noise and the hum of the air. "Nice to be out, you know? Like. really out. Not stuck in all the things that've been weighing on me."

Mitch smiled, his eyes softening with affection. "I'm glad to hear that," he said, reaching out to squeeze Angel's hand gently. His touch was warm, reassuring, but Angel hesitated for just a second before letting herself relax into it.

"I mean it, Angel," he continued, his voice low, steady. "I know things ain't been easy between us, and I know I got a lot to make up for. But I'm here. Whenever you need me."

Angel exhaled, glancing down at their hands. The past still lingered between them, heavy and unspoken, but there was something about the way Mitch looked at her—like he wasn't just saying what she wanted to hear, but what he needed her to know.

"You always did know how to smooth talk your way back in," she teased, a small smirk playing at her lips, but there was no bite to her words.

Mitch chuckled, shaking his head. "Ain't no smooth talking, Angel. Just facts."

She held his gaze, her heart tugging in two directions—one telling her to guard herself, the other reminding her that, no matter how complicated things got, Mitch had always been a part of her story. Maybe the ending wasn't written yet.

Before she could say anything else, their drinks arrived, and Mitch lifted his glass. "To fresh starts," he said, watching her closely.

Angel hesitated only a second before clinking her glass against his. "To figuring it out," she countered.

Mitch grinned. "I'll take that."

"So, what do you say we hit the dance floor?" Mitch suggested, a playful gleam in his eye. "They've got a live band tonight, and I don't know about you, but I'm itching to show off some moves."

Angel raised a brow, smirking. "'Show off some moves'? You make it sound like we're back at prom."

Mitch chuckled. "Come on, you love it."

She laughed, setting down her glass. "You got me there. Let's dance."

They weaved through the crowd and stepped onto the packed dance floor, where the music pulsed like a heartbeat. The energy in the room was infectious, a blend of nostalgia and something electric, something unspoken. Mitch's eyes never left Angel as she swayed to the rhythm, her body moving with an effortless confidence that made it impossible for him to look away.

The music wrapped around them, drawing them closer, and before either of them could overthink it, Mitch pulled her in. Their bodies fit together like a song they both knew by heart, every step, every turn a familiar yet thrilling game of push and pull.

Angel felt the tension ease from her shoulders as she let the moment take over. The past, the hurt, the uncertainty—none of it mattered here. Not when Mitch's hand rested on the small of her back, not when their laughter melted into the music.

For the first time in a long time, she felt light.

Mitch felt it too. This wasn't just dancing; it was something more, something unspoken but undeniable. Every glance, every touch was a quiet apology, a hesitant question: Are we still us?

As the night stretched on, they danced without thinking, without speaking, just feeling. And for a little while, it was enough.

Eventually, the band slowed things down, the once-thrumming energy softening into something more intimate.

As they sat down, the soft light of the club gently illuminating their faces, Mitch took a deep breath, preparing himself for what he knew would be a challenging conversation.

Mitch hesitated before speaking, his voice quieter now. "Angel…"

She looked up at him, something cautious in her gaze. "Yeah?"

He cleared his throat, eyes low like he wasn't sure how to start. "There's somethin' you need to hear."

Angel's expression shifted, the weight of reality creeping back in. The spell was breaking, the past rushing in to reclaim its place.

Mitch exhaled, running a hand through his beard. "Tonight… it reminds me of why I fell for you in the first place." He paused, eyes searching hers. "And why I can't let that go so easily."

Angel's chest tightened. "Mitch…"

"I know I fucked up, Angel," Mitch said, his voice thick with regret. "I was selfish, scared… and I took the easy way out instead of facing things like a man. And that woman… that night at the club…"

His head dipped, shame settling in his shoulders. "It meant nothing. A stupid, reckless mistake. Liquor and bad decisions, but no excuses."

Angel exhaled slowly, her fingers tightening around her glass. It was hard to hear, but she wasn't innocent either.

"You think I don't know about bad decisions?" she said softly. "I made one every day I didn't tell you the truth. I lied to you, Mitch. I let you fall for a version of me that wasn't real because I was scared—scared that if you knew, you'd look at me the way you did that night on the Strip."

Mitch's jaw clenched at the memory. He hadn't just looked at her—he had judged her, cut her down with nothing but a glare before driving off and leaving her standing under the neon lights like she was nothing to him.

"You didn't even give me a chance to explain," Angel continued, her voice trembling. "You just saw me, made up your mind, and left. Like all the time we spent together meant nothing."

"You were selling your body, Angel!" Mitch snapped before he could stop himself. "How the hell was I supposed to react?"

Angel flinched but held her ground. "You were supposed to love me enough to hear me out. To ask why before throwing me away like I was some damn stranger."

Mitch exhaled sharply, running a hand over his face. "And what would you have said?" he asked, quieter this time. "Tell me now."

Angel swallowed, forcing herself to meet his gaze. "That I never wanted that life. That I only did it to get enough money to open my own salon. That every time I was with you, that was the real me— not the girl on the Strip."

Mitch's eyes softened, but she wasn't done.

"And you wanna talk about secrets?" she continued, her voice rising. "You were out there running the streets, selling dope, living a whole life I had no clue about. You didn't trust me with your truth either, Mitch, and because of that, I ended up getting kidnapped by the Russians. So don't act like you were the only one who got lied to."

Mitch's face twisted with guilt. He had spent so much time feeling betrayed by Angel that he never really sat with the fact that he had done the exact same thing to her.

"You're right," he admitted, his voice raw. "I should've told you. Should've protected you instead of letting you walk into danger blind. I wasn't fair to you, Angel."

She let out a breath, her eyes glistening. "No, you weren't. But neither was I."

Silence stretched between them, thick with everything they had left unsaid for too long.

Mitch reached for her hand, gripping it tightly. "I need to hear you say it," he said, his voice low. "That you're done with that life. That you're not just telling me what I wanna hear."

Angel squeezed his fingers, steady and sure. "I'm done, Mitch. I've been done. I just didn't know how to fix everything after you found out."

Mitch studied her, searching for any trace of doubt. He didn't find any.

"Then I forgive you," he said, voice rough. "For the lies. For the secrets. For all of it."

Angel exhaled, her chest feeling a little lighter. "And I forgive you. For leaving me that night. For not letting me explain. And for keeping your own secrets."

Mitch nodded, brushing his thumb over the back of her hand. "So where does that leave us?"

Angel smiled, small but real. "I guess that depends… Are you ready to try again?"

Mitch's lips quirked, that old familiar spark flickering back to life. "I think I've been ready, Angel. I was just waiting on you."

Maybe they weren't perfect. Maybe they never would be.

But for the first time in a long time, they were finally on the same page. And that was enough.

The weight of her past life—those nights on the strip, the emptiness, the fear—seemed to drift further away, like a bad dream she couldn't wake from. But a sliver of doubt still gnawed at her.

"Can you promise me something?" Her voice cracked slightly, barely above a whisper. "Can you promise me that you won't look at me like... like the woman I used to be? Even if there are things I haven't told you yet? Things from that life… things I never had the courage to share?"

Mitch's eyes softened, but the pain in his expression never fully left. He reached out, his hand hovering for a moment before he gently placed it over hers. "Angel, your past ain't gonna change how I see you. It's your past.

His grip tightened, but not too tight—just enough to remind her that he was here. "I'm not going anywhere, Angel. All I need from you is honesty. No more lies, no more pretending."

A fragile, uncertain bridge began to form between them—thin, but real enough to make Angel wonder if there was still a way back. If what they had wasn't completely gone. But before she could speak, a sharp voice from a stranger cut through the air, dragging her right back to the cold reality around them.

<u>Tiana</u>

Mitch's jaw tightened, and Angel's heart sank. It was a reminder that no matter how much they wanted to heal, the weight of the past—and the people who would never let them forget it—was never far behind.

Tiana was built crazy—waist snatched, hips sittin' wide like a two-lane street, and that ass? Man, it sat high like it had its own ego. She didn't need to try—every curve hit like a punchline.

Walked in and bodies twisted like necks owed her somethin'. She wasn't just fine, she was *built*—heavy where it mattered, soft where folks prayed to land. Men couldn't help but stare, and even the women caught themselves lookin', quick glances when they thought no one was watchin'.

Her skin, the color of rich caramel, glowed under the dim lights, almost as if it had its own magic. Her hair, dark and luscious, fell in thick, perfect curls that framed her face with just the right amount of sass. Every detail was on point—nails meticulously done, and a strut that told anyone within a five-mile radius that she knew her worth.

But beneath the beauty was a woman with sharp edges. She didn't shy away from using that beauty to her advantage. Tiana's smile could disarm or cut deep, and if you crossed her, her tongue could bring you down faster than you could blink. She wasn't afraid of a little drama, either. No, she thrived on it. And tonight, she was about to stir up a whole lot of it.

As she walked toward the table, her eyes caught Mitch's, and she didn't bother masking the smirk that crept onto her lips.

Mitch blinked. For a quick second, everything around him blurred. His mind flashed back—Tiana's bare body twisted beneath him, back arched, her moans bouncing off the walls as she whispered his name like a prayer. She had him gripping the headboard, sweat dripping, her thighs locked around him like a trap he didn't want to escape. The way she used to ride him all night, making promises with her hips—yeah, it wasn't love, but it damn sure felt like a sin.

Damn, he thought, half-laughing in his head, **Tiana had that fire. Just a fuck buddy, but she had some *good* pussy.**

Then he snapped back, jaw tightening, eyes settling.

"Mitch! What a surprise to see you here!" Her voice was smooth, confident, like honey, but there was an edge to it that Angel felt immediately.

Angel's head whipped around, her eyes locking onto the woman standing there. She could feel her blood pressure rising, a storm brewing in her chest. Who the hell was this woman? And why was she acting like she owned Mitch?

Tiana stood with all the grace of a queen, her long curls cascading down her back like she'd just walked out of a hair commercial. Angel's forced smile was cool, but there was an icy edge in her eyes—like she knew exactly what was going on here.

"Who is this?" Angel's voice was deceptively calm, but there was a quiet fury simmering just below the surface.

Tiana glanced at Mitch, then back at Angel with a smile that barely hid her smugness. "Tiana. Nice to meet you." She extended a flawless hand toward Angel, her gaze lingering on their entwined hands a second too long. "Mitch hasn't mentioned you before."

Angel's smile faltered, but she forced herself to respond, taking Tiana's hand with a firmness that almost matched the woman's own. "Nice to meet you too, Tiana. We were just… catching up." The words tasted bitter as they left her lips, but she wasn't about to let this woman see how much she was rattling her.

Tiana's eyes bounced between them, like she was peepin' game and tryna clock the vibe. "Catching up, huh?" she said, smilin' just enough to play nice—but it ain't touch her eyes.

She glanced toward a vacant booth on the other side of the dance floor, the look in her eyes an unspoken invitation, a subtle nudge for Mitch to join her. "You two look like you have a lot to talk about," she purred, her voice dripping with just the right amount of venom.

Angel's jaw tightened. She could feel the rage bubbling up, her fingers curling around the edge of the table, nails digging into the wood. She was done with this woman, and done with Mitch for not handling it better. He was supposed to be leaving all of this behind— why was it still so easy for this woman to worm her way into their lives?

Mitch, looking caught between a rock and a hard place, finally spoke up, his voice strained. "Actually, Tiana, Angel and I were about to head out. We've got plans for the rest of the night."

Tiana raised an eyebrow, the sweetness in her voice disappearing. "Plans?" She let the word hang in the air, heavy with disbelief.

"Mitch, we had something planned for tonight too. Remember? That client meeting?"

Angel's chest tightened. She wanted to scream, wanted to throw her drink in Tiana's face, but she bit her tongue. Mitch hadn't even thought to tell her about a "client meeting." That wasn't the Mitch she'd been dealing with. Was he still playing these games?

Tiana's eyes never left them, calculating, watching. Angel couldn't decide if she wanted to slap her or throw her out of the club.

Mitch's voice was strained as he glanced at Angel, a silent apology in his eyes. "Right, right. I forgot about that." He cleared his throat and added, "But I think I can push it till tomorrow. Angel and I haven't seen each other in a while, and we were catching up."

Tiana's perfect façade cracked just a little. The frustration in her eyes was clear, but she forced out a tight smile. "Mitch, that client's not gonna reschedule. You know how these things go."

Angel, still feeling the weight of the situation, leaned in, her voice low and steady. "Maybe we all need to be more honest here," she said, the words sharp enough to cut through the tension.

Mitch shot her a quick look, something close to admiration flashing in his eyes before he turned back to Tiana. "Look, Tiana," he said, his voice firmer now, "I appreciate the reminder, but I'll take care of it tomorrow. Angel and I have some things to talk about."

Tiana's smile faded, and her eyes flicked from Mitch to Angel with an unmistakable challenge. "Well, maybe Angel wouldn't mind if I joined you both?" Her voice was a calculated suggestion, but there was a flicker of frustration in her eyes that Angel didn't miss.

Angel straightened, refusing to back down. "I think Mitch and I would prefer some privacy," she said, her tone cool but assertive. "Maybe you should reschedule that meeting."

Tiana stood at the table, a smile on her lips that didn't quite reach her eyes. Her gaze lingered on Mitch, the disappointment in her chest gnawing at her, even as she kept her composure. It stung to hear Mitch introduce her as just a colleague—it was a slap in the face she wasn't ready for. But she couldn't show it. Not here. Not now.

She glanced at Angel, feeling a rush of irritation bubble up but swallowed it down. "Fine," she said curtly, her eyes glaring at Angel before she turned to walk away. "Enjoy your night."

Angel watched her go, a feeling of victory swirling in her chest, but it didn't last. Mitch's attention was back on her, and there was an undeniable warmth in his eyes. "So," he said, a sheepish smile tugging at his lips, "where were we?"

Angel couldn't suppress the small laugh that escaped her. "Well, Mitch," she said, leaning back in her chair, "that was... something."

Mitch scratched the back of his neck, looking uncomfortable but also relieved. "I swear, I wasn't planning on that," he said. "But I guess I owe you an explanation."

Angel raised a hand, stopping him. "No need for explanations, Mitch. I think her little performance did all the talking."

Mitch exhaled, his shoulders relaxing. "I appreciate you for being so understanding."

Angel softened, her expression gentler now. "There's still a lot we need to talk about, Mitch," she said, her voice quiet. "But for now…" She let the silence fill the air, both of them aware of the unspoken weight between them.

Mitch leaned closer, his voice low. "For now," he echoed, his hand brushing a stray lock of her hair behind her ear. The gesture sent a wave of warmth through her, the connection between them undeniable.

Angel smiled, the weight of the evening's tension lifting. "Mitch, I've been trying to turn my life around since we got to Chicago. Photography, a possible salon… I'm trying to move forward."

Mitch's face lit up. "That's amazing, Angel!" he said. "I always knew you had it in you. You've got the strength to do anything you set your mind to."

A warmth spread through Angel at his words, but there was still that lingering anger. "I'm angry, Mitch," she admitted softly. "Angry that I'm in this situation because of you."

Mitch gave a small nod, his face softening with understanding. "I get it, Angel," he said quietly. "I've told you before, and I'll keep saying it—I want to fix things between us."

Angel's breath caught as he took her hands in his, his grip firm but warm. "I want to be there for you," Mitch added, his voice full of sincerity.

Angel blinked, feeling a spark of hope flicker inside her chest. "What do you mean?" she asked, her voice soft, almost unsure.

Mitch's smile was reassuring, his tone calm. "What I mean is, if you're serious about starting your business in Chicago, I'm all in. I want to help. I want to invest in you, Angel. I want to turn your vision into reality."

Angel's heart swelled as she looked at him, the gratitude and surprise filling her chest. "Mitch, I... I don't know what to say," she stammered, her voice thick with emotion. "Thank you. Thank you for believing in me, for giving me this chance."

Mitch reached up, brushing a tear from her cheek with a tenderness that took her breath away. "You don't have to say anything," he said quietly. "Just promise me one thing—promise me you'll leave the streets behind. Promise me you'll focus on your future, on making your dreams come true."

Angel's heart felt steady, and she nodded, her voice calm but resolute. "That life was never meant to last," she said, her eyes meeting his with determination. "The goal was always to have enough to open my business and leave it behind. And with your help, I know I can. I promise you, Mitch, that's behind me now. It ended the day we left Vegas."

Mitch's chest tightened with pride, and he gave her a soft but sure smile. "I believe you, Angel," he said, his words carrying weight. "I'll do whatever it takes to help you make your dreams real. We'll build something that lasts, something bigger than we ever imagined."

Angel felt a lump rise in her throat as tears threatened to spill again, but this time they were tears of hope. Mitch pulled her into a tight hug, holding her like he never wanted to let go. "I'll always be here for you, Angel," he whispered into her hair. "No matter what happens, no matter where life takes us, I've got you."

Angel buried her face in his chest, letting his words wash over her. For the first time in a long while, she felt like she wasn't carrying the weight of the world on her shoulders.

As they walked out of the club and into the crisp night air, Angel felt a new sense of determination settle in her. The road ahead wouldn't be easy—there would be struggles, doubts, and hard times—but with Mitch by her side, she felt ready to face whatever came their way.

When the chauffeur opened the door to the black car, Angel turned to Mitch with a soft smile. "Thank you for tonight," she said sincerely. "I really had a great time."

Mitch smiled back, his eyes warm with a hint of affection. "The pleasure was all mine," he replied, squeezing her hand. "I'm just glad you had a goodtime."

Angel's heart fluttered, emotions swirling in her chest. No matter how complicated things had been between them, tonight had reminded her just how much Mitch mattered to her.

As they parted ways, she felt a tightness settle in her chest, like she was leaving a part of herself behind. She didn't wanna go, didn't wanna let the night slip away. But watching Mitch stand there as the car pulled off, she knew it wasn't goodbye. For now, she'd carry the fire of tonight, let it simmer till they crossed paths again.

As the car peeled off into the night, Angel sat back, a crooked smile sneakin' across her face. Things were far from perfect, but for once, it felt like somebody was really ridin' with her.

She stepped out, heels tapping against the pavement, the night air still buzzing with everything that just went down. When she pushed open the front door, that loud smell hit her instantly—sweet, earthy, and thick. Momma Rose was at the kitchen table, a half-burnt blunt in hand, smoke drifting up slow while her eyes followed Angel like she already knew the whole damn story.

"Are you smoking weed, Momma Rose?" Angel asked, her eyebrows lifting in disbelief.

Momma Rose let out a soft chuckle, taking another slow drag from her blunt before releasing a thick plume of smoke.

"Yep, this is my medicine," she said, her voice raspy yet warm. "Keeps me feeling young, you know?"

Angel laughed, shaking her head in amusement. Despite the initial shock, there was something about Momma Rose's words that made sense. The woman had lived a life full of ups and downs, and if anyone deserved to unwind, it was her.

Sinking into the chair across from Momma Rose, Angel let the tension of the night start to fade.

"Tonight was amazing," she said with a smile. "I can't remember the last time I had so much fun."

Momma Rose's eyes softened, a hint of pride shining through. "You and Mitch, huh? You two make a good pair," she said warmly. "It's nice to see you smiling again, Angel. You deserve it."

Angel's heart warmed at her words, and she smiled wider. "Thank you, Momma Rose," she replied, her voice low but sincere. "I'm just lucky to have you and Mitch. You both mean everything to me."

They sat together in silence for a moment, the only sound the soft crackle of the blunt as Momma Rose took another puff. Angel let her eyes wander around the kitchen, feeling an unexpected peace settle in.

After a long pause, Momma Rose leaned back, eyes half-lidded, voice gritty with age and truth. "Life don't play fair, baby," she said, slow and steady. "It'll snatch the rug from under you soon as you think you standin' tall. But long as you don't let this world harden you too much, and you keep movin' like you got sense, you'll be just fine."

- Chapter Twenty-Seven -

"Heat Between the Sheets"

The next morning, Angel awoke in the guest room at Momma Rose's house, the sunlight filtering softly through the curtains. The warmth of the previous night lingered in her chest, and she couldn't help but smile at the memory. Mitch had been a breath of fresh air after everything she'd been through—laughter, easy conversation, and a connection that felt almost effortless.

She stretched out, the soft sheets rustling beneath her, and for a brief moment, she allowed herself to linger in the peacefulness of the morning. After everything, it felt good to be still.

But as her thoughts drifted back to Mitch, she knew she couldn't stay here forever. There were still so many unanswered questions about what was next, what had happened, and—more than anything—what she and Mitch were.

"Angel?" Momma Rose's voice floated up from downstairs. "You up, girl?"

"Yeah, I'm up," Angel called back, easing out the bed. The day was already weighin' on her shoulders, but for once, she ain't feel pressed. Maybe 'cause she wasn't duckin' nobody. Wasn't runnin'. Wasn't out here feelin' alone.

She hopped in the shower, lettin' the hot water hit her skin like a reset. Threw on her hoodie after, caught a glimpse of herself in the mirror. No makeup. Hair all twisted up in a messy bun. Just a woman holdin' it together while the world stayed on some bullshit and never gave her room to breathe.

Angel slid out her room, eyes still low, feet hittin' the cold floor soft as a whisper. The smell smacked her quick—bacon poppin', grits cookin' slow—draggin' her toward the kitchen like muscle memory.

Momma Rose stood over the stove in her robe, movin' like she'd been up talkin' to the day before it even started.

"Mornin', baby girl," she said, throwin' a look over her shoulder with a slow smile. "Go on and sit down. Your plate waitin'. Fixed it just how you like."

Angel grinned, belly talkin' loud as she dropped into the chair at the table. "You stay spoilin' me, Momma Rose," she said, reachin' for the plate stacked with pancakes, eggs, and that crispy bacon she loved.

Momma Rose gave a small laugh, her eyes crinkling with warmth. "Somebody's got to. I know you've had a rough time, child, but you deserve some peace. Especially after what all you've been through."

Angel's smile faltered, just for a moment. "Yeah, well… I'm trying to figure out what peace even looks like these days."

"Well, you've got to take it when it comes, baby girl," Momma Rose said, her voice gentle but firm. "And if peace looks like a quiet morning with pancakes and bacon, you take it. Don't question it. You deserve it."

Angel's thoughts wandered back to Mitch, and her stomach twisted. She hadn't been this at ease in a long time, not even in Vegas. Mitch had moved her out of there after everything with the Russian mob. It had been chaotic, dangerous, and there had been too many nights where she couldn't sleep without her gun under her pillow, too many moments where she feared for her life.

Chicago felt different. The weight on her shoulders wasn't gone, but it was lighter. For the first time in forever, she could breathe.

Momma Rose placed a warm mug in front of Angel, then sat down slow with a little sigh like her bones felt the weather. "You still got that boy Mitch sittin' on your mind, huh?"

Angel didn't say nothin' right away. She stared into her coffee like it might give her answers. "I just… I don't know if I'm enough for him," she said low. "Too much has happened. And me? I come with baggage."

Momma Rose gave her that look—gentle, but firm. "Baby, we all come with somethin'. That don't mean we don't deserve good love. Mitch ain't never been the type to waste his time. And trust me, he calls more than bill collectors."

That got a little smile outta Angel. "For real?"

"For real," Momma Rose nodded. "He don't say much about his feelings, but I know a man who cares when I see one. So if you sittin' here wonderin'… stop. Go visit that man. You don't need a reason. Just go."

Angel took a breath, heart thumpin' a little louder now. "You think he'd want that?"

"I know he would," Momma Rose said, reaching over and patting her hand. "Ain't nothin' wrong with showin' up for somebody who's been showin' up for you."

Angel got up slow, still kinda on the fence, but her gut was talkin' louder than her doubt. "Okay… I'ma go see him."

"Mmmhmm," Momma Rose leaned back in her chair, grinnin' like she already knew how it was gon' go. "Told you—he call more than bill collectors. And I bet he gon' light up soon as he see you."

Angel shook her head, pullin' on her shoes while tryna fight off the lil' smile creepin' up. She ain't wanna say it out loud, but Momma Rose had a point. Mitch had done more for her than most—without wantin' nothin' in return. He ain't crowd her or ask for explanations. He just *held it down*. Moved her out here, made sure she had room to breathe, room to figure things out without pressure. And deep down? She felt that.

Maybe it was time she stopped running from whatever this was.

"I'll be back later," Angel said, grabbing her keys.

Momma Rose waved her off. "Take your time. But don't overthink it, Angel. Love don't wait on nobody."

Angel froze for a second, her heart skipping an uncomfortable beat. Love?

She didn't respond. She just nodded, pushing open the front door and stepping outside.

She wasn't ready for that word. Not yet.

A short drive later, Angel pulled up to Mitch's place, the house looking as grand as it had the first time she saw it. There were no guards, no intimidating security, just the quiet calm of a place that felt oddly like home.

As Angel pulled into the circular driveway, she couldn't help but feel a little out of place. The mansion was the kind of home you only saw in movies—impossibly perfect landscaping, massive windows that reflected the morning sun, and a grand entrance that practically screamed wealth.

Angel parked out front, lettin' the engine run a second while she looked up at them tall double doors. She'd seen nice houses before, but this was different—this was *his*. And for some reason, that made it hit a little deeper.

She finally cut the car off and stepped out. Before she could even touch the door, it clicked open. Mitch had them cameras all around—of course he knew she was comin'. Probably watched her the whole way up.

Inside hit her with a blast of cool air. The spot was big, clean, real modern—looked like somethin' rich folks flex on the 'Gram. But it didn't feel all uptight…it felt lived-in, real. Like somebody with a story called it home.

A half-empty bottle of whiskey sat open on the bar, a jacket thrown lazy over a chair, and one sneaker stickin' out from under the couch like it got kicked off mid-step.

She was still takin' it all in when his voice cut through.

"Angel?"

She turned—and there he was. Not in his usual suit and tie. Tonight, it was a clean, fitted tee clinging to all that chocolate muscle in his chest and arms, and designer sweats sittin' just right.

He smelled good, like cologne mixed with his own scent—something that hit her in the chest and threw her off balance. She wasn't tryin' to react, but her body didn't get the memo. And them sweats? She tried to keep it cute, but her eyes dipped low—right to that print showin' out. She ain't mean to stare, but it was sittin' loud. Her lips parted slightly, her mind blankin' for a beat before she snapped herself out of it.

He leaned in the doorway, quiet, eyes steady like he was tryin' to figure her out… like she caught him off guard just by bein' there.

"Hey," she said, suddenly feeling self-conscious. "I, uh... I was in the neighborhood and—"

Mitch smirked. "And you figured you'd just stop by unannounced?"

"Something like that," she admitted, shifting on her feet. "Sorry if it's weird."

"Weird?" He let out a soft chuckle, shaking his head. "No, not weird at all. Nice surprise, actually."

He stepped in close, and when they moved through to the front room, his fingers brushed against hers—It was barely a touch, But still, it did somethin'. Made her catch her breath a little, spine straightenin' like her body noticed before her mind did.

They settled onto the couch, the kind of silence that wasn't awkward but instead carried a weight of unspoken things. The television was still on, blasting the chaotic sounds of an action movie.

"Sorry about that," Mitch muttered, grabbing the remote. "Just needed something loud enough to shut my brain up."

Angel arched a brow, smirking. "Your cure for overthinking is car chases and explosions?"

He chuckled, turning the volume down. "Works better than therapy."

He looked at her, eyes narrowing with curiosity. "So... what's the real reason you're here? You in some kind of trouble?"

She stepped closer, her voice light. "No trouble. Maybe I just missed you. Is that so hard to believe?"

A slow grin spread across his face. "Well, damn. If that's the case, consider me pleasantly surprised." He leaned back, watching her with an expression that made her stomach tighten. "Though, I have to admit... I was almost hoping for a little excitement."

Angel laughed, shaking her head. "Who says there can't be excitement without trouble?"

Mitch gave a slow nod, pretending to consider it. "Fair point." He patted the spot next to him, a teasing look in his eyes. "Your visits do tend to shake things up."

She rolled her eyes but moved closer, letting her shoulder brush against his. "I'll have to keep that in mind for next time."

As the conversation flowed, Mitch eventually led her through the house, showing off rooms she hadn't seen before. The place was as extravagant as she'd expected—marble floors, chandeliers, modern furniture—but it was the little details that caught her off guard.

Framed photos, a well-used leather chair in the corner, a vinyl collection that hinted at a man who still had a soul buried under all that power and polish.

"You sure know how to live," she commented, running her fingers over a polished wooden banister.

Mitch chuckled. "It's not all for show. I actually live here, believe it or not."

They ended up back in the living room, wine glasses in hand. Mitch poured them both a generous amount, the deep red swirling in his glass as he looked at her.

"So what you been on lately?" he asked, leaning back, trying to keep it casual.

Angel exhaled slowly, swirling her wine. "Besides missing you?"

Mitch cracked a small smile. "Obviously."

She rolled her eyes but smiled. "Work. Tryna piece life together, figure out my next move. You know how it is."

He nodded slow. "Yeah… grown-up questions. You got any answers yet?"

"Nah. Not really," she said, her voice dropping a little. "But I'm done chasin' what don't serve me. I want something more solid. Not just the same ol' grind."

Mitch took a long sip, let it sit on his tongue like he was weighing her words. "I feel that. Ain't nothin' worse than feelin' empty at the end of the day."

The convo lightened up after that—some laughs, some stories from way back, stuff that made them both relax for a minute. **As the day slipped away**, the room dimmed, and a calm settled between them.

Mitch glanced at the clock, then leaned back on the couch, eyes drifting back to her with that cocky lil smirk.

"Nah, you ain't leavin' yet. Not before you get a taste of my legendary cookin'. That's part of the Mitch experience."

Angel hit him with a side-eye, legs tucked up under her, tryna hold back the grin creepin' on her lips.

"Legendary? Boy, quit playin'. The only thing legendary was that expensive-ass plate they dropped in front of us last night. You ain't touch no stove—you touched the menu and let the chefs do the work."

Mitch laughed, not even phased. "Aight, that's fair," he said, smirkin'. "I ain't out here tryna be Gordon Ramsay or nothin'," he added, eyes softenin' as he looked at her. "But tonight? I'm feelin' kinda inspired. How 'bout a lil homemade gourmet action? On me."

Angel's smile broke through, full this time. Somethin' about seein' Mitch like this—laid back but lowkey sincere—had her curious.

"Oh, so you tryna switch it up on me, huh?" she said, a playful spark in her eye. "Bet. Challenge accepted, *Chef.*"

Mitch got up, hand extended, smirking like he knew he had her locked in. "Aight then, let's get it, *Chef Assistant.*"

She slid her hand into his, and just like that, the noise outside? Gone. His grip wasn't doin' too much—just firm enough to let her know she was good right there. Like her hand had been waitin' on his.

They didn't say nothin' on the walk to the kitchen, but the energy between 'em? Heavy. This wasn't just dinner. This was two people tiptoein' around something bigger, deeper.

They'd been takin' it slow, real slow—tryna piece somethin' back together that once got damn near shattered. No rush, no fake smiles, just two people meetin' each other halfway, flaws and all.

What started as a quick link-up turned into... this. Somethin' warm. Unexpected. And realer than she was ready to admit.

The kitchen was spotless, top-tier—everything polished up and lookin' expensive. Stainless steel appliances caught the light, granite counters smooth like they ain't seen a spill in years, and that pantry? Looked like a whole Trader Joe's lived up in there.

But all that fancy shit? That ain't what settled her nerves.

It was Mitch.

It was the way he moved—chill, unbothered, like he ain't had to say too much to still run the room. That lowkey confidence. That grown-man vibe. The kind that said, *"I ain't perfect, but I got you."* That type of energy that couldn't be faked.

She watched him from behind while he dug through the cabinets, and right on cue, he tossed her a quick lil wink like he already knew she was watchin'.

And yeah, she tried to play it cool... but deep down, she was feelin' all of it.

Angel leaned against the kitchen island, watching Mitch move with a ease that was fucking sexy. This ain't the same guy she met at the casino, all suited up and serious. This Mitch was chill, like he didn't give a fuck about anything but the moment.

He grabbed the olive oil and his hand slipped, brushing mine. Damn, that little spark hit like a live wire-electric as hell. Mitch just froze mid-reach, his eyes wide and locked on mine. The kitchen went dead quiet, the air so thick neither of us dared to blink.

"Shit," she whispered, cheeks heatin' up like her body already made the choice. The space between them? Tense. Like one more look might push her over.

Mitch stepped closer, his voice low, rough. "You feelin' this, Angel?"

She nodded, tongue swipe across her lips. "Yeah, I'm feelin' it."

He grinned, hand coming up to cup her cheek. His thumb slid across her skin just below her ear, and she shivered. It was a simple touch, but it got to her. Her heart skipped a beat.

"Good," he murmured, leaning in to kiss her neck. His lips were soft, but the roughness of his face against her skin sent a rush through her. She leaned in, eyes closed, gettin' lost in that fire between them.

Mitch's hands roamed her body, tentative at first, but growing more confident with each passing second. He gripped her hips, pulling her against him, and she could feel his hard-on pressing into her stomach. She ground against him, a soft moan escaping her lips.

"Fuck, Angel," Mitch groaned, his mouth moving to her ear. "You're driving me crazy."

She laughed softly, her hands ran through his fade. "That's the plan, baby."

He let out a low grunt, grabbin' a handful of her ass, squeezin' and workin' it like he'd been thinkin' about it all night. He lifted her with surprising ease, setting her on the kitchen island. Pans and dishes clattered to the floor, the sound echoing through the kitchen, but neither of them gave a shit.

Angel rocked them brown biker shorts, hoodie slippin' off one shoulder like it had a mind of its own. Chill fit, but still had him stuck. Hair tossed in a messy bun, bare face with that kind of glow no filter could touch.

Mitch just stood there for a second, takin' her in real slow, eyes movin' like he ain't wanna miss nothin'.

"So you really gon' post up like that? Hoodie half off, thighs out, lookin' like temptation? Don't start nothin' if you ain't tryna finish it."

Angel smirked, leaned back on her hands. "You starin' or steppin'? 'Cause I'm ready if you are."

That was all he needed.

He stepped up between her legs, slid the hoodie off like he was undressin' a gift. His hands gripped her thighs, rough but careful, like he was tryin' not to lose control.

"Say less," he breathed. "You already know I'm with the smoke."

Then he kissed her—it wasn't gentle or soft. It was greedy, like they'd both been holdin' back way too long. Tongues tangled, wet and wild, breathin' hard like neither of 'em wanted to come up for air. Angel's hands slid up under his shirt, fingers draggin' slow over his smooth skin, feelin' every muscle and curve like her hands couldn't get enough.

She pulled back just enough to catch her breath, eyes locked on his—those hazel eyes burnin' into her like he could see every damn thing. Her nails raked down his abs, and the low sound that slipped from his throat made her thighs press together.

"Keep touchin' me like that, and dinner's off the table. We gon' be way too busy," she teased, voice low and full of heat.

Mitch's hands were everywhere—grippin' her thighs through tight biker shorts, hoodie bunched up as he slid one hand underneath.

He hooked his fingers into the waistband and yanked those shorts aside, his fingers findin' her soaking wet like he was a fucking expert. As he slipped one finger in, Angel let out a soft moan, her head fallin' back, breath catchin' as her hips ground against his hand, matching his rhythm.

"Damn, you're dripping," Mitch groaned, voice low and rough, feelin' just how wet she was. He curled his fingers, hittin' that sweet spot that made her eyes roll back and her body tremble.

"You know I ain't got no self-control when it come to you, right?"

He added another finger, pumpin' them in and out, thumb circlin' her clit. Angel was breathin' heavy, gaspin' for air as she chased that high, body tight, teeterin' on the edge.

He pulled his hand out of her shorts, brought it to his mouth, suckin' her juices off his fingers, eyes never leaving hers. "Sweet as hell," he mumbled.

Angel's eyes flashed with desire. She reached for his belt, undoin' it with purpose, pushin' his pants and boxers down, freein' his dick.

Strokin' him slow, watchin' how his body responded with a look that said she knew exactly what she was doin'.

The second his body jumped, she licked her lips and gave him that look—pure tease, no hesitation, like she owned the moment.

"Always ready for me, huh?" she muttered, voice low and heavy.

He leaned into her ear, voice rough like gravel. "You already know. Now you got me past the point of playin' nice."

She leaned close, breath warm on his ear. "Good... 'cause I ain't tryna play nice no more."

Mitch groaned, dick throbbin' in her hand, eager for more.

He laid her back on the island, takin' a second just to admire her—full, thick, beautiful like art he wasn't tryin' to rush.

"Damn, Angel," Mitch muttered, eyes tracin' every curve, unable to look away. "You're perfect. Thick in all the right places... every inch got me hooked, ma."

"All this?" he said, hands grippin' her thighs tight. "Mine tonight. You feel me?"

She gave him that look—no fear, all fire. "Then act like it. I ain't here for half-steppin'."

He popped open the fridge, grabbed an ice cube and a can of whipped cream, turnin' back with a crooked grin.

"You trust me?"

Angel nodded, a playful smile on her lips. "Always. Just don't waste my time."

He ran the ice cube down her neck, over her collarbone, between her breasts, makin' her gasp and arch into him. He leaned down, took one nipple into his mouth, suckin' and bitin' gently—the cold ice and his hot mouth drivin' her wild.

"Mitch… don't stop," she gasped, nails grazin' his scalp, fingers clutchin' his fresh fade tight like her life depended on it. He moved to her other breast, givin' it the same treatment, slidin' his free hand back into her shorts, findin' her clit, circlin' it slow. Angel bucked her hips, tryin' to get more friction, but Mitch set a slow, torturous pace.

"Quit playin' and put it in already… I need to feel you deep in me."

He chuckled low and sexy. "Patience, baby. I'm just gettin' started."

He popped the cap off the whipped cream, shakin' it with that little grin.

"Don't move," he said, voice deep, sprayin' a cold line from her neck down. Angel sucked in a breath, body twitchin' from the chill.

He dipped his head low, tongue hittin' her skin slow and messy. He licked the cream off her warm skin, takin' his time like it was somethin' sweet he didn't wanna rush.

Angel let out a soft moan, back archin', hand findin' the counter's edge. He worked down—neck, shoulder, arm—kissin', slowly suckin', makin' her squirm with every pass.

"You taste better than all this cream," he muttered against her skin, voice rough, breath warm. "And I ain't even halfway done."

He moved lower, sprayin' whipped cream on her stomach, hips, thighs, takin' his time—slow, deliberate. His tongue chased every drop, lickin' and suckin' like he was tryin' to memorize her taste. Angel was already a mess beneath him, breath catchin', body shiftin', a moan slippin' out every time his mouth found a new spot. She squirmed, beggin' without sayin' a word, and he was eatin' it up.

Then he slid lower, breath hitchin' like he second-guessed himself— but his hands didn't stop. He grabbed the can again, sprayed a cold line further down, and when it hit her skin, Angel flinched—just a little. A soft gasp spilled out, body twitchin' under all that heat.

Mitch paused, eyes searchin' hers, hands hoverin' like he didn't wanna go too far. She didn't say nothin'—just gave him that look, lowkey and locked in, like yeah… keep goin'.

So he did.

His tongue followed the trail he made, lappin' up the sweetness, mouth draggin' slow across her skin like he was learnin' her one breath at a time. His fingers came right behind, touchin' spots he didn't know could make her breathe like that—soft, shaky, deep from the chest. It wasn't perfect, but it was honest. Him tryna give her everything, even if his hands still trembled from wantin' it too much.

Angel's chest rose and fell slow, fingers slid onto the back of his neck, holdin' on—not just for the feel, but for the closeness.

"Mitch, yes," she moaned, hands grippin' his hair, urg-ing him on. "Right there. Don't stop."

"Mitch, please," she begged, voice desperate. "I need you inside me."

He smirked, positionin' himself at her entrance, dick hard and ready. "With pleasure, baby."

He thrust in, fillin' her completely, both moanin' at the feelin'. He started movin', hips thrustin' against hers, dick hittin' that sweet spot inside her. The kitchen filled with the sounds of their lovemaking—skin slappin' skin, ragged breaths, wet sounds of their joinin'.

"Mitch, you feel so good," she moaned, body tremblin' with pleasure.

He increased pace, hips movin' faster, dick drivin' deeper, fingers circlin' her clit—the dual stimulation sendin' her into a frenzy.

"Mitch, I'm gonna cum, I'm gonna cum!" Angel panted, body tremblin' on the edge.

Mitch leaned down, mouth capturin' hers in a deep, passionate kiss, tongue mimickin' his hips. "Cum for me, baby," he groaned. "Let me feel you come all over my dick."

Those words pushed her past her limit. Angel let out a raw cry, body tremblin' as pleasure hit like a tidal wave. She tried to hold it back, but it was too late—she was gone. Mitch kept strokin', ridin' out every shaky breath, every twitch. Jaw clenched, brows furrowed, tryin' to hold on but losin' it quick.

"Damn, girl," he grunted, voice thick, body tight as hell, chasin' his own moment like a man hangin' on by a thread.

With that last deep stroke, Mitch let out a low grunt, body lockin' up as he busted inside her. His dick throbbin', hips pressed close, like he didn't wanna let go yet. Angel sat on the island edge, legs gripped tight, breath shaky as her body tried to come down.

He leaned close, forehead on hers, both breathin' heavy, sweat mixin' like they just been through it. Her fingers slid down his neck, holdin' him there—silent, just feelin' him.

Mitch finally pulled out slow, glancin' down—her thighs glistenin', body twitchin' from the pressure he just put on her.

"You good?" he asked, voice low, almost shy.

Angel smiled, wiped a stray hair from her face. "Better than good. I'm damn near perfect."

Angel slid off the counter, adjusting her clothes, still tryin' to catch her breath. She gave him a sideways grin as she brushed past, steady but quiet, like she didn't have nothin' else to prove.

He grabbed her wrist gently, pullin' her back in for one more kiss— deep and unhurried, like he wasn't ready to let the moment slip just yet.

They ended up back on the couch, bodies tangled, breaths slower now. The mood shifted—less heat, more hush. They talked low, laughed a little, let the silence do some of the heavy liftin'. Wrapped up in each other, time just drifted.

Sleep found them like that.

But when Angel opened her eyes the next morning, she wasn't in the living room.

She was in his bed.

Soft sheets, his scent still hangin' in the air. Her brows knit tight as she turned her head—Mitch wasn't there. The other side of the bed was cold, barely touched. He must've carried her here after she knocked out.

She sat up, confused and a little thrown. The crib was too quiet now, like all that warmth from last night just dipped with him.

Then she saw it. A folded note sittin' on the nightstand.

Her name written bold.

She reached for it, heart twitchin' as she unfolded the paper, eyes scanning the words he left behind.

Angel,

Woke up to an empty bed (big letdown, honestly) but I'm hoping you're still asleep. No rush to leave if you don't have to—had an early meeting, but wanted you to take your time this morning. Coffee and breakfast are ready in the kitchen. Last night was amazing. You left me with a dumb grin on my face as I drifted off. (I'd apologize for my questionable kitchen dance moves while cooking, but, well... I'm not sorry!) There's more I want to say, but for now, enjoy your breakfast. I'm looking forward to seeing you again soon.

Yours, Mitch

P.S. This house feels a lot bigger without you in it.

A blush crept up Angel's cheeks as she reread that last line. Unforgettable. It felt right—what they'd shared had been raw, real, something beyond what either of them expected. It wasn't just the heat of the night that lingered; it was the connection that made her feel like she'd been seen, in a way that was both surprising and a little overwhelming.

The smell of coffee slid into Angel's thoughts like a slow jam on a Sunday morning. She blinked, lookin' down at the note in her hand, snatched straight outta her daze.

The house didn't feel all staged and stiff like before. That coffee scent danced in the air, smooth and deep, makin' the place feel cozy in a way that messed with her head.

She let out a breath and got up, movin' quiet through the hallway. The kitchen was straight love—fruit cut up pretty, pastries sittin' like they came from some bougie spot, and that carafe of coffee steamin' like it knew she needed it. She poured a cup, watchin' the steam swirl as the pot gurgled low in the background. Took a sip and closed her eyes, lettin' that heat sit right in her chest.

She wasn't about to rush nothin'. If this peace had an expiration date, she'd still take every drop. After a hot shower, she came back feelin' brand new, takin' her time with breakfast before slippin' into one of Mitch's big robes. It swallowed her whole—soft, heavy, smellin' like him—and for a second, she let herself melt into the moment.

Curled up on the chaise lounge by the window with a book in hand, she allowed herself to drift, the sunlight casting a golden glow over everything. Part of her wanted Mitch back, but another part found this unexpected alone time just as important—an opportunity to process everything that had happened, to explore the side of him she hadn't known before, the quieter, more sincere one.

As she sat there, the world outside moving quietly in its own rhythm, Angel felt the weight of what they'd shared. It wasn't just a fleeting passion; it was something more. Something that hinted at deeper possibilities—like the simple pleasure of a quiet breakfast, or the way Mitch's absence filled the house with a new kind of longing.

Chapter Twenty-Eight

"Jealousy Ain't Cute"

Angel's stomach twisted when she saw Tiana's face pop up on the doorbell camera. She blinked, wondering if her eyes were playing tricks on her. This had to be a joke.

With a deep breath, she opened the door just enough to block the entrance with her body. Her voice was sharp, laced with irritation. "What the hell do you want, Tiana?"

Tiana smirked, stepping forward like she owned the place. "Oh, look at you. Answering Mitch's door like you got a title." She tilted her head, her eyes scanning Angel with slow, deliberate judgment. "Mitch always did love a good project."

Angel's fingers curled into fists, but she kept her face blank. "Why are you here?" Her voice was low, steady, but strained with barely contained frustration. Tiana let out a short, humorless laugh. "Damn, you really don't know, do you?" She leaned in slightly, lowering her voice like she was letting Angel in on a secret. "I came to see *my* man."

Angel arched an eyebrow, unbothered by the weak attempt to rattle her. "Your man?" she repeated, her tone dry. "Funny, 'cause last time I checked, Mitch wasn't running back to you."

That hit a nerve. Tiana's eyes darkened, but her smirk stayed in place. "That's what you think. You really believe you're special? You're just a damn seat-warmer. A temporary distraction till Mitch gets his head on straight."

Angel's lips curled into a smile, but her patience was running thin. "Right," she said slowly. "Because a real woman shows up uninvited, pressed over a man who already moved on."

Tiana let out a hollow laugh, flipping her hair over her shoulder. "You must not be too important if Mitch didn't bother telling you the truth about me," she sneered. "You think you're the first chick he's brought up in here? Girl, I had a key before you even knew his damn address."

Angel tilted her head, unimpressed. "A key?" she mocked. "That's what you're bragging about? Girl, get a hobby."

But Tiana wasn't done. She stepped closer, her voice dripping with venom. "Look at me, then look at you! Do you really think he's gonna leave all this—" she gestured to herself with an arrogant smirk "—for that?"

Angel let out a sharp laugh, her head tilting back. "You know what?" she said, shaking her head. "That's real cute. But let me tell you something, since you clearly don't get it." Her voice lowered, every word hitting like a hammer. "If ass and pussy was all it took to keep a man, you wouldn't be standing here begging for leftovers."

Tiana's face twisted with rage. "Bitch, who the hell do you think you're talking to?"

Angel stepped forward, toe to toe with her, her voice calm but deadly. "I'm talking to a bitter, pressed-ass female who can't handle the fact that she got replaced."

Tiana's chest rose and fell, her fingers curling into fists. "Oh, I dare you to hit me," she growled. "I'll drag your ass right off this porch."

Angel smiled, but there was nothing friendly about it. "Try me, bitch. See how fast you get dragged right back to that lonely ass apartment Mitch left you in."

Tiana's nostrils flared, her fists shaking at her sides. But before she could say another word, Angel turned, snatched the door handle, and slammed it in her face.

Inside, Angel leaned against the door, her heart hammering. Her hands trembled, but not from fear. It was anger—pure, red-hot rage.

She closed her eyes, took a slow breath, and pulled out her phone. Mitch's name glowed on the screen before she even had the chance to dial.

She answered, her voice tight. "Hey."

Mitch's deep voice came through the line, warm and affectionate. "Hey, baby. I was just thinking about you. How's your day been?"

Angel let out a sharp laugh, full of disbelief. "Oh, you know. Just had a real nice chat with Tiana."

Silence.

Then, "What?"

"You heard me," Angel snapped. "She just showed up at your damn doorstep, talking about her man."

Mitch exhaled through his nose. "Damn. I'm sorry you had to deal with that."

Angel's blood boiled. That's it? Sorry?

"That's all you have to say?" she demanded. "Mitch, you need to handle this. Because if you can't tell her that y'all are done, for real, then I won't be part of your little twisted triangle."

Mitch sighed. "Angel, I—"

"No, listen to me!" she cut him off, her voice shaking with frustration. "You lied to me, Mitch! You sat there, on our date, and told me she was just some chick from work. Not someone you were fucking."

Mitch ran a hand down his face. "It's not like that."

Angel let out a sharp, bitter laugh. "Oh, it's not? Then why the hell does she think she can still claim you? Because from where I'm standing, either you're lying to her or you're lying to me."

Mitch stayed silent, his jaw tightening.

Angel took a deep breath, her voice steadier now. "Look. I've been nothing but honest with you. I trusted you. And right now? That trust is hanging by a damn thread." She paused, then delivered the final blow. "If you're still messing with her, tell me now. Because I refuse to be anybody's damn second choice."

Mitch's voice was low. "Angel, I don't want her. I want you."

Angel scoffed. "Then you better make that real clear to her. Because I ain't got time for this high school shit."

Mitch tried to respond, but Angel had already made up her mind.

"You know what?" she snapped. "Matter of fact, go ahead and keep her."

And with that, she hung up.

Mitch stared at his phone, his stomach sinking. He'd played this whole thing wrong. He knew Angel had every right to be pissed, but damn… he hadn't expected her to shut the door on him like that.

Meanwhile, Angel stormed out of the house, her head spinning.

"Finessed," she muttered, gripping the steering wheel as she sat in her car. Played like a damn fool.

By the time Angel pulled up to Momma Rose's house, her emotions had settled into a slow-burning anger. She slammed the car door shut, storming up the steps like a woman on a mission.

Inside, Momma Rose barely had time to look up before Angel kicked off her shoes and collapsed onto the couch.

"I hate men," Angel muttered into a pillow.

Momma Rose chuckled, setting down her glass of sweet tea. "Let me guess—Mitch?"

Angel turned her head just enough to glare. "He lied. About **everything.**"

Momma Rose sighed, shaking her head. "Men lie, baby. That's what they do."

Angel sniffed, rubbing a hand down her face. "I don't even know why I let myself believe it could be different."

Momma Rose patted her leg. "Because you *wanted* to believe it. Ain't nothing wrong with that."

Angel swallowed hard. "I just… I don't know what to do."

Momma Rose studied her for a long moment before leaning back with a knowing smile. "Oh, baby girl. Yes, you do."

Angel stared at the ceiling, heart heavy, mind racing.

Did she give Mitch a chance to fix this?

Or did she walk away before he broke her completely?

The answer was right there.

She just had to be strong enough to choose it.

Chapter Twenty-Nine

"Drama on the Menu, No Dessert"

Mitch had been pacing his damn living room for the last twenty minutes, rolling his shoulders, exhaling like a bull about to charge. He had dealt with a lot in his life—snakes in the streets, shootouts, even betrayal from his own people—but dealing with a scorned woman? That was a different kind of battlefield. And Tiana? She was the general of petty warfare.

With a deep breath, he snatched his phone off the coffee table and dialed her number, his fingers pressing the screen harder than necessary.

She answered on the third ring, her voice dripping with fake sweetness. "Mitch? What a surprise."

He rolled his eyes. "Tiana, we need to talk."

A pause. Then a slow, knowing chuckle. "Oh, so now you got time for me? I was starting to think I was just your entertainment when you got bored."

Mitch clenched his jaw. "Meet me at L'Vere. Seven-thirty. Don't be late."

"Oh, so now you're setting the schedule?" she taunted. "I don't know, Mitch… I might be busy."

"Tiana." His voice was low, warning.

She let out a dramatic sigh, like this was all some big inconvenience. "Fine. But this better be good."

Mitch ended the call and tossed his phone onto the couch. He knew this wasn't going to end well, but one thing was certain—Tiana needed to hear the truth, whether she liked it or not.

The restaurant was one of those fancy outdoor spots, candles flickering on tables, expensive wine flowing like water. Too romantic for the kind of conversation they were about to have. Mitch sat at a corner table, swirling his glass of whiskey, mentally preparing for the storm that was about to walk in wearing designer heels.

And then she arrived—Tiana, in a body-hugging red dress, her hair in soft waves, like she hadn't just been causing chaos in his life. She strutted toward him, her stiletto heels clicking against the pavement like a countdown to destruction.

"Wow," she smirked, sliding into the seat across from him. "All this effort for little old me? You must really miss me."

Mitch exhaled sharply, already exhausted. "Cut the act, Tiana. You know why we're here."

She pouted, stirring her drink with one manicured finger. "Oh, let me guess. Angel?"

His grip tightened on the glass. "You showed up at my house unannounced, in front of her. What the hell was that about?"

Tiana leaned back, crossing her arms. "I was just stopping by to check on you. Since when is that a crime?"

"You don't just stop by after months of me telling you it's over," he shot back. "That was a game, and you know it."

Her expression darkened. "So, what? You're really throwing me away for her?"

"Tiana," Mitch said, his voice firm, "we were never together. It was what it was. We were just fucking, and I was honest about that from the start."

"But we had a connection!" she blurted, her voice cracking just slightly. "You don't just sleep with someone like that and feel nothing!"

Mitch sighed, rubbing a hand down his face. "Tiana... I'm sorry if you thought it was more. But I've moved on. You need to do the same."

Tiana's nostrils flared. "Oh, I need to?" she repeated, voice rising. "You really think Angel is some upgrade? Like I'm just some expired coupon you can toss out?"

He didn't answer. He didn't have to.

And that's when it happened—before Mitch could even blink, Tiana slapped the hell out of him.

The crack echoed through the restaurant, making the nearby patrons freeze mid-bite. A few gasps rippled through the air. Even Tiana looked a little surprised at herself, her chest rising and falling as she stared at the red mark blooming on his cheek.

Mitch exhaled slowly, his jaw tightening as his hand hovered over his face. The sting was sharp, but the heat in his chest? That was something else.

The old him—the street-bred, fight-first-think-later Mitch—would've snapped. But this? He wasn't about to lose his cool over someone who lived for drama.

He leaned in slightly, voice low and deadly. "The only reason I'm not losing my damn mind right now is because you're a woman."

Mitch let out a slow breath, rolling his jaw. Then he laughed. A deep, mocking laugh that made Tiana's face twist in fury.

"See, this is exactly why I can't stand you," he said, his voice laced with contempt. "Nothing but drama—just noise and problems with nothing real to offer."

He scanned the restaurant, the curious eyes of the other patrons making the scene even worse than it already was. He could feel the weight of their stares, like a spotlight he couldn't escape. He weighed his options: walking out without paying would make him look small, but staying felt like swallowing his pride too easily. With a frustrated sigh, he grabbed his wallet, throwing down enough cash to cover both meals and leave a decent tip for the waiter who had nothing to do with this mess.

Tiana stood up so fast her chair scraped against the floor. "You'll regret this, Mitch. You don't get to treat me like some disposable side chick and walk away clean."

Mitch leaned back, smirking. "Watch me."

Tiana huffed, grabbing her purse and storming out. Mitch exhaled, shaking his head. He had no doubt this wasn't the end of it, but one thing was for sure—he was done with Tiana.

And now, he had to make sure Angel knew that too.

Back at the crib, Mitch stared at his reflection in the bathroom mirror. The slap on his face still lingered, just barely, but that wasn't what really got to him. It was the fact that Tiana wasn't finished. She was the type to drag things out, keep the chaos alive just for the drama of it. And it hit him—this wasn't just some argument; this was a show for her.

He grabbed his phone, dialing Angel's number without thinking twice.

"Yo," he said when she picked up, his voice low, like the weight of the day was catching up with him.

"Hey," Angel's voice was soft, but there was concern in it. "What's up? You good?"

Mitch exhaled a long breath. "Yeah, I'm straight."

"You sure?" she pressed, sensing something was off.

He paused for a moment before answering. "She... she lost it tonight. Said some wild stuff. Even got physical."

A heavy silence hung between them before Angel spoke, her voice sharp. "She hit you?"

Mitch let out a frustrated sigh. "It's nothing, Angel. Don't trip."

"Mitch." Her tone had a bite now, more stern than he expected. "That is something."

Mitch ran his hand through his hair, sitting down on the edge of the bed. "Look, I just need you to know I didn't lead her on. That's been over. But you know how some people act when they can't let go."

There was a pause, and then Angel's voice broke the silence, dry but not unkind. "So, I'm the 'new model,' huh?"

A small, almost reluctant smile crept onto Mitch's face. "Guess so."

"I believe you," Angel said quietly, but there was an edge to her voice now. "But you gotta know... she's not done with this."

His chest tightened. "What you mean?"

Angel's voice dropped lower. "She was outside my job today. Just... watchin' me."

Mitch's heart sank. A cold rush of anger and concern hit him all at once.

He stood up quickly, grabbing his keys. "I'm on my way."

There was a breath of relief from Angel. "I knew you'd say that."

And just like that, Mitch knew the storm wasn't over. The mess Tiana started? It wasn't finished yet.

One hot afternoon, Angel was just leaving work when she spotted a flash of red. Tiana, all decked out in stiletto heels and designer sunglasses, strutted across the street with that same smug look she always wore. Angel's stomach twisted. Not today, Lord. Not today.

Tiana spotted her too, and with all the grace of a runway model, she made her way across the street. Her expensive purse swung from her arm like it was a weapon.

"Well, well," Tiana drawled, her voice oozing fake sweetness. "Look who it is, the little side chick who thinks she's the main one now."

Angel's stomach turned. She had no time for Tiana's games today. "Mitch was never yours, Tiana," Angel shot back, locking eyes with her. "He was always mine, even when you were around."

Tiana snorted, not fazed. "Please, girl. You think Mitch will actually choose you over me? You're nothing but a pit stop. I'll always be his real girl. You're just here for the ride."

That was it. Angel's blood boiled, and before she could stop herself, her hands balled into fists. "I'm done with your mouth, Tiana."

Tiana's eyes narrowed as she took a step forward. "Oh, you wanna do something about it?"

Without a second thought, Angel swung her fist, landing a punch to Tiana's jaw. Tiana staggered back, shocked, but quickly recovered, her hands reaching for Angel. They went at it—slapping, scratching, kicking.

"You don't know who you're messing with!" Angel growled as she slammed her knee into Tiana's side.

Tiana retaliated with a nasty swipe, nails raking across Angel's cheek. Angel hissed, but she didn't back down. With a powerful shove, she forced Tiana into a nearby car. The crowd around them murmured, some cheering, others trying to pull them apart, but

Angel was too far gone. All she wanted was to make Tiana understand who was in control.

Tiana screamed in frustration, pushing back with all her strength, but Angel twisted her wrist and slammed her into the car once more, a sick satisfaction curling in Angel's gut.

"Enough!" The voice came from behind them—security had arrived. Two officers rushed in, quickly breaking up the fight and pulling the women apart. Tiana was yelling, fuming, while Angel was still seething with anger.

As they were separated and led away, Angel barely registered the officers' words. Her chest was still heaving with adrenaline, her mind racing.

A few moments later, Angel sat on a bench, catching her breath and trying to calm the fire inside her. Her phone buzzed in her pocket. Mitch. She hesitated but answered.

"What the hell happened, Angel?" Mitch's voice was steady, but there was an edge to it, like he was ready for trouble.

Angel let out a bitter laugh. "What do you think happened? Tiana's got a mouth on her, and I'm done letting her talk to me like that."

Mitch sighed, the sound low and almost disappointed. "I told you to stay away from her, but you never listen." There was a pause, and then he added, "I'm on my way. Stay put."

True to his word, Mitch showed up a few minutes later, his black SUV pulling up in front of her. He got out, his presence commanding, like he was ready to take control of whatever had happened.

Angel stood, brushing herself off. Mitch didn't say anything at first, just gave her a sharp look that said everything.

"Get in the car," he said.

Angel slid into the passenger seat, and Mitch started driving. For a while, neither of them spoke. The car moved, the engine steady, but neither of them had figured out how to break the silence between them.

Finally, Mitch broke the quiet. "What the hell were you thinking? You know what kind of mess you just made."

Angel exhaled hard, her fingers tapping against her knee. "You know what? I let a lot slide, but I'm done. Done with her, done with the back and forth. She think she can say whatever, do whatever— nah, not anymore. I ain't the one."

Mitch's grip tightened on the steering wheel. "It's not just about her, Angel. It's about you. You're letting your temper get the best of you. You know what happens when you act like that—people take advantage. They'll try to use it against you."

"I can handle myself," Angel said, her voice cold. "I don't need anyone to step in. Especially not you."

Mitch shot a glance at her, his expression hard. "You think I stepped in for you, Angel? Nah. I'm telling you because I care. You might not need me, but you sure as hell need to stop letting your emotions control you. We've both got enough problems without you adding fuel to the fire."

Angel folded her arms, her glare cutting through him. "You ain't the hero in this situation, Mitch. So don't act like you are."

He stayed steady, his voice low but firm. "I never said I was. But I'm not about to watch you let Tiana pull you down to her level."

Angel stared out the window, feeling the weight of his words. "I didn't want to hurt her. I just wanted her to shut up."

"I get it," Mitch said softly. "But you've got to be smarter than that. You've got to pick your battles."

The rest of the ride passed in silence, and by the time Mitch parked in front of momma rose's place, Angel wasn't sure what to feel. Angry? Relieved? Exhausted?

Mitch turned to her, his gaze intense. "Don't make me come down here again, Angel. Not like this."

She gave him a small nod, the weight of his warning sinking in.

"Thanks for picking me up," she muttered, opening the door. "But I'm not your responsibility, Mitch."

Before she could get out, Mitch's voice stopped her. "You're always my responsibility. Whether you like it or not."

Angel paused for a moment, then stepped out, the door slamming shut behind her. As she walked up to her door, she couldn't shake the feeling that no matter how far she pushed Mitch away, he wasn't going anywhere.

Chapter Thirty

"Kingpin's Playbook: Jamal and Tiana's Rise"

<u>(Jamal King)</u>

Jamal had always been a problem. Not just a street hustler—he was a king in his own right. His name rang out from the South Side to the West End, and anybody who was about their business knew better than to cross him. He wasn't just rich; he was ruthless. His hands weren't just stained with money—they were stained with blood.

Diamonds sat heavy on his fingers, catching the dull club lights as he twisted the big ass ring on his pinky. His teeth, gold-plated with diamond cuts, gleamed every time he spoke. But it wasn't the ice that had people shook when they saw him. It was the way he carried himself—calm, like a man who didn't have to raise his voice to end a motherfucker's life.

Mitch? That nigga was a clown to him. A roach that kept crawling back no matter how many times he stomped on him.

Their war went back to high school, when they were just two young niggas trying to be top dog. It started with fists, then knives, then bullets. Years later, they still fought over the same corners, the same money, same bitchs, the same damn city.

Jamal wasn't about to let that slide.

That's why, when Tiana slid up to him at the club, he wasn't quick to trust.

(Tiana)

Tiana had been played before, but not like this. Not by a man who knew damn well she was riding for him. Mitch had used her up, made her feel like she was his, only to toss her aside the second Angel came in the picture.

That hurt.

But Tiana wasn't the type to cry about it—she was the type to get even.

She had one name on her mind: **Jamal King**.

Mitch's enemy. The only man in the city who could hurt him worse than she ever could.

He was in his usual spot, posted up in the back of the bar like a damn kingpin, his people surrounding him in all black. The way he sat back, ice dripping from his wrists and neck, exuding that aura of "fuck with me and die" energy, she knew this was the man she needed.

Tiana wasn't stupid. She knew Jamal and Mitch had history, knew they had been fighting over these streets forever. But now? Now she was the perfect weapon, and she was about to make sure Mitch felt every ounce of it.

She took a deep breath, straightened her dress, and walked over. She wasn't scared—she had too much anger in her for fear.

Jamal barely glanced at her when she approached, just took a slow sip of his drink before finally letting his dark eyes settle on her.

"You lost?" His voice was rough, laced with amusement.

Tiana smirked. "Nah. I'm right where I need to be."

Jamal leaned back in his seat, looking her over like he was sizing her up. "What you want?"

She licked her lips, her voice smooth. "A conversation."

Jamal chuckled, low and dangerous. "See, I got a problem with bitches that come up to me talking 'bout conversations. That usually mean they on some bullshit. So tell me—" He leaned in, his voice dropping to a near whisper. "—how do I know I can trust a bitch like you?"

Tiana didn't flinch. She met his gaze head-on. "Because I hate Mitch more than you do."

That caught his attention.

He studied her, then smirked. "That so?"

Tiana knew Jamal wasn't the type to move on no petty revenge. If she was gonna get his attention, she had to hit him where it mattered—business.

She leaned in, voice low but steady. "Mitch been eating off your plate, Jamal."

That made him pause, just for a second. His people got real quiet, listening now.

Tiana kept going. "He been making moves on your side of town. Pushing weight through spots that answer to you. And it ain't just small-time—he got boys collecting on your corners, setting up shop where your name used to hold weight."

Jamal leaned back, eyes cold. "You better not be wasting my time."

"I ain't." She met his gaze, unflinching. "Mitch got greedy. Thought you got too comfortable to notice. He running his product through your old connects, moving silent, keeping it clean so it don't raise no alarms. But I know where. I know who's running it for him. And I know exactly where he keeping the money that should've been in your pocket."

Jamal swirled the liquor in his glass, quiet for a beat. Then he smirked, but there was nothing friendly about it.

"You telling me," he said slowly, "Mitch been getting fat off my turf, and you just now bringing this to me?"

Tiana leaned forward, fire in her eyes. "I'm bringing it to you now 'cause I got nothing left to lose. Mitch used me, lied to me, threw me out like I was nothing. But I ain't no pawn. And I sure as hell ain't gonna sit back while he plays you like one, too."

Jamal let out a low chuckle, dark and knowing. "See, now that's something I can work with."

(Weeks Later: The Rise of a Queen)

What started as a business arrangement turned into something else real quick.

Jamal ain't just take Tiana—he claimed her.

She wasn't just his sidepiece, his plaything. She was at his right hand, rolling with him like she had always been part of the crew. Niggas in the streets started talking. Mitch's old girl was now Jamal's queen.

And she played the part well.

Where Mitch saw her as a liability, Jamal saw her as an asset. Tiana was smart—smarter than most of the fools Mitch kept around him. She knew how to read people, how to move undetected. And she had secrets—shit about Mitch that Jamal could use to his advantage.

But shit was about to get real.

One of Jamal's biggest shipments had been intercepted. And not by just anybody—by Mitch.

Jamal was livid. His fist slammed down on the table, sending glasses flying. "This motherfucker think he can keep taking from me?" His voice was razor-sharp, his crew already bracing for war. "I'm gonna kill him. Let his people know what happens when you fuck with a king."

Tiana, standing beside him, placed a hand on his shoulder. "Nah, baby," she purred. "Killing him right away? That's too easy. Too quick. We make him suffer first. Let him think he got one up on you… then we burn his whole operation to the ground."

Jamal turned to her, eyes dark. "You really on some cold-blooded shit, huh?"

Tiana smiled, tilting her head. "I learn from the best."

Jamal chuckled, running a hand down her thigh.

"Let's go to the devil's den pay Mitch a visit."

The tension in the air was thick as Jamal and his crew prepared to pay Mitch a visit. The news of Mitch's latest betrayal had set everything in motion. Jamal was a calculated man, never rushing into anything without careful thought, but Mitch had pushed him too far this time.

His eyes were locked on Tiana, standing beside him, watching as the wheels of his mind turned. She wasn't just a pretty face; she was a mastermind in her own right. The way she spoke, the way she thought—it was like she was born for this world. And now, she was part of it.

Jamal had learned early on to never underestimate anyone, but Tiana? She wasn't like anyone else. Her loyalty was earned. Mitch, on the other hand, had made a mistake. He thought she was just a woman to use, a pawn in his game. But Jamal? Jamal knew better. He'd seen what she could do.

The plan was set, and they moved fast. Jamal's crew was ready, weapons tucked in holsters, eyes sharp, moving with the kind of efficiency only years on the streets could teach. They weren't here to talk—they were here to send a message. And Mitch was about to learn the hard way that Jamal King wasn't the type to forgive and forget.

The ride to Mitch's territory was silent. Jamal's mind was focused, calculating every possible move. He wasn't about to let this be another failed operation. This time, Mitch was going to feel the weight of his betrayal. And Tiana? She was the perfect tool to make sure Mitch's downfall would be slow and agonizing.

As they pulled up to the speakeasy, Jamal's eyes narrowed. He could see the security guards patrolling the outside, but it wasn't enough. Not for him.

"You ready?" Tiana's voice broke through his thoughts, smooth and confident, like she had no doubt they'd walk out of here unscathed.

Jamal looked at her, his lips curling into a smirk. "I was born ready."

Chapter Thirty-One

"Respect the Hustle or Get Handled"

The alley outside Momma Rose's spot was dark, cold, the kind of place where the city swallowed you whole if you weren't careful. The sound of distant traffic was drowned out by the murmur of low voices and the occasional shout from the streets. Jamal King stood in the shadows, his crew just behind him. He didn't need to say a word—they knew what time it was. This wasn't a visit. This was a statement.

Tiana stood next to him, her black dress tight, the kind of dress that screamed danger without saying a word.

The deep, thumping bass of Curtis Mayfield's "Pusherman" spilled out from the club's doors, and Jamal's jaw clenched at the familiarity of the track. It was a damn soundtrack for his life—gritty, grimy, with a little funk in the struggle. But tonight, it wasn't the music that had his blood running hot. It was Mitch.

"Let's go," Jamal said low, his voice like a knife in the night.

The door to the speakeasy creaked when they pushed it open. The place reeked of stale whiskey, cigarette smoke, and bodies too close for comfort. The usual crowd was there—small-time players trying to act bigger than they were, hustlers, lowlifes. But when Jamal walked in, everything went still. The music didn't matter, the games didn't matter. All eyes were on him.

His crew moved through the room with the kind of purpose that made people nervous. Nobody said shit. Nobody dared to look too long. Jamal didn't have to talk to make people feel him. He was a presence, and they all knew it.

Mitch was easy to spot. He was sitting at a back table, one leg propped up on the chair, like he owned the joint. The smirk on his face was all bravado, but Jamal wasn't fooled. Mitch was the kind of guy who thought he could talk his way out of anything. But tonight? Tonight, Jamal wasn't listening to any excuses.

Jamal moved toward him, his footsteps slow, deliberate. Mitch looked up, his smile flickering for just a second, before it went back to that cocky grin.

"Jamal King, what's really good?" Mitch asked, his voice smooth, like he was just bumpin' into a long-lost homie, but there was no mistaking the watchful tension in his eyes. He leaned back in his chair, acting like it was business as usual, but inside, he was already sizing up the situation. Mitch knew when something wasn't right, and Jamal standing in his spot? That wasn't no coincidence.

Mitch didn't flinch or try to front like he wasn't aware of what time it was. He'd seen enough to know that Jamal didn't roll up on his turf unless shit was about to hit the fan. But Mitch wasn't stupid, either. He wasn't gonna let Jamal think he could intimidate him in his own house.

"Yo, you got the nerve to walk in here like you runnin' shit?" Mitch's words were sharp, but there was a certain calm in his tone that told Jamal Mitch wasn't shook. He wasn't scared, not one bit. He had too much respect for the game, and for himself, to let anyone walk in and dictate how things were gonna go down.

Jamal's crew was deep, but Mitch had his own hitters right there, and he knew the lay of the land better than anyone. If it came down to it, Jamal wasn't the only one who knew how to make moves. But Mitch wasn't about to make this personal unless he had to.

"Come on, man. What's this really about?" Mitch pressed, his eyes narrowing just slightly, like he already knew Jamal had something he was holding back. He wasn't about to give Jamal an inch. Not in here.

"What's good?" Jamal repeated, his voice cold. "You wanna know what's good? You been movin' all over my territory, Mitch. You been taking food off my plate. That's what's good."

Mitch's grin didn't fade, but Jamal saw the shift. He could feel Mitch trying to stay confident, trying to act like he wasn't about to get swallowed whole by the man standing in front of him.

"Man, come on. You know how this works. I'm just tryna make my bread," Mitch said, leaning back like he didn't have a care in the world. But there was an edge to his voice now, a crack. He was starting to get uncomfortable.

Jamal didn't sit down. He just stayed standing, towering over Mitch. "Yeah, I get it. I really do. But you makin' bread off my shit. And that ain't how this works."

Mitch scoffed, like Jamal was being extra for no reason. "You actin' like we ain't all out here tryin' to eat. I ain't disrespectin' you, Jamal. We doin' business. You should know that. Ain't no need to make it personal."

"Don't tell me it ain't personal," Jamal shot back. "You think I run this city out of charity? Nah, Mitch. I run it 'cause I built it. I put in work for this, and you think you're just gonna slide in and take it? Nah, that ain't how it goes."

Mitch's face hardened, the cockiness starting to slip, replaced with something else. Maybe fear, maybe respect, but Jamal wasn't sure yet. He could see Mitch's wheels turning, calculating. He wasn't ready to back down yet, but the fight was already over in Jamal's mind. He had Mitch right where he wanted him.

"You really think you can just shut me down like that?" Mitch's voice had a bite to it now, like he was looking for a way out, trying to bluff his way through the situation.

Jamal didn't flinch. His eyes locked onto Mitch, unshaken. "I ain't shutting you down, Mitch. I'm giving you a choice. Stay off my turf, or there's gonna be consequences."

Mitch's smirk twisted into something more sinister, like a lion sizing up its prey. "Consequences, huh?" he said, voice oozing with disbelief. "You think you can scare me with that weak shit? Nah, man, lemme give you some advice, Jamal—don't start no war you ain't ready to finish."

He leaned back in his chair, the sarcasm thick in his voice. "I know you mad 'cause I'm cutting into your hustle. But guess what? I don't give a fuck." His eyes narrowed as he sized Jamal up, watching for any sign of weakness.

Jamal's jaw clenched, his patience running thin. "You think you're untouchable just 'cause you got a few muscle heads backing you? You ain't running shit in my spot, Mitch. Keep pushin', and you'll find out real quick."

Mitch chuckled, low and dangerous. "Your spot?" He shook his head, his tone sharp, almost mocking. "This ain't a damn playground, Jamal. It's business. And right now? I'm doing better business than you. If you can't handle that, maybe you're in the wrong game."

Jamal slammed his fist on the table, rattling the glasses. "You crossed the line, Mitch. This ain't just about money no more. This is about respect. And you ain't got none."

"Respect?" Mitch scoffed, leaning forward, his eyes cold. "Respect's earned, not handed out. And from where I'm standing? You ain't earned a damn thing."

Mitch's lips curled into a smug grin as he leaned in closer. "Your territory? Please. This land is free. I answer to no man. And if you think you're the king of this block, maybe you should take a better look. You're in my world now."

The tension was thick enough to cut with a knife. Jamal's grip tightened on his jacket, his face a mask of controlled anger. He leaned in, his voice low but lethal. "You love your family, Mitch? Then you better think real hard about your next move. Don't fuck with me."

For a second, Mitch's muscles tensed. He could feel the weight of Jamal's threat. The man wasn't playing, and the stakes just got real. But Mitch wasn't about to show any fear.

His voice dropped to a menacing whisper. "My family is off-limits. You touch a hair on their head, and I promise you'll regret it. You know who the fuck I am. You know what I'm capable of. Keep testing me, and you'll see real quick what happens when you push the wrong man."

Jamal's laugh echoed in the room, cold and biting. His gold teeth flashed in the dim light, but his smile was pure malice. "Nobody's off limits, Mitch," he said, his tone dripping with danger.

Mitch didn't flinch. He met Jamal's gaze with an icy glare, voice hard as steel. "Mark my words, Jamal. Touch my family, and hell's coming for you."

The room felt like it was on the brink of exploding, both men standing toe to toe, each one daring the other to make a move. The air crackled with tension, every second stretching out like an eternity. But neither one blinked, both knowing the battle between them was far from over.

Jamal's hands balled into fists, frustration boiling over as Mitch kept pushing. His hand brushed against the cold metal of his gun, the temptation to end it right here rising in his chest.

But before anything could pop off, a voice cut through the heavy silence, clear and firm.

"Enough."

Everyone's eyes shot to Tiana as she stood next to Jamal, her face giving nothing away. She was calm, but there was something about her, a quiet strength that made everyone take notice.

"This ain't the time or the place," she said, her voice steady, like she was the one in control. "We're not gonna do this now. You two need to chill before this turns into something none of us want."

Jamal scanned the room, his eyes moving to every corner, every shadow, every thug Mitch had stationed in the place. His crew was outnumbered, and no matter how hard he wanted to put his foot down, he knew when to back off. This wasn't the fight he needed. Not today.

Tiana leaned in close, her breath warm in his ear. "It ain't worth it, Jamal," she murmured, her voice low but steady. "We'll handle Mitch another way, but not like this. Not now. Let's just keep it cool and get outta here."

Jamal exhaled, slow and heavy, like the air had been knocked outta him. She was right, he knew it. Pushing things further now would only set them up for something worse down the line. "Yeah, you're right," he grunted, a bitter edge in his voice. "But this ain't over. Mitch might think he won this round, but trust me—he'll regret it. I'll make sure of that."

Tiana gave him a look, steady and sharp. "I got no doubt about that," she said, her confidence unwavering. "But we'll hit him harder when the time's right. For now, we lay low. We plan." She gave his arm a quick squeeze, a silent promise.

They walked out into the night, the city streets stretching dark and empty in front of them. Mitch watched them go, the sharp pain of Tiana's betrayal hitting him harder than any of Jamal's threats. After everything, he hadn't expected her to turn on him like this. But then again, as the old saying went, "never trust a bitch." Anger welled up inside him, burning through his chest, but he swallowed it down, pushing it back. He wasn't about to show weakness now.

Inside the speakeasy, Mitch slammed his fist down on the table with a force that made the wood groan under pressure. Sarah, the bartender, nearly jumped outta her skin, the glass she was holding sloshing liquor all over the bar. Mitch glared at her. "Another drink," he growled, the words coming out like poison. His mind was racing, the scene with Jamal replaying over and over. The smug grin on his face, the cocky swagger. Mitch couldn't let that shit slide. Not now. Not ever. "Make it a double."

Outside, the night air hit Mitch's face, sharp and cold. His crew fell in line behind him as they walked down the empty streets. The city felt alive, the silence a thick weight pressing down on him. Mitch's instincts were firing—something was off. He scanned the street, his eyes flicking back and forth, trying to sense anything outta place.

Then, he saw it—a black car parked a little too close. Too still. The hairs on his neck stood up. His heart started thumping, quick and heavy in his chest. He couldn't shake the feeling that something was about to go down.

He tried to keep walking, but every shadow seemed to creep closer, every noise felt amplified. His hand instinctively went to his waist, his fingers brushing over his gun, ready for whatever came next. He wasn't going down easy.

Just then, the screech of tires ripped through the night. Mitch barely had time to react before three guys in ski masks piled outta the black sedan, guns raised and pointed straight at him. Time seemed to slow, and Mitch's pulse went wild. Fear shot through him, but he wasn't gonna let it take over. Not tonight.

He ducked for cover behind a car, heart pounding, mind racing. This wasn't just a random hit—it was a message. From Jamal. He'd sent his goons to send him a clear warning: back off, or else.

Mitch's breath came in quick bursts, his hands shaking as he pulled his own gun from its holster. He had one shot at this. He wasn't gonna die here in some alley, caught slipping.

The black car shot forward, tires squealing. Mitch's finger hovered over the trigger. No hesitation. This was do or die.

The gunfire tore through the air, deafening in the silence of the night. Mitch fired back, his shots ringing out, his eyes locked on the moving targets. His heart raced, every bullet that missed him a miracle, but he didn't stop. He kept his cool, firing when he had to, ducking when it was necessary. Survival was all that mattered now.

When the smoke cleared, the street was silent again. Mitch stood there, chest heaving, sweat slicking his brow. None of the bullets had hit him, but he knew this was far from over. The message had been sent loud and clear, and now it was his turn to send one right back.

He took a deep breath, steadying himself. Jamal was playing a dangerous game, but Mitch wasn't backing down. He wasn't about to let some punk ass nigga with gold teeth think he could run shit in his city. Mitch had fought too hard to get to where he was.

Without a second glance, Mitch walked away, his crew close behind, the rage simmering inside him, burning hotter with every step. He knew it was only a matter of time before they clashed again. And next time? He'd be ready.

Chapter Thirty-Two

"No Way Out, But Together"

Mitch leaned back in his chair, the dim light from the lamp barely cutting through the darkness of the room. The hustle had been non-stop, but tonight, something felt off. He couldn't shake the feeling that he needed something more—needed to hear her voice, feel that connection. So, without thinking too much, he grabbed his phone and made the call.Angel pulled up a few minutes later, the engine of her car rumbling down the street, and Mitch didn't waste any time. As soon as she stepped inside, he was on her—holding her close, feeling the familiar warmth of her body, trying to push everything else out of his mind. For a minute, it was just them. No streets, no enemies, no danger—just two people trying to survive.

They didn't speak right away. It wasn't necessary. Mitch wrapped his arms around her, letting the tension in his shoulders relax as he breathed her in. He'd been through hell, but right now? This felt like peace.

But even in the silence, Mitch knew this wasn't gonna be easy. His life wasn't a simple one, and Angel deserved to know what she was getting into.

After a few moments, he pulled away, just enough to look her in the eyes. "Angel, I gotta ask you somethin'. You sure you wanna be with a man like me? Tomorrow ain't promised for me. And if somethin' happens... I need to know if you can handle that."

Angel exhaled slowly, her gaze steady. "Mitch, I've thought about this a lot. I love you with everything I got, and yeah, I'm sure. I know what comes with being with you, and I'm willing to face it, because you're worth it to me. I'm in this, all the way."

Mitch felt something tighten in his chest. She was real, no front, no games. He wasn't used to it, but he couldn't deny it—he needed it. He reached for her hand, his voice low. "Don't talk like that, Angel," he said, his eyes searching hers. "I can't promise you forever. But you gotta understand—I'm tryna give you the best I got. I'm tryna build somethin' for us."

Angel squeezed his hand, her grip firm, not just with love, but with a kind of resolve Mitch could feel in his bones. "I don't like hearin' you talk like that," she said, her voice steady. "You're not goin' anywhere, Mitch. You hear me? I can't picture life without you, and I won't. We're in this together, all the way. No matter what."

Mitch looked at her, the raw honesty in her words cut through the layers he'd built around himself. He rubbed the back of his neck, trying to find the right words. "I've made my mistakes, Angel. Done shit I regret. Walked some dark roads that I can't erase. But through all that, you've been the one steady thing, the only thing that kept me from fallin' apart."

Angel's touch was gentle, her fingers tracing the line of his jaw as if to remind him that none of that mattered now. "Mitch, we all got our pasts. Hell, I ain't perfect either. But it's about how we move forward, how we learn and grow from what we've been through. And I see you, Mitch. I see the man you're trying to be. You're doing better, for yourself, for me, for us."

Mitch's heart swelled. He had always been the one trying to hold it all together, never trusting anyone enough to let them see the cracks. But Angel? She saw him for who he was, all of him, and still stood by him.

"I don't deserve you, Angel," Mitch murmured. "But you've always believed in me, even when I didn't believe in myself."

Angel smiled softly, her voice quiet but sure. "That's what love is, Mitch. Seeing the best in each other, even when the world's only lookin' at the worst parts. And I'll always be here, no matter what. That's my promise to you."

Mitch pulled her in closer, his hands gripping her tightly like he was scared to let go. "You've been through so much with me, Angel. I can't lie... my life ain't easy. But I'll move heaven and earth to make sure you're safe. To keep you out of harm's way. I'm not leavin' you in the dark."

Angel's voice was steady, her words cutting through the doubt swirling in his mind. "And I'll do the same for you, Mitch. We're a team, you and me. We ride or die together, you know that. Ain't no one or nothin' that can break us."

Mitch chuckled dryly, squeezing her hand. "I like the sound of that. Bonnie and Clyde, huh?" He grinned, despite everything, as the weight of their situation softened, just for a moment.

Angel's smile was full of mischief. "Well, if we're Bonnie and Clyde, then we're gonna need some wild rides and plenty of love along the way. But promise me, Mitch—no matter what happens, we stick together. We ride this out like true partners, no matter the storm."

Mitch leaned in, pressing a kiss to her forehead, the words rough but sincere. "Look, Angel. I ain't great with words. But you keep me grounded. You pull me back when everything's spinnin' outta control."

He took a deep breath, his expression serious. "There's one more thing we need to talk about. I gotta handle this situation with Jamal. And the way it's lookin', it could get ugly. But I need you to know—whatever happens, I'm seein' this through to the end."

Angel's eyes flickered with concern, but she didn't flinch. "I understand, Mitch. You gotta do what you gotta do. Just... promise me you'll be careful."

Mitch took her hand again, his grip strong, unwavering. "I promise. I'll make sure I stay safe. But there's one more thing I need from you, Angel."

She leaned in, meeting his eyes with all the trust in the world. "Anything, Mitch. You know I got you."

Mitch paused, the weight of the world on his shoulders, but a sense of resolve building inside. "I want you to start lookin' for your business location. I want you to have somethin' that's all yours, Angel. A place you can call your own, that you can be proud of. And I'm gonna make it happen for you. I believe in you, and I owe you this."

Angel's eyes widened, surprise written all over her face. "Mitch, you don't gotta do that. I can find a spot on my own."

Mitch shook his head, his tone final. "Nah, Angel. You've been down for me through all this madness. I owe you more than that. We talked about this. Consider it my way of sayin' thank you for not givin' up on me. For always believin' in me, even when I didn't believe in myself."

Angel's hand reached up, cupping his face softly. She was overwhelmed, but her eyes were steady. "Mitch, you don't owe me anything. But I appreciate this more than you know. I'll start lookin' today."

Mitch smiled, a deep sense of pride swelling in his chest. "I know you will. And when you find that spot, when it all comes together, it's gonna be the start of something big. Something real."

Angel leaned in and kissed him gently, her lips soft against his. "I love you, Mitch. And I'll always be here. No matter what."

Mitch pulled her in, holding her close, not wanting to let go. "I love you too, Angel. And I'll do whatever it takes to make sure you get the future you deserve."

Chapter Thirty-Three

"Pressure Makes Diamonds"

Mitch could feel the pressure creeping up on him like a drumbeat in his chest, steady and unrelenting. The beef with Jamal King, the ruthless boss of the Southside, was spiraling out of control. There was no more pretending that the danger wasn't right on their doorstep.

The corners of the block, the rundown spots, all whispered danger. But Mitch, staying true to his gritty nature, kept his eyes locked on the prize— Angel's dream.

It had started as a faint wish, like something that could easily slip through your fingers, but now it was slowly taking shape.

"Just picture it," she said, tapping the condensation on her iced tea, looking lost in the thought of it. "A place where women can come in beat down by life and leave feeling like queens. Nails on point, hair fresh, ready to take on whatever the world throws at 'em."

Mitch smirked, half-amused. "Sounds good, but dreams need more than just a wish to make 'em real. They need something solid."

She didn't flinch. Her eyes locked on his, full of fire. "This time, Mitch," she said, steady like she knew something he didn't, "I'm gonna build that foundation."

And those words hit him like a shot to the chest. They stayed with him, even as the world seemed to close in around them.

Every day, Angel hit the pavement. Searching, scouring, checking out spot after spot. There was no layout for this kind of hustle, but she dove in like it was second nature. Each location had potential. Some had that old-school charm, others the foot traffic she could build off of, and some... well, they had that quirky vibe.

Mitch? He was there every step of the way, pushing through the headaches of budgets and dead-end offers, helping her navigate the business side of things. He spent evenings breaking down financials with her, using street smarts he learned the hard way to give her guidance on the tough stuff. And when they walked into places together, his eyes were sharp, catching flaws she might've missed – the broken plumbing, the cracked wiring. He was her rock, even when the ground beneath them kept shifting.

Rejection after rejection came in—"no's" that felt personal—but Angel didn't bend. With each "no," she just burned hotter. Mitch watched as that stubborn streak of hers kept her pushing forward, always talking about the vision, never backing down.

There were times she'd be frustrated, sitting in a park bench, trying to work out what came next, her voice trembling with uncertainty. And Mitch? He'd just listen. He didn't always know what to say, but he always knew how to be there. A squeeze of her hand, a quiet presence, and it was enough.

Then one day, after weeks of frustration, they found it. A small storefront that barely stood out from the street, but something about it called to her. Angel, with her fingers brushing the weathered brick, knew right then: this was it.

"It's perfect, Mitch," she whispered, a spark in her voice that Mitch hadn't heard in a while.

Mitch took it all in—sure, the place had its rough edges, but damn, the location was solid. He pushed the door open, and the smell of dust hit him. But still, the place felt like a possibility. Angel turned around, arms wide, her eyes sparkling with the wild energy of a dreamer.

"Mitch, this could be my canvas. A place to create something amazing."

Mitch chuckled, the smile softening his usual hardness. "Yeah, it's got potential. But getting it's gonna take more than a dream."

A week later, they were sitting across from Mr. Davis, the loan officer with a buzzcut that screamed "by the book." Angel's presentation was crisp, all the numbers in place, everything lined up perfectly. Mitch wasn't much for the paperwork part, but he knew how to back up a deal.

"I'm sure you've seen this before, Mr. Davis," Angel said, voice steady but tight, "but I need this. We need this." She slid the folder over to him, full of market research and financial projections.

Mr. Davis was skeptical. Small businesses were always a risk, and this one had plenty of red flags. Mitch leaned back in his chair, studying the guy. It wasn't his first rodeo; he knew how this worked.

And when the questions started, Mitch slid in to clarify a few things, showing that Angel wasn't just some hopeful dreamer—she had the plan. The kind of plan that could make this work.

After a few tense exchanges, Mitch broke the ice. "Look, we appreciate the offer, but paperwork ain't really our style." His voice was casual, but there was a raw edge to it that made Mr. Davis' brow twitch.

Angel tried to hold it together, but she couldn't hide the grin that slipped out. She was starting to see Mitch's different side—the side of him that was all about getting things done, no matter what it took.

The loan officer wasn't impressed at first. But Mitch didn't let up. He leaned forward, voice low but steady. "We're not here for a loan. We're here for something else. You've got a piece of property that fits exactly what Angel needs. So, let's cut to the chase: what's the price? Give us a number, and we'll close this right now."

There was a shift in the room. Mr. Davis looked thrown off—he wasn't used to clients who flipped the script like this. But Mitch? He was steady as hell, showing no fear.

Mitch reached into his jacket and pulled out a leather folder. He dropped it on the table with a thud. The papers inside? Bank statements, records—everything that proved they were ready.

"Mr. Davis's eyes flicked to the folder, his posture stiffening as he took in the evidence. 'Well, now that's a different story.'"

The tension was thick, but Mitch didn't budge. The room felt suffocating, the only sound the ticking of the clock, stretching the silence.

Mr. Davis slowly flipped through the papers, his brow furrowed. He took his time, processing every detail.

Finally, after a long beat, he leaned back in his chair, shaking his head with a half-smile. "You really don't play by the rules, do you, Thompson? This... this is straight-up bold."

Mitch leaned forward, grinning. "I call it thinking outside the box."

Davis chuckled, shaking his head as he reached across the table to shake Mitch's hand. "Guess it worked. We've got a deal."

Angel let out a breath she hadn't realized she was holding. "Thank you, Mr. Davis," she said, her voice full of relief and excitement.

Outside, Mitch pulled her close, kissing her hard. It was a kiss that said everything—pride, relief, and the promise of what was to come.

"You killed it in there, Angel," Mitch muttered. "Straight fire."

Angel smirked, a little flustered. "You weren't too bad yourself, Mr. Thompson." She laughed softly. "That 'outside the box' thing? Definitely got me hooked."

Mitch chuckled, his usual cool demeanor slipping just a little as he pulled her in for a tight hug. "Seems like we make a good team, huh?" he whispered, his voice dropping low. "And this? This is just the start."

Renovation became the grind that kept them going. Weekends were spent scraping paint, hauling junk, and turning the old storefront into something new. Mitch, more accustomed to a different kind of hard work, found satisfaction in the DIY world—sanding, fixing, building. He hit flea markets for furniture, finding pieces that added character to the space. And Angel? She was on her grind too, researching, dreaming, planning, making sure every detail was perfect.

And then it happened. The place came together. It was no longer a shell; it was a vision realized. Angel's Haven was born.

The opening day was electric. The neighborhood buzzed with excitement. Women came in—some regulars, some curious—and they all left looking like a million bucks. Angel's face lit up with pride as she worked behind the counter.

Mitch, standing back and watching it all unfold, knew one thing for sure: this wasn't just about the business. It was about them. About what they could do together when they pushed, when they believed.

It wasn't just a victory—it was a new chapter. And Mitch, in his own way, had laid the foundation for Angel's dream to become a reality.

- Chapter Thirty-Four -

"Blood in the Streets"

Chicago's early morning light did little to soften the city's hard edges. Mitch stood by the window of his South Side hideout, blunt burning between his fingers, watching Angel disappear into the distance. A quiet storm brewed in his gut—he knew the streets were shifting, the power tilting in Jamal King's favor. Sitting on the sidelines wasn't an option anymore.

The streets had always been a game of chess, and Mitch wasn't about to be a pawn. He made the call. One by one, his crew assembled—men who'd bled with him, men who had bodies on them, men who didn't flinch at war. T-Money was the last to arrive, stepping into the warehouse with his usual cocky grin, though Mitch could see the tension behind it. They sat at a metal table littered with throw away phones, maps, and half-empty bottles of Hennessy.

Mitch took a drag, exhaled slow. "We tear Jamal down from the inside out—his drug spots, stash houses, his top guys. One by one, we dismantle everything he's built."

T-Money nodded, cracking his knuckles. "And then?"

Mitch met his gaze, unwavering. "We take his fucking head."

No one spoke. They didn't have to. This wasn't a debate—it was a death sentence for somebody. The only question was who'd be left standing when the smoke cleared.

The War Begins

The war started that night.

Mitch and his crew moved like phantoms, striking Jamal's empire with precision. Trap houses went up in flames, drug runners found themselves at the wrong end of a Glock, and bodies stacked up faster than the city could clean them. Every hit sent a message—Jamal King wasn't untouchable.

But Jamal wasn't the type to go down easy. His retaliation came fast and merciless, bullets raining in broad daylight, catching Mitch's men slipping at red lights, in grocery store parking lots, even in their own damn homes. Nobody was safe.

Mitch barely slept, barely ate. He moved through the chaos like a man already dead, fueled by anger, loss, and the cold knowledge that once you start something like this, you don't stop until one side is buried.

The Cost of War

It wasn't just the bodies that haunted Mitch—it was the collateral damage.

A little girl, no older than eight, caught in the crossfire outside a corner store. A mother screaming over her teenage son's body after he got mistaken for one of Jamal's runners. The way the streets whispered that this war was getting out of control.

T-Money was the first to say it out loud.

"This shit's gettin' reckless, man," he muttered, leaning against a beat-up Impala outside their latest raid. His knuckles were bloodied, and the barrel of his gun was still warm.

Mitch wiped the sweat from his brow. "You think we stop now, Jamal's gonna shake our hands and let it slide?"

T-Money shook his head. "Nah. But I'm sayin'... how many more bodies 'til we just ghosts walkin' around, waitin' for our turn?"

Mitch didn't answer. Because he already knew.

They were past the point of no return.

The call

His phone vibrated on the table, snapping him out of his thoughts. T-Money.

Mitch let it ring once more before picking up.

"Yo."

"Meet me at the spot, man. We need to talk."

No jokes. No bullshit. Just straight to it. That wasn't like T-Money.

"Bet. Give me ten."

Mitch tucked his piece in his waistband and pulled off.

The streets were quieter than usual as Mitch drove. Too quiet. The war had pushed the city into paranoia—everyone watching their backs, everyone waiting for the next body to drop. As he pulled into the alleyway, T-Money was already there, leaning against his car, blunt lit in his hand.

Mitch stepped out, his hand instinctively resting near his hip. "What's going on, T?"

T-Money exhaled, watching the smoke curl into the night air. "I ain't gonna lie, Mitch... I'm tired, man. Tired in a way I ain't never been before."

Mitch frowned. T-Money was always the wild card, the one who laughed in the face of danger, who never let fear creep into his voice. But tonight, something was different.

"T, what you saying?"

T-Money hesitated, rubbing his hand over his face. "I mean... how long we gon' do this, man? How long before it's our bodies in the street? I keep waking up feeling like I'm already dead, like I'm just waiting for the bullet that's got my name on it."

Mitch stayed quiet, letting T-Money talk.

"I ain't scared of dying, Mitch. Never have been. But the way we living... this ain't life. This ain't even survival. It's just waiting. You ever feel that?"

Mitch sighed, looking past T-Money, past the city skyline that had seen them rise up from nothing. "Yeah," he admitted. "More than I wanna say."

T-Money laughed, but it was hollow. "Man, when we started this, it felt like we was building something. Like we had control. But now? Now it's just blood for blood. A cycle that don't stop till there's nobody left."

Mitch clenched his jaw. He wanted to tell T-Money they were different. That this war had a purpose. That all this killing meant something. But did it? Or was it just revenge feeding revenge, a never-ending hunger for power neither of them could ever truly hold?

"You ever think about leaving?" Mitch finally asked. The words felt strange in his mouth, like he wasn't supposed to say them.

T-Money scoffed. "Leave? And do what? Flip burgers? Work some nine-to-five where a boss talk down to me like I ain't a man? Hell nah." He shook his head. "I just... I just want it to mean something, Mitch. If we gotta go out, I want it to mean something."

Mitch nodded. He understood. The streets weren't just a battleground. They were home. And walking away wasn't as simple as leaving town. The streets lived in them.

"We take out Jamal," Mitch said, his voice steady. "And then we figure it out."

T-Money looked at him for a long moment, then nodded. "Alright. But I need to know something, Mitch."

"What's that?"

"When this is over... you really think there's a way out for us?"

Mitch didn't answer right away. He wanted to lie, to say yes, to promise a future neither of them were sure existed. But he couldn't.

Instead, he clapped a hand on T-Money's shoulder. "We make our own way out, T. One way or another."

T-Money exhaled, then flicked his roach to the ground, crushing it under his boot. "Then let's finish this."

They weren't just fighting for power anymore. They were fighting for something more.

A way out—or a way to die on their own terms.

- Chapter Thirty-Five -

"The Setup Ain't Always Sweet"

The bar was dim, thick with smoke and the murmur of low voices. In a shadowy booth, Mitch and T-Money nursed a bottle of whiskey, its condensation pooling on the worn table. The door creaked, and a young man stepped inside, eyes darting like he expected a bullet any second.

Mitch barely lifted his head. "You lost, kid?"

The young man hesitated, fingers twitching against the brim of a frayed baseball cap. "I, uh… got some information you might want."

T-Money leaned forward, studying him. "Information about what exactly?"

The kid licked his lips, voice dropping. "Jamal. I know where he's at."

Mitch exchanged a look with T-Money.

"We don't take intel from just anybody. Especially not some kid who looks like he still got a curfew."

The young man squared his shoulders. "I ain't just anybody. I used to run with Jamal. Till he did me dirty."

T-Money scoffed. "Join the club. What makes you different?"

The kid's hands curled into fists. His voice turned raw. "That motherfucker stripped me in front of everyone. Took my clothes, my respect, had me walk out with a gun at my head. I ain't forgot that."

A silence settled between them. Mitch studied the kid, looking for any hint of bullshit.

"Alright. Talk."

The young man leaned in. "He's holed up in that abandoned warehouse on 5th. The old Briggs spot with the busted windows. Thinks he's safe there, but I been watching."

Mitch's jaw tightened. "How many he got with him?"

"Five, six guys. They rotate shifts. But Big Ron's always there, strapped."

T-Money nodded. "What they packing?"

"Heavy. ARs, shotguns. But they get sloppy, especially late. Jamal been feelin' untouchable."

Mitch exhaled through his nose. "Entry points?"

The kid's eyes gleamed. "Back alley's usually unguarded. And there's a fire escape that leads to the second floor. That's your way in."

T-Money smirked. "You sure about all this?"

The young man's voice turned ice cold. "I been watching for weeks. Just make sure that bitch don't walk out alive."

Mitch stared at him, then gave a slow nod. "We'll handle it."

T-Money slapped the table. "Now that's what I like to hear."

The kid took a breath, like unloading his grudge had lifted a weight off him. He nodded once and slipped out the door, swallowed by the night.

Mitch watched him go, a bad feeling curling in his gut. "You trust him?"

T-Money took another swig. "Don't matter. His hate's real, and hate makes people useful."

Mitch wasn't convinced. "Something about him's off. Too eager."

T-Money shrugged. "Then we send a couple guys first, see if he's feeding us bullshit."

Mitch exhaled, rolling his whiskey glass between his fingers. "Yeah… and we dig into who he really is. Find out why Jamal humiliated him like that."

T-Money grinned. "Now you talkin'. But first…" He raised his glass. "To ending this shit."

They clinked glasses, the quiet clatter echoing like an omen.

5TH STREET WAREHOUSE

The South Side was quiet in that eerie, middle-of-the-night way, the streetlights flickering over wet pavement. Rico and Darnell rolled up in a beat-up Impala, chrome bumpers catching just enough light to look out of place in the decay.

Rico, built like a wrecking ball, climbed out first. Cornrows, cauliflower ear, and a scar slicing through his eyebrow—he looked like he'd been through war and walked out grinning. He slammed the car door, the sound loud in the empty street.

Darnell, younger, twitchy, pulled his hoodie tighter. "This the place?"

Rico grunted, scanning the warehouse. "Yeah. Same spot the kid gave us. Jamal been holed up here ever since his last play went left."

The Windy City Warehouse stood like a forgotten beast—brick walls tagged up with gang symbols, busted-out windows glaring like empty eye sockets. A sour wind carried the stench of garbage and something metallic, making Darnell's stomach turn.

They moved in, gravel crunching under their boots. Rico shoved against the rusted door—it groaned open, revealing pitch-black inside. The air reeked of mildew and old oil.

Guns drawn, they stepped inside. The warehouse swallowed them, their flashlights cutting through the gloom. Towers of rusting shelves loomed around them, cobwebs dangling like abandoned dreams.

BANG.

The sound slapped against the walls, making them both freeze.

Darnell's breath hitched. "The fuck was that?"

Rico didn't answer. He crept forward, light sweeping the darkness.

They reached an open space. A single crate sat in the middle like bait in a trap. Rico hesitated. "Something ain't right."

Then—

BANG!

A shot rang out. Sparks exploded. Rico barely ducked in time.

"Move!" Darnell hissed, scrambling for cover.

High above, a red ember glowed in the dark—someone smoking, watching.

Then, laughter. Low, taunting.

They weren't alone.

Darnell swallowed hard, his fingers tightening around his gun. The air was thick with smoke and the sharp scent of gunpowder. Bullets kept raining down, splintering wood, kicking up dust.

Rico peeked around the crate—two on the catwalk, another two moving in from the far end of the warehouse. No way out but through.

"I'm dumping left, you go right," Rico ordered, reloading fast. His shoulder throbbed, but adrenaline kept him moving.

Darnell nodded. No hesitation. Just action.

"Now!"

Rico swung out first, unleashing a wild spray of bullets toward the catwalk. The metal railing sparked as slugs ricocheted, forcing their attackers to duck. Darnell burst right, firing as he ran. The two men on the ground scrambled for cover, but he caught one in the thigh—POP! The man hit the floor, screaming.

The second one fired back. A shot whizzed past Darnell's head—too close.

Rico rushed forward, ignoring the burn in his shoulder, and put two slugs in the guy's chest. He dropped like a sack of bricks.

Above them, one of the shooters leaned over the railing—BANG. A bullet slammed into Rico's crate, inches from his head.

"Staircase!" Darnell barked.

They sprinted toward the exit, weaving between rusted barrels and broken pallets as gunfire chased them. Rico's shoulder burned like hell, but he pushed through.

One of the shooters from above jumped down, trying to cut them off—bad move.

Darnell caught him mid-air with a shot to the gut. The man crumpled, coughing up blood. No time to finish him.

The warehouse doors were just ahead.

Rico rammed into them first, shouldering them open. Cold night air slapped them in the face as they bolted outside.

The getaway car sat in the alley, engine running.

They weren't even halfway there when the warehouse doors slammed open behind them.

More shots cracked through the night. Bullets ripped into the brick walls, glass shattered nearby.

"Go, go, go!" Rico barked as he yanked the passenger door open and dove in.

Darnell barely made it in before Rico floored the gas. Tires screamed against the pavement as they peeled off down the alley.

In the rearview, shadows moved near the warehouse entrance. More shooters spilling out.

Darnell twisted in his seat, rolling down the window. He leaned out, letting off a few rounds to keep their pursuers back.

An engine growled down the block, loud and mean—somebody was peelin' out, and the chase was on

"They followin'," Darnell muttered, ducking back inside.

"Not for long," Rico gritted.

He hit a hard right, then another, weaving through the streets. The car behind them stayed on their ass, headlights bouncing in the rearview.

Darnell reloaded, cursing under his breath.

Then—an opening.

Rico spotted a narrow alley and cut the wheel hard. The car fishtailed before slipping into the alley's shadows. He killed the lights, pressing the brake just enough to let them coast.

The other car sped past the alley entrance, missing them completely.

Rico waited a beat. Two. Then he gunned it in the opposite direction.

Darnell exhaled, rolling his shoulders. "Shit."

Rico didn't say anything. He was too busy thinking.

The kid set them up.

As they slid into that back alley behind Momma Rose's speakeasy, the chipped-up walls and tired lights overhead gave off just enough comfort to breathe easy. Stepping out of the car, the beer-soaked air that hit them felt almost like home. They knew what they were walking into, even if the night had already gone sideways.

The moment they stepped inside, Mitch's sharp gaze landed on Rico's bleeding shoulder.

"The fuck happened?"

Rico tossed a bloody chain onto the table, his voice like steel.

"That little punk set us up!"

Big Mike, a mountain of muscle with a permanent scowl and a cigar between his teeth, sat hunched over a poker table. T-Money, always quick on his feet, was in the middle of a dice game, eyes sharp, always on alert.

Rico and Darnell's entrance was met with silence. The laughter died, the clink of glasses stopped. The room went still, every pair of eyes landing on them. Mitch, sitting at the back of the bar, looked up from behind a haze of cigar smoke. He didn't need to say a word. The slight jerk of his head told them to come forward.

"Spit it out," Mitch growled, his voice low, rough.

Darnell cleared his throat. "It's a setup, Mitch. The whole thing was a trap."

Mitch's cigar dropped, hitting the table with a soft thud. His eyes darkened, his jaw tightening. His fist clenched. T-Money, who had been in the middle of his game, froze, his focus now completely on them.

Rico stepped forward, wincing as pain shot through his shoulder, but he forced it down. "They had us good. Shot me, led us on a wild goose chase. The place was crawling with Jamal's guys."

Mitch slammed his fist on the table, sending poker chips scattering. "That damn kid. Should have known it was a set up."

The room exploded with shouts and curses. What was supposed to be a quick job turned into a setup. They'd been at war with Jamal for months, each move another punch in a long, brutal fight. But now? It was time to end it, end him. No more waiting, no more second chances. Enough was enough.

Darnell's stomach sank. They'd walked right into it. The intel was trash, the plans were all wrong. Jamal had outplayed them—and made sure they bled for it.

The tension in the air was thick. What now?

T-Money leaned in, eyes sharp. "You catch a face? Anybody look familiar?"

Rico hesitated, jaw clenching. "It was dark... but I ain't blind. One of 'em had that limp—walk like his shoes too heavy. I'm pretty sure it was Rizzo."

Mitch's whole vibe shifted. He bit down on his cigar, smoke curling from his nose like a dragon about to breathe fire. "Rizzo?" he said slow. "That snake still crawlin' around?"

T-Money's face twisted. "Ain't he with Jamal?"

"Yeah," Rico nodded. "Ain't no doubt now. This wasn't no random hit. That setup? Jamal signed that shit in blood."

Vinnie, damn near slidin' off the edge of his seat, finally spoke up. "So what's the move, Mitch?"

Mitch didn't even blink. He slammed a wad of hundreds on the table so hard it echoed. "We done playin' defense. Double the men. We go straight for Jamal. Tomorrow."

Darnell and Rico locked eyes—rattled, but ready. That warehouse ambush had been too close, but they weren't backing down.

Mitch leaned back, eyes on fire. "Rizzo wanna show his face? Cool. He just signed his own death warrant."

The whole room fell quiet.

They knew what was coming.

The city was about to bleed.

- Chapter Thirty-Six -

Grief's Embrace

The days after the ambush moved slow and heavy—like time was draggin' its feet. Rico's shoulder stayed wrapped up, blood still crusted on his hoodie, but he ain't complain. Darnell was movin' like his ribs was still screamin', but he kept it pushin'. They ain't throw hands in the shootout, but it felt like they got jumped by life itself. Tired sat deep in their bones—past sleep, past rest.

Jamal made this personal, so now it wasn't just about takin' back turf—it was about makin' a point.

It wasn't just blocks and corners no more. It was ego, pain, and pride—all mixed up. Rico ain't just want his spot back, he wanted Jamal to feel it. To know he crossed the wrong line. And Darnell? He was right there with him—loyal, hurt, and mad as hell. Turf meant somethin', yeah… but now it was about who gon' bleed for it.

Word on the block was Jamal wasn't just peddlin' weight no more—dude had his hands in everything: From bookin' bets to extortion, dude was runnin' it all. The big money was in them underground spots—gambling dens, dirty bars, and hidden backrooms where cash got counted like it was the air they breathed.

That's where Frankie "Fingers" DeMarco came in.

Frankie wasn't built like no heavyweight, but don't get it twisted — his hands worked faster than a dealer slingin' aces. They say he got the name "Fingers" not just from cleanin' out suckers at cards, but from a trigger finger so quick, folks barely heard the click before they hit the ground. Dude was jittery, nerves always tight, eyes dartin' like he was waitin' for a hit that might come at any second. That twitch? Saved his ass more times than he could count — and got him in some messes too. Frankie knew how to move money through any backroom in Chi-Town and keep it all countin' out loud.

He's the one who dropped the info—three spots, locked down tight, but weak if they hit 'em all at once. Learned that from late-night talks, whiskey whispers, and a couple side chicks who just couldn't keep quiet. Mitch trusted him. Hell, everybody did. Frankie earned that trust—been ten toes down for years.

So when the crew ran up on those spots—Division, Clark, and the docks—Frankie rolled with it. He led the charge on Clark, laughin' like the devil in a tailored suit, finger on the trigger and a cigar hangin' out his mouth. Bullets flew, chaos broke out, and Clark got shut down just like the rest.

But Jamal ain't take that lightly.

Two days later, they found Frankie laid out cold in an alley on the South Side. One to the head, execution style. A single red rose behind his ear. No wallet, no piece, no mercy. Just silence and a message louder than gunfire—Jamal don't forget betrayal.

Mitch took it hard. Sat in the back of the speakeasy, eyes glued to the floor like he could still see Frankie walkin' through it. T-Money?

He ain't say much, just lit a Black & Mild and stared out the window like he was tryna set the city on fire with his thoughts.

"Frankie was family," Mitch finally muttered. "And Jamal just signed his death warrant."

After that, it wasn't just a war—it was vengeance wrapped in strategy. Rico and Darnell started diggin' into who sold Frankie out. Took to the streets like bloodhounds, chasin' whispers and leanin' on snitches. That's how they found out about Lucky Luciano—a washed-up boxer turned junkie, talkin' too much for too little.

Turned out Jamal's crew caught wind of Frankie's involvement from Lucky, who ran his mouth after losin' big and owin' even bigger. They used that info to set Frankie up.

Mitch could've smoked Lucky right then—but instead, they flipped him. Used his weakness for cash and coke to bait Razor Riley, Jamal's number two.

That warehouse meeting? A straight setup. Razor walked in cocky, thinkin' it was just business. He left bloodied and broken, singin' like a bird with no wings. Gave up everything—drop spots, stash houses, even Jamal's diamond move comin' in from overseas.

Now with Frankie gone and Razor flippin', Mitch and T-Money knew the end was near. Every move they made after that was for Frankie—for loyalty, for brotherhood, for the streets.

Because when you lose someone like Frankie? You don't heal—you get even.

The Final Conflict

They moved through the shadows of the warehouse, navigating past rusted machinery and piles of junk. It was like stepping into the belly of the beast, the smell of sweat and old gunpowder hanging in the air, thick as a cloud of smoke. Then—bang. The gunfire came at them like a wave, but Mitch and T-Money didn't flinch. They returned fire, fluid and fast, moving with a deadly kind of rhythm.

The whole place felt alive with bullets flying, chaos in every corner. Mitch's heart was racing, but his mind was locked in—focused. He was here for one thing: Jamal. One way or another, it ended tonight.

Out of the smoke, Mitch saw Jamal, his figure lit up by the flickering light of a fire. A snarl twisted Mitch's lips. This was it. With a roar, he rushed forward, gun blasting, dodging the bullets flying in his direction. Jamal fired back, the air crackling with the violence between them.

But just as Mitch was closing in, T-Money moved in front of him, taking the brunt of a barrage of bullets. Mitch's blood froze in his veins. Time slowed. He watched his best friend go down, blood blooming around him like a horrible flower.

"T-Money!" Mitch screamed, his heart breaking open. But there was no time for that. Not yet.

With a burst of raw anger, Mitch unloaded on Jamal, rage turning his hands to fire. Jamal went down, but not before he managed to squeeze off a final shot, one that caught T-Money right in the chest. Mitch didn't know how to breathe for a second. Everything stopped.

As Jamal crumpled, Mitch's world felt like it was coming undone. He dropped to his knees beside T-Money, holding him, trying to make sense of it all. The man who had been his brother, his partner in every twisted hustle, was gone. And all Mitch could do was watch his life slip away.

The rain started coming down in sheets as Mitch and the crew fought their way out of the warehouse, the streets of Chicago turning into a war zone. But Mitch felt like he was moving in slow motion, numb, like the fight had left him. He wasn't thinking about survival anymore. He was thinking about how empty his life was now that T-Money was gone.

He drove through the night, the black Impala cutting through the rain-slick streets like a knife. Neon lights blurred into a watercolor of pain. The car radio played a sad, soulful tune, the saxophone wailing like it knew Mitch's heart was torn apart. He could still hear T-Money's voice, his laugh, the way he'd always act like nothing could touch him.

Mitch pulled over by a park, the swings creaking in the wind like ghosts of their younger selves. He sat there, the engine off, the weight of everything settling on him. This wasn't just another day, another job. This was the end of something he could never replace. He closed his eyes, the memories flooding him—T-Money was the reckless one, jumping headfirst into everything. Mitch was the one who planned. They balanced each other, completed each other. But now half of him was gone, and all that was left was a hole so deep it felt like it would swallow him whole.

Mitch couldn't shake the sight—T-Money laid out on that cold warehouse floor, blood spillin' like a busted pipe, eyes already slippin' into that empty stare. His voice, cracked and low, still echoed in Mitch's head: *"Finish it, Mitch... don't let that motherfucker walk."*

Mitch gave him a nod—one of them tight ones, the kind where you ain't got no words left. He did what had to be done. Put Jamal in the dirt. But now? With the smoke cleared and the city dead quiet? Shit felt empty.

Ain't no W in this. Ain't no celebration when your brother ain't there to see it. All that blood, all them moves, all that rage—what it really get him? Just more ghosts.

His hand slammed down on the steering wheel, the anger flaring before it bled into sorrow. Mitch hadn't cried in years. But tonight— tonight, he couldn't hold it in. The tears came like a dam breaking, and he let them fall. The grief, the loss—it was all too much.

Eventually, he wiped his face, staring out into the night. The weight of what he had to do next loomed over him. He had to go to T-Money's mom. He had to tell her her son was gone. The thought twisted his gut. She had treated Mitch like family, and now he was the one who had to break her heart.

The rain had finally let up by the time Mitch got to T-Money's mom's apartment. He sat in the driveway, staring at the dim light coming through the window, gathering the strength to face her. This wasn't something you were ever ready for. Hell, nothing in this life ever prepares you for this kind of loss.

He climbed the steps to the apartment, every creak of the old wood echoing like a drumbeat in his chest. When he knocked, it felt like he was knocking on the door to his own future, uncertain and heavy with regret.

Mrs. Johnson opened the door, her tired face lighting up for a second before her eyes went to Mitch's expression. She saw it before he said a word.

"Mitch, baby, what's wrong?" Her voice cracked, but there was still hope in it. She thought he was here to tell her something good.

Mitch swallowed hard, his throat thick. "Ms. Johnson, I... I need to talk to you about Terrence."

Her face froze, her hand flying to her chest. "What... what about my boy?" she whispered, her voice small.

"He's gone, Ms. Johnson," Mitch choked out, his voice barely making it past the lump in his throat.

Her scream tore through the air, raw and painful. It didn't even sound human, just a mother's heartbreak laid bare. Mitch stood there, feeling like a shell of the man he used to be. She lashed out at him, fists pounding against his chest in frustration, in pain. But Mitch didn't flinch. He just stood there and took it, holding her as she sobbed against him.

"I'm sorry, Ms. Johnson. I'm so sorry," Mitch whispered, the words feeling like they would never be enough.

She pulled away, wiping her tears. "What are we gonna do, Mitch?" Her voice was broken, empty.

Mitch could only offer her a weak promise, the weight of it sitting heavy on his heart. "We'll get through this together, Ms. Johnson. I'll take care of everything. I'll make sure Terrence gets the funeral he deserves."

She nodded, her eyes filled with both pain and some strange, quiet gratitude. But then she looked him dead in the eyes. "Promise me, Mitch. Promise me you'll get out of this life. Promise me T-Money's death ain't gonna be in vain."

Mitch squeezed her hand, his jaw tight. He wasn't sure if he could keep that promise, but for her, for T-Money, he would try. He had to.

Chapter Thirty-Seven

"Lost but Never Forgotten"

Mitch stood at the front of the church in a suit that felt like it belonged to someone else, his body stiff with discomfort. Mrs. Johnson leaned heavily on his arm, her frail body trembling with grief. The preacher's loud voice echoed through the room, but Mitch barely heard the words. The mention of T-Money's name, spoken in wonder, was a slap in the face.

A single tear was able to slip down Mitch's cheek as he fought to keep his cool. The heat clung to the air, thick and wet, as if the air itself mourned. His black suit clung to his sweating flesh, each square inch a reminder that life went on, regardless of whether he was ready or not.

Around him, the Greater Hope Baptist Church was overflowing with people—men dressed in sharp suits, their faces lined with sorrow and lived-in hardship, and women in bright dresses, trying to hold it together while dabbing at their eyes with handkerchiefs. The smell of lilies mixed with the too-sweet perfume of expensive cologne, making Mitch feel like he was choking.

Reverend Jackson stood up there at the pulpit, his voice loud and full of that rehearsed compassion, but Mitch wasn't feelin' it like everyone else was. "We're here today to remember our brother, Terrence, aka T-Money," the preacher started, steady but heavy in his tone. "He was taken from us too soon, but not before he left his mark. A smile that could light up the darkest room, a spirit as warm as the sun… But the Lord, in His wisdom, calls us home when it's our time."

Mitch gritted his teeth, swallowing hard as the preacher kept talkin', paintin' T-Money as a man who messed up, but always had a good heart. "None of us are perfect," Reverend Jackson said, his words echoing around the church like they were supposed to mean somethin'.

"But even in the darkness, a good heart can shine through."

The reverend went on to share memories of T-Money—stories of him as a young boy, full of curiosity, always getting into something. He talked about how, despite the trouble he got into, T-Money had always tried to be there for those he loved, like the time he'd cleaned up a neighborhood lot or bought his sister the biggest stuffed animal he could find, even if it meant going hungry for a day.

Mitch's chest tightened as the words washed over him. The images of a young T-Money, full of dreams and life, felt like a bitter reminder of what had been lost. A ripple of soft sobs filled the room as the preacher's words finally sunk in. Mitch blinked hard, trying to keep his focus on the pulpit, but his thoughts kept slipping away.

As Reverend Jackson's voice trailed off, Aunt Beatrice, T-Money's aunt, stepped up to the podium. She was a small woman, her face wrinkled with both age and sorrow. But her love for her nephew was written all over her. "Terrence wasn't perfect," she said, her voice shaky at first, but growing stronger as she spoke. "He made mistakes, but he had a heart of gold. He could light up a room with just his smile."

Her eyes flickered with the weight of the memories as she spoke of T-Money, telling stories from his childhood, moments that made Mitch's chest tighten. She spoke about how he'd looked out for his little cousin, how he'd helped a neighbor when no one else would. The whole church was locked in, feeling her every word, as she painted the picture of a young man who, despite the grind of the streets, never lost that fire deep inside.

When she hit the end of her eulogy, her voice cracked, "We lost him too soon... but his memory's gonna live on—in the laughs of kids on the court he built, in the kindness he showed... in the love he gave."

She stepped back from the podium, and the air got thick, like her words hit everyone in the chest. A heavy silence dropped, only broken by the sound of sniffles and tissues rustling. It was that kind of silence that made the loss of T-Money feel like a punch to the gut.

Then the hymn "Amazing Grace" kicked in, and the congregation sang slow and heavy, voices thick with raw emotion. Mitch joined in, his voice thick too, his eyes burning, fighting back the tears he wasn't ready to let go.

When the hymn finally faded, the pallbearers came forward, their faces a mix of pain and that silent strength you only get when you've lost someone close.

Darius, Malik, Andre, and a few of the homies from way back moved up on the casket, all of 'em in black suits—fresh, sharp, but the pain in they eyes said it all. This wasn't no regular goodbye. This was war loss. Street loss. Family loss.

Mitch stood off to the side, dark shades on, jaw tight. Voice low, but it cut through the silence like a blade.

"Bro went out like a savage. Stood tall. No duckin'. No runnin'. He knew what it was."

Darius, broad frame barely holdin' it together, gave a slow nod. "Man... I still remember when them Southside boys tried to rush us in that back alley. T ain't run, ain't hesitate. Took more hits than he gave, but never backed down. Told me, 'We die together or walk out together—ain't no in between.'"

Malik, the one who never said much, looked down at the ground. "T ain't have it like that all the time, but he moved like he did. Man could be dead broke and still hand out his last dollar like it ain't hurt. That's just who he was… heart too big for the streets he was in."

Andre, young but scarred by this life, swallowed hard. "Y'all remember when Miss Jackson roof fell in after that storm? Everybody turned they back 'cause they was broke. But not T. He pulled up with them tarps like it was a whole new roof. Said, 'It ain't much, but it's better than nothin'.' That's who he was."

Silence crept in. The kind that make your chest feel hollow.

Mitch took a breath, voice low and real. "World ain't got room for too many like T-Money no more. Streets gon' feel colder without him walkin' 'em."

Darius wiped his face, voice cracking just a little. "Colder... and a whole lot meaner."

Andre looked to the sky, like he was tryin' to find T somewhere up there. "Maybe a little safer now. He was always a target, man."

Malik shook his head slowly, teeth clenched. "Nah, it ain't safer. It's just quieter. Empty. 'Cause when a lion dies, the jungle don't sleep—it starves."

They fell into silence again, the weight of their loss hanging over them like a thick fog.

The heat hit them hard as they stepped outside, the sun beating down mercilessly. The procession moved slowly toward the grave, the air thick with humidity and the scent of freshly cut grass. Mitch felt the weight of T-Money's absence pressing on him, each step a reminder that his friend, his brother, was gone.

As they reached the graveside, the crowd quieted. T-Money's little cousin stepped forward, a small basket of white doves in her hands. She released them one by one, each dove rising into the air like a silent tribute to the man who had once been a beacon of light in their lives.

Then, they all stood still, watching as the last shovelful of dirt fell onto the casket. The earth swallowed T-Money whole. But just as the final prayer was said, a single shot rang out. It was sharp, jarring—a cold reminder that the streets never forget.

Mitch stood still, his expression hard. He knew it was a message, a warning, a way of saying that T-Money's name, his legacy, wouldn't go forgotten.

When the mourners began to leave, Mitch, Darius, Malik, and Andre remained, lingering under the shade of the oak trees, their grief wrapped around them like a heavy cloak.

Bottles of whiskey got passed 'round, the burn hittin' like a harsh reminder of what they'd lost.

Mitch stood with his homies, just lookin' at that fresh grave, the pain creepin' deeper into his soul. The world felt way more empty now. The block, the laughs, the good times—everything felt distant, like the noise had faded out.

But T-Money was gone. And the silence around him, that was something Mitch would carry with him forever.

Mrs. Johnson, T-Money's mother, approached them, her face aged with grief.

Her eyes had that deep pain in 'em, like no words could fix it. Mitch stepped up, voice heavy with emotion, but nothing came out. He just grabbed her hand, tryin' to offer what he couldn't say.

She nodded, one tear slidin' down her face, shining like it was the only thing left to say.

"He was a good boy, Mitch," she whispered. "He had a good heart."

"He did," Mitch choked out, the sob he'd been holding back breaking free.

The others circled around her, hands on her shoulders, no words needed—just letting her know they got her. After a minute, Mrs. Johnson stood up straighter, wiped her tears, and her voice got steady. "But y'all gotta go now," she said. "He gone. Let him rest."

The crew shared one last look, no words, just that quiet understanding that this was it—this spot was done. The streets might feel colder, emptier now—but T-Money's name, his stories, his love—ain't none of that ever gonna fade.

- Chapter Thirty-Eight -

"The Cost of Letting Go"

A month passed, and the calendar only reminded Mitch of T-Money's absence. Each day reopened the wound, leaving him with that same hollow ache, the one that followed loss—sharp, relentless, impossible to ignore. The war against the Southside Serpents was over, but the victory felt like nothing more than a cruel echo.

Chicago, once his battleground, now felt like a cage. Every corner whispered of gunshots, every alley held the ghosts of people he couldn't save. G, T-Money, too many others to name—they were all gone, victims of choices he had made. And now, every life lost weighed on him like a suffocating cloud.

He'd never been naive about the life he'd chosen. He'd embraced the thrill of danger, welcomed the risk. But lately, that rush had soured, replaced by a gnawing anxiety—not for himself, but for her.

Angela. The woman who had somehow slipped past his defenses. She brought light into his life, a light he didn't know how to protect. The woman who saw more in him than he could see in himself, who unknowingly became his anchor in a world of chaos.

He couldn't deny how much she had changed him, how much he'd grown because of her. She was everything this world was not: bright, hopeful, real. But the night he saved her from the Russian mob, something inside him broke. He couldn't keep her in this world, not with him. Not when every step he took felt like it would drag her deeper into the dark.

A framed picture on his shelf caught his eye—one of them, laughing together. She was leaning into him, her eyes sparkling in the warm summer light. It was a snapshot of a life he couldn't imagine anymore, a life that felt like it belonged to someone else.

He longed for peace, for a life where the danger wasn't always lurking, where the quiet moments weren't just temporary respites before the next storm. He thought of the beach in Costa Rica, where he'd once walked with his grandfather. The rhythm of the waves, the sunlight—it was all a world away. A dream he could never quite reach, until now.

The letter from his father sat in his hand, its weight heavy with a promise of escape. Costa Rica. A life away from the bloodshed. He knew it was selfish, but what other choice did he have? Angel had found something here—something real. Her salon was thriving, her dreams coming to life. And he was about to rip it all away.

But he couldn't let her live like this. Not knowing the constant threat that hung over them, the danger that followed him like a shadow. The idea of her in harm's way, because of him, was unbearable.

He grabbed his phone, the cold weight grounding him as he dialed her number. This wasn't something that could be said over text. He needed to see her face, to feel the raw emotion that would spill from her. He knew it would break her, but it was the only way.

"Hey, stranger!" Her voice, warm and easy, sent a pang of guilt straight through him.

"Hey, Angel," he replied, his voice rough. "Can I meet you at the shop after closing?"

There was a pause, the silence thick with unspoken questions. "Sure," she finally said, her voice hesitant, a crack in its usual cheerfulness.

"Alright, see you in a bit," he murmured, the weight of his decision pressing down on him.

He hung up, and the reality of what he was about to do sank in. The next few hours dragged on, each second heavy with dread.

He paced his house, his feet leaving creaks in the wooden floors. His eyes kept drifting to the photo of them, frozen in a moment of happiness. He could feel it slipping away.

Finally, as the city darkened outside, he forced himself to shower. The hot water didn't wash away the guilt, but it numbed it just enough to get him through. He dressed, but the new shirt didn't mask the turmoil inside.

With a deep breath, Mitch stepped out of his house, his heart weighed down by the inevitable heartbreak that awaited him. At Angel Haven, everything would change. And it had to.

Chapter Thirty-Nine

"A Love Left Behind"

The sun was dipping low in the sky, throwing a golden light through the windows of Angel's Haven. It wasn't the harsh city light that had once filled this space with shadows; it was softer now, kinder, like everything was at peace—even if it wasn't.

Mitch pulled his car up to the curb, staring at the place that used to look like it was barely holding itself together. But now? Now, it was solid. Fresh paint, a bold sign that screamed this was Angel's. No more empty promises or shattered dreams. This was her heart, bleeding out in the form of a business. A space made with sweat, hope, and a whole lotta fight.

He sat still for a minute, trying to shake the nerves crawling up his spine. There was no avoiding it now—the talk he'd been dodging for weeks. The thing that felt like it was gonna tear him apart the moment he said it. But it had to be done. He couldn't keep running from it.

He opened the car door, the bell above the entrance jingling when he stepped inside. Angel looked up, her eyes lighting up like the damn sun was shining just for her. Damn, that smile. It had always done something to him.

"Mitch!" she called, voice high and warm, as she rushed toward him. Her arms were already open wide, and before he knew it, she was pulling him in, her lavender scent mixing with vanilla and everything that felt like home.

For a second, he didn't know if he was more relieved to be in her arms or terrified of what he had to do next. She pulled away, her hands still on his shoulders, her face shining with that damn smile. "Didn't think I'd see you so soon," she said, voice soft but excited.

"Had to check on my girl," Mitch said, his voice coming out rougher than he'd planned. He sucked in a breath, then forced a grin. "This spot? Looks real good. You did that."

She grinned, standing tall like she owned every inch of it, 'cause she did. "It's been a grind, but yeah... it's finally starting to feel real." She took in the space, her eyes glowing with pride. "Feels like it's all mine."

Mitch nodded, feeling that genuine respect.

"You earned this, Angel. All of it. This is you."

They sat down together, Angel talking about her day. It was the usual stuff—meetings, orders, new challenges. Mitch gave his own updates, but the conversation was light. Easy. Until it wasn't.

A shift in the air. Mitch could feel it—the way everything in the room suddenly felt too tight. Too heavy.

Angel must've sensed it too because her smile started to fade, just a little. "Mitch… What's going on?" she asked, her voice a soft lilt of concern.

Mitch could feel the weight of his chest. His words didn't come easy, but he couldn't keep dodging it. "I gotta tell you something."

Angel's eyes narrowed, the concern deepening in them. "What is it?"

He reached for her hand, fingers brushing over hers, warm and familiar. He swallowed, throat dry. "I gotta leave Chicago," he said, his voice barely above a whisper.

Silence dropped between them like a hammer. She froze, her hand tightening around his like she was holding on to the last thread of a dream. "Leave?" Angel's voice cracked, the hurt slipping through. "What do you mean leave?"

The words stung, like they were slicing through him. He couldn't meet her eyes. "I can't stay, Angel. The life I'm living... It ain't safe. It ain't just for me anymore. It's... it's dangerous for you too."

Angel's face twisted like he slapped her. She pulled her hand away, staring at him with disbelief. "You knew this was coming?" Her voice was shaking, like she wasn't sure if she wanted to believe him.

He nodded, every muscle in his body aching with the truth. "Yeah. I knew. I just didn't want it to go down like this."

A tear slid down her cheek. She didn't say anything, just wiped it away, trying to hold it together, but the hurt was there, raw and real.

"I knew there was more to you," she whispered, her voice small. "But you kept your walls up so high. I thought... maybe one day you'd let me in."

Mitch's chest tightened. Guilt swallowed him whole. "I tried, Angel. I really did. But this life? I can't let you into it. I can't let it drag you down too."

Her hand shook as she wiped another tear away. "I didn't ask for you to protect me," she said, voice small but sharp. "I asked for you to be real with me. I asked for you to be here, Mitch."

He closed his eyes, pain crawling up his throat. "I'm not good enough for you. Not like this. I never was."

Her eyes shot up to his, a crack in her voice. "Don't say that. Don't do that to me."

He stood, slowly, like he was trying to pull himself together. "I'm not leaving you because I don't care. I'm leaving because I do. I can't keep you trapped in this mess. I can't drag you down with me."

She was quiet for a moment, but the silence felt heavier than any words. "So... that's it? You're just gonna leave and I'm supposed to be okay with that?"

He swallowed hard, his voice low. "You deserve more, Angel. You deserve peace. A life where you're not constantly looking over your shoulder. A life where sirens don't wake you up in the middle of the night."

She shook her head, her eyes wild. "You really think I can just let you go? You think you can just walk away from me like we were nothing?"

Mitch rubbed his face, struggling to breathe. "I'm not walking away because of us, Angel. I'm walking away because I don't want to see you destroyed by the world I'm in. I can't give you a future, not like this."

She didn't say anything, just looked at him like she couldn't understand what he was saying. Like she couldn't wrap her mind around the idea that he was leaving.

"You wanna know why?" Mitch took a step forward, his voice cracking. "I wake up every damn day with a gun under my pillow. Every phone call, every knock on my door, it could be the end. That ain't living, Angel. That's survival. And I won't drag you into it."

Her eyes were wide, tears streaming down her face now. "You're really leaving me. Just like that. You think you can just disappear?"

Mitch closed his eyes, fighting the tears of his own. He pulled out a small velvet box, and for a second, it felt like the weight of everything was pushing on him. He opened it, showing her the diamond necklace inside. A piece of him he couldn't say with words.

"This is for you," he whispered, pressing it into her hand. "A piece of me."

Angel looked at it for a moment, her fingers trembling as she held it. "I don't want this," she said quietly. "I don't want jewels, Mitch. I want you."

Mitch shook his head slowly, his heart breaking all over again. "I can't be what you need. I can't be the man you deserve."

She reached up, cupping his face with both hands, her touch gentle but desperate. "Mitch, don't do this. Please. Don't leave me here. Don't leave me in this."

He closed his eyes, the weight of it all pressing down on him. "You're gonna be alright, Angel. You have this place. You have your future. You built this from nothing."

She laughed, but it was bitter. "And what about you, Mitch? What about everything we were?"

He shook his head. "I built my life on broken pieces. And now it's all falling apart. I'm just trying to walk away before I drag you down with me."

She stared at him, her eyes searching his, looking for any trace of the man she thought she knew. "I thought we were supposed to be forever."

Mitch reached into his jacket pocket and pulled out an old photograph, worn and faded. It was of them—laughing, smiling, untouched by the world. He handed it to her, fingers trembling.

"I wanted forever, Angel," he whispered, "but forever's not promised in my world."

She looked at the photo, then back at him, her eyes full of unshed tears. "You built everything on lies, Mitch. And now you're walking away from it all."

"I never wanted this for you," he said, his voice barely audible. "But I can't drag you down with me. I love you too much for that."

Angel held the photo to her chest, her body trembling. "You can't just disappear, Mitch. You can't just walk away like you were never here."

Mitch turned, his heart breaking all over again. But this time, he didn't look back. The door swung closed behind him, and Angel was left standing there, holding the broken pieces of their love.

And in the quiet, under the weight of their shattered dreams, Angel finally understood. Forever wasn't something they could hold on to.

It was something they had to let go.